La Vida Segunda

The Second Life

Andrew Benzie Books
Martinez, California

Published by Andrew Benzie Books
www.andrewbenziebooks.com

Printed in the United States of America
First Edition: December 2019

10 9 8 7 6 5 4 3 2 1

Escott, Esther
La Vida Segunda: The Second Life

ISBN: 978-1-950562-25-1

Cover and book design by Andrew Benzie
www.andrewbenziebooks.com

I wish to thank my husband, Charles Escott, MA in Metalsmithing, the actual creator of Jonas's urn and a great help in writing this book.
Thanks also to my wonderful editor, Paul Weisser, Ph.D.

FOREWORD

In the early 1970s, California's Santa Cruz Mountains and the Santa Cruz city area became known as the "Murder Capital of the World." I lived in those mountains for eighteen years, including the 1970s, and remember well that grim history. Three demented killers were active there at the time: John Linley Frazier, Edmund Kemper, and Herbert Mullin. The murders were well documented in the *Santa Cruz Sentinel*, the *San Jose Mercury News*, and other newspapers. Since then, they have been open to research in many sites online.

The religious John Linley Frazier became known as the Killer Prophet. Edmund Kemper, with his murders of female hikers and other young women, was called the Co-ed Killer. Herbert Mullin considered his killings sacrificial, believing that they were preventing earthquakes.

A total of twenty-seven murders were committed within thirty months. At first, many people blamed hippies, thinking the killings stemmed from their world of peace, sex, and mind-altering drugs. But local hippies reported Frazier to the police.

In *La Vida Segunda*, the protagonist enters this dangerous world seeking a peaceful life in the redwood forests.

CHAPTER 1

The bus carrying Will McKeen from San Francisco through the Santa Cruz Mountains crept up Highway 17 behind a heavy truck. Leaning forward in his seat, near the front of the bus, he watched the truck's back end through the bus's windshield as the bus driver maneuvered the winding road. Having driven his own car on this road twelve years ago, Will wondered why he didn't remember the sharp curves.

His eyes shifted to the forests passing beside him as he watched for redwood trees. He had spied a few, not large, maybe a foot in diameter. Standing amid dense underbrush and small-leafed trees that were unfamiliar to him, the redwoods were easily distinguishable by the straight columns that were their trunks.

As Will leaned forward, his well-cut suit fit him loosely. Recent weight loss had sharpened his cheekbones and crooked-ridged nose, and his gaze into the forests was weary and uncertain.

Judas Priest, where are the big trees?

Through the intervening twelve years, he had kept a memory of real giant trees. Just a few, but he thought he had actually stood among them. Or had his memories become tangled with photos of redwoods he had seen?

Finally sitting back, he tried to rest. When his plane from New York had landed in San Francisco, he had stood in the crowded aisle and suffered a spell of dizziness. Then, stepping up the ramp at the airport, he had staggered and had to catch himself. All through this day of travel, his physical condition had been on his mind. Will, a thoracic surgeon, was still recuperating from a severe heart attack.

After the attack, while he was still in the hospital, an old dream of his had risen anew. When his wife was still alive, they had talked of retirement in redwood forests on the land he had bought on his earlier trip to California.

His friend George, an orthopedic surgeon, had been aghast, warning him against moving into such dangerous isolation. The flight alone, he had insisted, would be risky for a man in Will's condition. Thinking of George now, Will checked his pulse. Steady, just slightly fast. He had survived the flight.

It's going just as I planned, George. Here I am, safe and sound, riding a bus.

Finally, the climbing road leveled as the bus started across a wide, open mountaintop that actually had a cafe and a gas station, where, to Will's pleasure, the truck pulled off the road. Then he watched through the windshield as the bus started downhill and back into the woods. Far ahead and below, layers of forested ridges extended southward toward Monterey Bay. The farthest horizon, he discovered, was different from the nearer ones, which were topped with small, rounded humps of trees. This distant skyline was formed of pointed spires, each one an individual tree.

Will smiled to himself.

At last.

He was feeling a little brighter by the time the bus entered the streets of Santa Cruz. After it had arrived at the terminal, he stepped into the aisle to leave and noticed a newspaper lying on the seat across from him. One of the smaller headlines caught his eye: "Another Murder in the Santa Cruz Mountains."

The words barely registered in his brain as he moved toward the door with passengers pressing behind him. While he stepped carefully down from the bus, the headline hovered in his mind. Another Murder in the Santa Cruz Mountains? New York had murders. Plenty of them.

But *another* one?

While he waited for his luggage, the full impact of the headline struck him.

A new murder had occurred here, in addition to earlier ones. How many murders had there been?

There were two taxis parked at the curb, with both drivers

climbing out, watching him. One looked middle-aged, wearing a blue uniform jacket. The other appeared to be just a kid, with straggly, dark hair nearly to his shoulders, and wearing a faded, smudged-looking t-shirt. Will started automatically toward the blue jacket.

But the kid was heading straight toward him, and speeding up, cutting between Will and the other driver. Will paused, frowning.

The kid spoke. "Doc McKeen, right? I'm your ride. I'm Jonas Schumann."

He extended a work-roughened hand. Dark eyes and wide, angular jawbones: he looked increasingly foreign.

Will was slow to reach for his hand.

"I've been waiting for you," Jonas said. "C'mon, I'll give you a ride up the mountain."

The youth glanced down at Will's two expensive new suitcases, a parting gift from George. Then he picked both up and started for his cab.

"Just a minute!" Will called. "How do you know who I am?"

"Berriman told me you were coming. You know, the realtor who sold you the cabin? He's a friend of mine."

"Strange, he didn't tell *me* I'd be met!"

Jonas looked bewildered. "Well, he's like that. He's pretty half-assed as a realtor. I told him I'd meet your bus. I live just up the road from your place." He paused to set one suitcase down. "By the way, I brought my key to the cabin with me. You have yours with you, I trust." He held up a ring with a key on it. "Berryman thought I should have one, too, to keep an eye on the place. I've had it for years. Do you mind if I keep it? You can have a copy of my house key, too, if you like. You know, as neighbors."

Will brought out his key from a pants pocket to show that he had it. The strange, tough kid had a key to the cabin! Feeling powerless to prevent this intrusion, Will stood watching Jonas load his luggage into the trunk.

Then Jonas climbed into the driver's seat, looked through the car at Will, and waited.

Will stood as if rooted to the ground.

Presently, Jonas climbed out of the cab, sighing heavily, came around to Will's side, and opened the front passenger door. He looked sweaty, tired, and exasperated. "Look," Jonas said, "You can find your own damn ride if you want to. Berriman didn't know which bus you'd be on, and I met the noon bus, too. I missed a three-hour class, waiting for you."

Will, chastened and wordless, climbed in.

Jonas navigated a few blocks of Santa Cruz traffic as Will looked out the window. The cabin was north of Santa Cruz; would they retrace the route the bus had just come down on, Highway 17? But, to Will's great appreciation, Jonas started out into grassy hills. After they passed a street sign, "Arroyo Road," the way became winding. In a mile or two, they entered woods, which gradually became deeper and darker.

Glancing over at Jonas, who was steering smoothly hand-over-hand, Will guessed that he was about 22, maybe a little older. Probably a college student. Did they dress like that out here?

Trying to rest as he stared out at brushy woods, he suddenly spied a few larger redwood trunks, which reached so high that no craning of his neck at the window could let him see their tops.

"Looking for redwoods?" Jonas said, chuckling. "You and every tourist I bring in here." He shook his head in a mildly contemptuous manner. "Sorry to disappoint you. There are still a few nice groves, but most have been logged off, over the years. Then all this brush moved in."

Speaking with his head tilted toward Will, Jonas seemed in a better humor now, apparently having forgiven him for the long wait and for his reluctance to climb into the cab.

"You could get lost in this undergrowth for days," Jonas went on. "This is a great place to hide from the police, or hide a body, or hide just about anything. There have been a bunch of murders around here lately. Do you know about them?"

Will stirred out a husky reply: "I saw a newspaper on the bus that had an article about it, but I didn't get a chance to read it."

"There've been three..., actually three psychopaths, working independently of each other in these hills. Santa Cruz County is being called the Murder Capital of the World."

Will stared silently straight ahead.

As if he possessed a little tact after all, Jonas changed the subject: "Do you know what most of this thick brush is?"

Will murmured, "I think I see a little blackberry."

"True. Tons of blackberry. But the most prevalent ground cover is poison oak. You have a lot of it on your land. I'll show you what it looks like, in case you don't know. By the way, if you don't mind me asking, how did you ever come to buy land out here?"

"Well…, I was in San Jose for a conference, and had an extra day, so I rented a car and drove down here to see the redwoods. Just another tourist." He glanced over at Jonas, who stayed silent. "When I found a beautiful grove with a For Sale sign, I got out and explored a bit. I climbed a hill, and the view from up there pretty well decided it. I went back down and copied Berriman's phone number off his sign. It was more land than I wanted, and the owner wouldn't split it. So I bought it all, ten acres, with the cabin."

Jonas whistled. "Ten acres? Wow! Have you been back since then to see it?"

"No. My wife died shortly after that, and I just kept busy with my medical practice. No, I haven't been back. I'm curious about what shape the cabin's in. Berriman told me it was empty, at least."

"Well," Jonas said, then paused as if deciding what to disclose. "The old tenant is out, yes. Berriman did have the electricity and water connected. He said he'd put in a phone. I hope he did. But you can sleep there tonight, if you can stand the bed. There's some furniture, but—well, you'll see soon enough."

"I'll make do. I'll need to buy a car in Santa Cruz. Do you think I can book a ride with you tomorrow?"

"Actually, yes. I have a seven-thirty class, and I can pick you up about a quarter to seven. How's that? You can get yourself a good hot breakfast in town."

"That sounds wonderful. Thanks. You're in college, then?"

"Yes. UC Santa Cruz. I'm working on my master's in Metalsmithing. Hollowware and sculpture, a little jewelry. Right now, I'm designing a large complicated piece in pewter and bronze. And a little—" He broke off. "Oh, damn!"

He slammed on the brakes, throwing Will forward. With squealing tires, the cab skidded to a stop, barely missing a man who was scurrying off the road.

Will drew back from the dashboard into his seat. He just dimly recalled seeing the man on the roadside, who had actually jumped out in front of the cab.

"Bill!" Jonas called out, still gripping the wheel. "You stupid fool!"

The man was large and bearlike, with a thick, black beard. He had hustled back to the front of the cab and now stood with his arms spread wide, preventing Jonas from driving on. Then he started sliding around the right fender, leaning down to peer in at Will.

Will was absorbed with his racing heart, which had missed a few beats, then given a hard thump, followed by pounding.

Easy…, settle down, he thought. *We didn't hit the guy. Nobody's hurt.*

Bill slid past, his large belly pressing against the window.

"What are you doing!" Jonas shouted as the man snaked along the car toward the back.

Scree-ee-ee, the tires squealed as Jonas pulled out, throwing Will back again. From the side of his eye, he had seen Bill get the rear door open and flop himself in. He had made it inside the cab!

"You imbecile!" Jonas shouted, furiously slamming the cab into a higher gear. "Are you trying to kill yourself?"

"It wouldn't hurt you none to give me a ride." Bill's loud voice sounded curiously youthful. "Is that any way to treat a neighbor?"

"Don't start that neighbor crap with me!" Jonas turned his head to glance at Will. "What's the matter? Is something wrong?"

Will's heart was still racing. "No, I'm alright. Just shaken up a bit. Keep going."

Jonas drove on, but at a slower pace. "That's Bill Santone." He motioned with his head toward the back seat. "Bill lived in your cabin the past few years…, him and his girlfriend, Lydia Bird. Berriman kicked them out recently, getting the place ready for you." He raised his voice to talk to Bill in the back. "This is Doc McKeen, the man who owns the cabin."

"That's what I thought!" Bill bellowed congenially, filling the cab with sour beer smell. "That's one reason I wanted to ride along!

Pleased to make your acquaintance, Doc."

Will nodded dully toward the back seat. The brute had been living in the cabin! He made no reply, needing to wait as his heart settled. Looking out, he saw that they were entering what appeared to be a genuine redwood forest. Still shaken, he gazed out at straight columns in a patch of bright sunlight, with trunks so ruddy that the dusty air they stood in seemed tinged with red.

The cab rounded a curve that seemed familiar, and then another. Then on the right came a sign he remembered, its letters now faded on the rough wood: "Live Oak Lane."

Jonas turned onto the dirt road, drove a short way, and let the cab settle into a rut.

Will was starting to worry about where Bill was getting out when Jonas called, "End of the line, Bill. You'd better get on up the road."

As the man clambered out of the cab, Jonas explained, "He and Lydia moved into a shack further up the hill. You might see Lydia now and then. She's a nice girl. Sort of a recluse. There's a road to the right further ahead of us, called the Arroyo Cut-off, that goes across to Highway 17. Bill can reach it directly from his place, so he doesn't use this part of Arroyo very much." A quick glance to Will added the silent message, "fortunately for you."

"Listen, you," Jonas said, raising his voice to Bill, who was watching him lift Will's beautiful luggage out of the trunk, "the next time you jump out in front of my cab, I'm gonna run you over. Hear me? When you see me coming, you'd better get the hell off the road."

"Jonas, you shouldn't talk to me that way," Santone said, pursing his plump lips and looking hurt. Hair as thick and black as his beard hung around his face. With heavy shoulders and arms, he stood half a head taller than Will's five-feet-eleven. His height surprised Will, who had seen him mainly leaning down and bobbing around.

"You ought to show a guy a little respect," Bill continued. "You could be nice, and give me a ride now and then."

"You know I'm not allowed to pick up freeloaders. Besides, you've got your own car."

"My car ain't runnin'!"

Ignoring him, Jonas started toward the path with both suitcases.

"You're about to get a look at your new home, Will."

"Yeah, it used to be *my* home!" Bill called out.

Will glanced back, catching a resentful look on the man's face.

Jonas handed Will the smaller suitcase. "Here, you'd better carry one, and mind it doesn't touch the bushes. There's poison oak in here. Get a good look at it..., three small oak leaves. They have a toxic oil that makes a terrible rash. You don't want it on your luggage."

Will positioned his suitcase in front of himself to become as narrow as possible as he followed Jonas on the path.

From higher up the road, Bill called again, "By the way, Jonas, give my regards to Amy."

Jonas stopped short, then turned sharply to look back in the direction of Bill's voice.

"What's the matter?" Will asked.

Jonas shook his head before walking again. "What did he mention Amy for? I don't even like him using her name!"

From farther up the road, they heard Bill laugh.

As they proceeded on the brushy path, thin fog was gathering. Gradually, the cabin came into view, with graying redwood siding, a narrow porch, one large front window, and a shingled roof covered with redwood needles. A glossy-leafed tree Will didn't remember had grown closely beside the cabin, with one red-barked branch reaching in over the porch.

As Jonas waited on the path, Will put down his suitcase and turned to look around. He nearly staggered, stepping back quickly to catch himself. In front of him, gigantic tree trunks were rising to tower over him, the closest one a few yards away, and two others near it. Looking up, he nearly lost his balance again as his eyes followed the massive trunks up until they were lost in greenery, and above that more greenery, dimming and finally disappearing into fog.

"Whew!" he said, stunned. "My God! These are mine?"

"They are."

Then the thought that he was standing on his own land, and these were actually his trees, caused Will's eyes to water. He turned his head farther to the side, to hide it.

"Don't be embarrassed," Jonas said quietly. "Nobody loves the redwoods more than I do. Except maybe you." He grinned. "Apparently, you don't remember them."

Will gave a short laugh and nodded, not trusting himself to speak. Then, while Jonas waited, he carried his suitcase onto the porch and moved the springy tree branch aside to insert his key into the lock. The door stuck a little. As it opened, a musty, saccharine odor met his nose. Mouse urine.

"Jonas, I want to—" He started to thank Jonas for all his trouble—for waiting for him, for the ride, for helping him to the door.

Jonas held up a restraining hand. "No need for thanks, Will. I live less than a mile further north on Arroyo. When you drive up there, watch for an open area and a Spanish-looking house with a red tile roof. My landlady lives there, Julia Harrington, and her son, Manny. Julia's a Mexican lady, very nice. You'll like them. Amy and I live in the small house in back."

Jonas was taking a quick look around. "You're gonna have plenty to do here. Do you plan to set up medical practice again?"

"No, no. I'm retired. I plan to loaf."

"You're retiring? Aren't you a little young?"

"I'm fifty-six. I had a heart attack recently, and decided it was time to quit. I'd planned to retire out here anyway. I'm just a little early."

Jonas's dark brows gathered sharply. "You've just had a heart attack? A bad one?"

"Yes. Massive."

"And you plan to live here..., alone?"

"Sure. I'm recovering well. I've had a lot of physical therapy, which I'll resume here. I'm in touch with Doctor Garrett, a cardiologist in Santa Cruz."

Jonas looked away, apparently assessing Will's chances of surviving here. His returning eyes held a brief look of annoyance.

Will caught the look, and through a moment of silence, his spirits sank so fast that he felt his face blanch.

"Well, I'll be nearby," Jonas said. "And Amy, and Julia. It helps to have good neighbors. I wouldn't worry about Santone. He shouldn't be any trouble."

Then they said goodbye, and Jonas glumly turned away.

Will watched him depart, his bare heels in sandals like white spots bobbing down the path in the fog. The kid hadn't expected a neighbor who might be a hassle for him.

I never asked for your help, Will thought. But he felt no better.

When he went inside, he poked around among his suddenly acquired possessions. Ignoring the dirty, odd-shaped kitchen, he noted two wooden chairs and a narrow bed with a thin mattress. He found his telephone, but there was no dial tone. Through dirty windows, the evening seemed to be darkening fast. In the fog high above him, the tops of the redwoods were still in dim sunlight, but he had no way of knowing that.

Still wearing his good suit, with a warm robe thrown over him, he stretched out on the bed. He tried to plan what he needed to do in the morning, but instead George came into his mind. George at the airport, with tears streaking down his fat cheeks. Will decided not to tell him about the murders.

I'm here, George, but I seem to be arriving in bits and pieces, still waiting for parts to catch up. I have beautiful redwoods, but the cabin is uninhabitable.

CHAPTER 2

The forest along Arroyo Road lay at the bottom of a northward-drifting ocean of fog: ferns freshening in the mist, blackberry leaves growing more velvety, poison oak leaves glistening and sometimes stirring with falling, sliding drops of water. High above, the giant trees were taking in through their tiny needles the moisture that had sustained them through a long summer without rain.

Farther north on Arroyo Road, a smaller lane, the Arroyo Cut-off, branched off to the right. Shortly after the Cut-off, the forest on the right side opened to a grassy meadow with two large, sprawling live oak trees. Then came a tile-roofed house with a garage, and a smaller building to the rear. From a back window of the large house, light was straying out into the fog.

Inside, Julia Harrington stood at her kitchen sink, rinsing dried beans. Her olive-skinned hands lifted them in the water as she strained them through her fingers, picking out an occasional shriveled bean. Black hair hung down her back in a loose braid, with a few strays curving past her cheeks.

Looking out the window, she gazed through the fog to another lit window, on the small house behind hers. She knew from its bluish glow that Jonas and Amy were watching television. She enjoyed seeing her tenants' lit windows at night, taking comfort in knowing that she and Manny were not alone. Although, at the moment, she *was* alone, because Manny was still outside, tramping around somewhere in the hills behind the Schumanns' house. She glanced at the clock. It was almost 8:30.

After drying her hands, she turned on the porch light and stepped outside. The fog sent back the glare of the light, so she couldn't see far.

"Man-n-ee!" she called, not too loudly, since she didn't want Jonas to come bustling over to see what was wrong.

"I'm right here!"

"*Dios*, Manny! You scared me! You popped out of the fog like a ghost!"

"Sorry." The 12-year-old grinned as he came stepping up onto the porch.

Julia swept back his black bangs. "You're wet! Wipe your feet, Babe." He ducked his head to wipe his shoes on the mat. "I don't like you being out this late. From now on, I want you inside the house before dark."

"*Why?*"

"Because! I worry! What if you got hurt up there somewhere? You could fall in a hole, and I'd never find you."

"There aren't any holes up there. I was just following the deer trails, leading down to the creek. I know all their trails, and their nests, too, where they sleep in the daytime." By now, he was preceding her into the house.

"Nests, eh? Deer nests." She shook her head.

"Sure. Nice, soft nests, with the grass all matted down."

"Then, there's the other thing, Manny. I read a piece about the murders in the paper today. There's supposed to be another deranged killer now. They've caught one, but more bodies keep turning up. At the university, the students aren't allowed to walk out alone at night."

"I know, the school kids talk about it. But I'm safe up in the hills. What would a killer be doing up in the hills?"

"Humph. Anyway, it's late. You'd better head straight for the tub. I still have to study my Teacher's Aid stuff."

The boy tilted his head in a bright-eyed, teasing look that reminded her of his British father, who had died eight years ago.

"I've got some news," he said. "But I guess you don't have time to hear it."

"What news?"

"I talked to Jonas. He came home just as I was going out. It can wait till morning, though."

"Don't fool with me, Manny."

"Jonas picked up the doctor in Santa Cruz today, and brought him to the cabin.

"The doctor! He's here?"

"Yep. He's a typical New Yorker, Jonas said, traveling in a dressy suit and tie. He's pretty rich, too. His suitcases were real leather."

Julia stood enthralled. "I wonder what he looks like."

"Tall and skinny, Jonas said. Kind of funny-looking. His nose looks like it was broken, or something." His eyes strayed to the refrigerator. "Mind if I get some milk?"

She reached distractedly into the cupboard for a glass. "Is he staying long, I wonder? Or just checking the cabin, or what?"

"He's here to stay. He's retired."

"To stay! *Retired?*"

Manny poured his milk with maddening slowness. "Yep, he's old. And he just had a heart attack. He's in bad shape, Jonas said."

Julia stopped short, letting her shoulders drop as she stared into space. After speculating about the New York doctor all these years!

With hands on her hips, she stared about her gleaming kitchen, with its olive-green appliances, the finest available when she and Thomas had built the house. She had taken such good care of them, they still looked brand new. Her pleasure in them seemed to give her a slight lift.

Tomorrow was Saturday. She had the Teacher's Aid meeting in the morning. She would put Manny to work in the garden, and in the afternoon, take him shopping. Maybe to the library. There were plenty of interesting things to do.

Manny drank his milk as he stared out the window. He had brought the good smell of the woods in with him, and something else—an energy, like a radiance. He seemed to collect it out there, more than just the shine on his smooth tan skin.

"I wonder," he said, "what the doctor's gonna do over there in all that poison oak."

"You've likely been in it yourself. Scrub yourself with soap. And lay your jeans on the washer, so I know which ones to be careful with. Move now, please, *muchacho*. Bedtime."

After the boy left for the back of the house, Julia rubbed her head. Her tired scalp ached to be brushed as she removed the rubber bands at the end of the braid. Combing her hair with her fingers, she smoothed the dark ripples. Heading for her bedroom and a hairbrush, she muttered, "Just what I need. A sick old man over there to worry about."

CHAPTER 3

Bill Santone picked his way on his own narrow trail through live oaks, bay trees, and brush, crossing the ridge between his shack and the Arroyo Cut-off. As he approached the paved road, it was growing dark, and fog was thickening in the trees. He had been counting the cars he heard going down the Cut-off—five already. Unusually heavy traffic.

Today, the old Doc had arrived and moved into the cabin that used to be Bill's home. Bill still had a door key, having had a third one made before the realtor could collect Bill's own two. He had buried that third key near the cabin, in a hollow beneath a burnt redwood stump, waiting for any time he might need it.

Two more cars now, all of them rushing down the Cut-off from Highway 17 to Arroyo Road. When he reached the Cut-off, he paused to check the road, peering out from the bushes. All clear. He strode forth.

Bill moved with a deceptively easy, rolling gait that ate up the miles. He liked the fog, liked the feel of it, and liked its concealment, feeling that it gave him a certain freedom of movement. Hearing was best in the fog, a secret he had discovered long ago. In the thickened air, earth sounds rose up and floated right into his ears.

He knew he heard things other people missed. He could hide in the bushes near a house and overhear whole conversations. And today he had played a trick on that mean-mouthed Jonas Schumann. He had planted a little seed of worry in Jonas's mind, informing him that he knew the name of the pretty wife Jonas kept in the little building behind Julia Harrington's place. How Jonas expected to keep a girl like that happy in a chicken house was beyond him.

Without seeing Jonas's face, Bill knew that the seed of worry he had planted had taken root when he heard the doctor ask the boy, "What's the matter?" From halfway up the road, Bill had heard that softly spoken question, and afterward, had sensed the fear and anger in Jonas's silence. Bill had to chuckle. Later tonight, he would make a trip over to the Schumanns'. Sometimes he could catch a glimpse of Amy through their lit bedroom window.

When he reached Arroyo Road, three cars in a row roared by, forcing him to step into blackberry bushes. He knew where they were going. Sal Marino, a bigshot lawyer from San Jose, lived farther ahead on Arroyo. He was the leader of a rock group that sometimes practiced at his home. Bill despised them for the harsh noise their speakers poured out into the woods. Sal was having a party tonight. Bill had heard about it in a bar. It smacked of big money and drugs.

After tramping along a short while, he heard the first strains of their music as they tuned themselves up—which was almost impossible, since they had blasted out their own hearing long ago.

Frowning to sharpen his eyes, Bill spied a movement on the road ahead. Just a thickening in the fog at first, then a dim, slight figure, moving steadily along in the gloom. Bill constrained his boots to land more softly and stepped faster. It had to be Denny Wheeler. There was no mistaking that snappy, short-legged walk. Denny lived on Tunnel Road, branching off Arroyo farther back.

Yep, pale at the top, blond hair. All dressed up in a tan suit, the little dandy.

Bill hated Denny's little dandy guts. He had been trying to get money from him lately, money he figured Denny owed him. The little runt had kept putting him off, mean and insulting about it as only a small man can be.

"Hey, Denny!" he shouted, his voice booming into the dusk. "Wait up! Where you hurryin' to?"

Denny didn't pause, so Bill broke into a lumbering run to catch up. He knew Denny had heard him, because with his head bent down and arms swinging, the little jerk was stepping faster.

"Slow down, will ya? I'll walk you up the road a ways."

The music swelled as they drew nearer the house.

Outrun and overpowered, Denny slowed down. "Oh, hi, Bill.

What're *you* doing out here, prowling around in the fog?"

"Just checkin' on what's happenin'. Christ, wait a minute!" Bill caught up with him and adjusted his legs to Denny's short, choppy stride.

Denny lifted his chin toward the woods ahead. "Marino's having a party tonight. That's his band playing now. Should be a good group. Friends of his from San Jose."

"Oh, Valleys, eh? And you're furnishin' the entertainment, I take it. Other than the music, I mean." Bill grinned and ducked to peer over at the shorter man, whose scrawny little face appeared stern.

"That's *my* business. I'll thank you to keep out of it, if you don't mind." His hand nervously patted his coat pockets and touched the coat again, higher.

Seeing the gestures, Bill laughed. "Now, ain't I always kept out of it? I never told anyone except people who was lookin' for a buy. And I never told a soul I didn't know, or know the reputation of."

As well as being a dealer, Denny had his own pot farm back on Tunnel Road, the plants mixed with toyon and coyote bushes in a hollow behind eucalyptus trees.

A chatter of drums wafted closer, and then throbbing tones from a keyboard. At the start of Marino's driveway, yellow lights glowed through the trees. As electric guitars started their screeching, Bill briefly covered his ears.

"I've sent a lot of buyers your way, Denny."

"Alright, so I slip you a bottle now and then, don't I? It's more than you deserve. Why I do it, I don't know. For old time's sake, I guess."

Bill took the insult with a grin, plodding beside the marching little man. "Well, and it's for old times' sake that I keep your secrets. I don't have to, do I? And when I steer a buy your way, I warn them to keep it quiet, 'cause you got good stuff, and you don't need publicity. That makes them anxious for your pot, Denny, and your angel dust. You're into that now, ain't ya? I hear you're making your own, you and some Bachman from over in Big Tree."

Denny didn't reply. Bill glimpsed his little face pinching in with spite.

"I think I'm worth somethin' to ya, Denny. Hell, you can afford it. How about slippin' me just a twenty now and then?"

Denny seemed not to have heard this, so Bill lightly touched his sleeve.

"Stop it!" Denny said, yanking his arm away. "Damn it, I've offered you grass, the best I've got! But, no, you have to have your stupid booze. So booze you get! I kept you in good bourbon all summer, better than you could afford."

He preceded Bill over a small footbridge that covered a trickle of water. As they neared Marino's driveway, Bill reached again for his arm.

"Now, Denny, I want ya to start slippin' me twenties instead of a bottle. That's all I ask. You can spare it. Cripes, we been buddies so long."

"Keep your hands off me!" Denny jerked away again, his tie flapping loose and a wave of light hair falling over his brow. "Look, get something straight! You do *not* work for me, so get it out of your head that you do!"

Bill took a better hold of the sleeve while Denny kept going, stretching the coat so hard that a thread snapped.

"Slow down, will ya? Shit, I'm tearin' your coat. Listen, you little runt, if I sic the police onto ya, they'll be damn glad to dig into that factory you got goin' back on Tunnel Road. Ain't that right?"

Denny spun around, so mad that his voice squeaked. "You don't dare talk to the police! You drive a stolen car, you numbskull! And the mess you made at that gas station, cutting a guy over a lousy tire. He can still identify you! You're a damn liability! So get lost. I'm cutting you off!"

Bill scrambled after him, trying to think, but suddenly drums exploded, shattering the peace. It was almost unbearable to ears attuned to the fine shades of quiet in the woods. He covered his ears again.

"No more bourbon?" he had to almost shout. "Denny, you don't mean it!"

"What did I say, Bill? Get lost!"

Bill was surprised at himself, staying so civil, when each beat of the music pumped his anger a notch higher. His throat ached from the injustice of it. He was big enough to squash the little flea and here he was, just taking it.

"What are you doing, Santone?" Denny looked halfway around, his sharp little nose in profile against the porch lights. "No use following me. Marino won't let you into his hou-hou-house." He faced front again and started trotting.

The light on the ground showed something ahead of Denny's scurrying little shoes. A short, broken branch—it looked like black oak—green and heavy. Bill's fingers flexed, yearning for the feel of that rough-barked grip, such a handy size. Another pale, scared flash of Denny's face, and his legs opened in a sprint. He skittered in confusion, not knowing where Bill was. He was running like a scared rabbit!

A flurry of drums and a high trill on the keyboard—Bill was bounding after him, charged by Denny's terror. He swooped down for the branch and continued on in one smooth motion. Only a few yards to the porch, with Denny fluttering helplessly as a butterfly. Bill was behind him swinging, throwing his back and shoulders into the swing.

Crack! A high fly! Denny was lifted slightly as the limb caught him just below the cranium. Then he fell forward, with arms spread out, landing on his face. Bill quickly bent over him, dragging him by the arms out of the clearing and into the trees. Then he stood erect again, catching his breath.

The music had stopped, but Bill hadn't even noticed. Sharp now, he peered over the line of cars. Silent. The night reeled in the aftershock of noise, with not a soul in sight. Then trilling laughter rose softly from the house.

Kneeling, Bill flipped the body over to see what he had done. The nose looked slightly mashed, with dirt in the nostrils pushing out in a little puff. Blood now, running down his cheek, so dark it looked black. Denny's eyes moved, touched with wonder at his life slipping away.

Bill straightened and looked around. All was quiet. He picked up the tree limb and hurled it far back into the brush. Then he slung the limp body over his shoulder and headed into the woods. He located an open space he knew of, where a stream and some buckeye trees lay below a hillside. Laying the body down, he gazed up the hill, its dry grass ghostly pale in the foggy dusk. Mt. Timothy Road crossed the hill somewhere up there. But no matter, even in broad daylight he couldn't see the road through the buckeye trees, and people up there couldn't see down here, either.

Denny's wallet interested him now, as he squatted to search the body. Blood had gotten on Bill's hand, and now on the wallet, where he wiped at it. Denny had peed himself, his crotch soaked and still warm. Bill could forgive him for that, which was just decently human.

Inside the suit coat, he found several pockets, containing a wad of bills and fat little plastic bags. He thrust the wad of bills into his own pocket along with the wallet money—followed by the wallet itself. No use helping the cops by leaving it here. Plus he might find a use for some of Denny's cards. Before rising, he cleaned his hands with dirt.

Standing up, he glanced around in the growing darkness. Then, bending down, he gripped the little body by an arm and a leg. Leaning back slightly with his burden, he swung his arms back to one side, then made a trial swing forward. Back again, and on the next, harder swing, he released it. The body sailed into a low buckeye tree drooping with pods, and landed, crackling down into the branches.

He watched the small round pods, which the falling body had set dancing. Funny how they bounced and bobbed around. Like kids' toys—balls on rubber strings.

CHAPTER 4

In gray morning light, Will explored his cabin. He was surprised at the chill in the air, for late July in California. Hunched and shivering, he kept his hands in his pants pockets, occasionally taking one out to examine something. Confirming that his cabin was a filthy hovel, he was trying to hold off shock, letting it touch him a little at a time. All this could be fixed.

In addition to the cabin's combined living room and bedroom, it had a kitchen-like area, and behind that, a tiny bathroom. The floor covering was linoleum, torn and patched with several patterns. In the small shower and under the kitchen sink, he found mold. The refrigerator door had a broken latch, requiring one of the chairs to prop it shut. Searching through drawers, he found a twelve-inch ruler, and used it to measure the small refrigerator so he could buy one that fit the space. Glancing at his electric stove, he knew without further scrutiny that he'd be replacing it. In fact, everything in the cabin would have to be replaced. He decided not to dwell on the fact that he had paid Berriman thousands of dollars over the years to keep the cabin in good shape.

Jonas arrived as planned, driving a battered-looking gray Volkswagen. As they rode into town, Will was glad the yawning and disheveled youth spoke only a few words, so he could contemplate his situation. After Jonas dropped him off in downtown Santa Cruz, it struck Will that, once again, he hadn't paid him for the nine-mile ride.

After coffee and a hot breakfast in a Santa Cruz restaurant, he felt a little better. It was nearly noon in New York, so he located a pay phone to call George, who wasn't in his office, but somebody ran to find him. When he finally answered, a heavy truck lumbered past the open phone booth, so Will had to shout over the noise. He wanted to tell George the truth, that the cabin was a wreck and he felt lost. But instead, he told him that all was well. The shouting was beneficial, as it stirred him out of himself and helped keep the weariness and disappointment from sounding in his voice.

That morning, he bought a new white pickup truck, and drove it through town to buy a refrigerator. He also bought a new telephone and arranged for it to be connected. Since he had to wait a few days for the refrigerator to be delivered, he bought bread, instant coffee, fruit, some canned goods, and a can opener. Carrying it all into the cabin, he told himself that food would make the place seem more livable.

Later, he explored his small yard, carefully avoiding the poison oak, which was rampant. Sometimes it blended devilishly with blackberry bushes. A few leaves were starting to turn red, causing him to speculate that they must be deciduous.

Are bare branches as toxic as the leaves? How can you keep out of it if you can't see it?

He stepped across the clearing to his closest redwood and laid his hands on its rough bark. Gazing up to the thick, dark green branches, he felt calmer, imagining that he was soaking up a little of the huge tree's strength.

★ ★ ★

After Will's first few days of puttering about the cabin, the weather changed. The fog vanished, and the mornings became dazzlingly bright and clear. While the onshore flow of ocean air had dropped, heat from the inland valleys was sweeping west. It was a regular phenomenon, but Will didn't know that. The first couple of bright days, the afternoon temperatures reached 90 degrees on the small thermometer outside his door. The air smelled of sweet, dried grass, and the tree that crowded the cabin surprised him by dropping sheets of thin, red bark over that half of his porch. He sat on the steps, fingering the strange, papery bark, listening to flies buzzing, and feeling heat bounce up at him from the sunbaked wood.

Then the daytime temperature climbed to nearly 100, and the cabin became an oven.

Suffering, he padded about in his underwear, placing pans of water to try to keep a little moisture in the air. With his nasal passages burning, he worried about an old sinus problem. An infection could prove more stress than his heart could stand. He dosed himself with aspirin and vitamin C. Then, along with the burning nose, came a scratchy sore throat.

Although his shower was so small that he could scarcely turn around in it, the plumbing worked, so he managed to take cooling showers. Between them, he lay naked on his bed with a damp undershirt over his face and chest. Heat filled the air, thick and suffocating. Breathing through his mouth to spare his nose, he tried to hold off fear, which he knew put great stress on his heart—and just knowing that brought on a new kind of anxiety.

On an evening of bright mental sharpness that seemed brought on by fever, he lay gazing up at two large, merging water stains on his ceiling. He saw various shapes in them: an old Chevrolet, two cows grazing, two seated women. The truth, which he had been trying to deny, became inescapable.

I can't make it here, George. I was wrong, after all, and you were right. I should have listened to you.

Tears squeezed out of his eyes and slid down his temples.

At last, he glanced over at the telephone, not yet connected. He'd have to find Jonas, and ask to use his. Such an easy way out, a direct line between himself and New York. Even though it would be like pulling his own teeth, tomorrow morning he would call George. Then he would pack up his clothes again. Shutting his eyes, he fell asleep while the hot day dwindled into a warm, dazzling evening.

In early morning, while half awake, he reached down to pull up the robe he had been using as a blanket. But it wasn't enough cover as he drew his cold knees closer to his chest. Puzzled, he took a testing swallow, and his throat felt smooth. Glancing toward the wide window over the porch, he saw nothing but solid white.

Rising quickly, he drew the curtain all the way open. The clearing was filled with thick, motionless fog. He hurried to unlock the door and open it. As cold, damp air rushed in, he took one deep breath after another. Then, shivering, he closed the door again.

Catching sight of himself in his little wall mirror, he stepped closer. His image there looked even worse than he had expected—hollow-eyed, with skin stretched white and shining over his cheekbones and crooked-ridged nose. The blue eyes staring back at him gleamed with uncertainty. His hair and whiskers both needed cutting. In fact, he had what appeared to be his longest-ever stubble of beard.

Frowning, he drew nearer the glass. In the stubble, he caught a glimpse of coppery red. Extending his chin, he examined it closely, and found other such bright hairs.

No, never, he thought. *But, was it possible? His beard was growing in red?*

He unlocked his door and, barefooted, crossed the porch and stepped gingerly onto the cold, rough ground. In dead silence his giant trees, fading away above him, seemed asleep.

Chuckling, he scrambled back across the porch, inside the cabin, and back to bed.

★ ★ ★

The Arroyo Cut-off, which connected Arroyo Road and Highway 17, was a quarter-mile of rough pavement winding around redwood and eucalyptus trees. On its south side rose a high mossy bank that never saw the sun. Across from this were the trees, some of which jutted out into the road.

On a sunny morning, Will drove his pickup eastward on the Cut-off, planning to take Highway 17 into Santa Cruz. Uncertain what day it was, he intended to buy a calendar, a battery-operated radio, and some newspapers.

In the cabin, he had resumed his exercise program, using small weights and running in place. Soon, he thought, he would start jogging along Arroyo Road. He'd had another talk with his Santa Cruz cardiologist, with a more thorough exam, and had left George's telephone number to be called in case he died or was brought in.

Steering carefully along the Cut-off, he was maneuvering a sharp curve when suddenly he was blinded by sunlight on his dirty windshield. Having drifted outside his lane, he suddenly saw a yellow car looming straight ahead. He hit the brake but couldn't avoid a collision. A scraping blow, and he veered off into a recess in the bank. His truck stopped with a crunch of metal, and he was thrown forward, his nose striking the top rim of the steering wheel.

Opening his eyes, he looked down through the wheel to see blood dripping, soaking into his pant leg. His heart was pounding.

Moderate fright—I can take this.

Now came the tightness, his heart unable to pump blood fast enough to meet the demand.

Stop the adrenaline. I don't need all these constricting vessels.

After a bit, he carefully sat back, then eased out his handkerchief and held it to his dripping nose.

"Manny! Oh, *Dios mío!*"

Dark eyes, filled with alarm, were suddenly close to his face. A woman had opened the door beside him and pulled herself up partway onto the seat, so that she was pressing against him.

Through half-open eyes, Will saw a smooth olive cheek with a crease of dimple. Then he was jarred alert as her hand touched his face. She was trying to press an eyelid open.

"Don't!" he grunted, turning his head away.

"Oh, no, please, you're not having another heart attack!"

Will reached out and found his hands full of her. After a moment of confusion, he drew back his hands, while she backed hastily down and out of the cab.

"Manny! Run home and call an ambulance! If Jonas is there, tell him to come!"

Tripping words, a Spanish accent.

Through the open door, Will saw a boy running past them toward Arroyo Road.

"No," he muttered. "Stop. I'm alright."

"Wait a minute, Manny!" she called again.

Having guessed who the couple were, Will said, "Hello, Julia," using the Spanish J sound as Jonas had, "Hoolia." He leaned out to extend a hand toward her. Then, as she reached to take it, he had to jerk his hand back to grab his nose. While he applied the handkerchief again, a laugh escaped from her. He found himself chuckling with her through his pain.

Then she looked chagrinned. "What's the matter with me? I know you, of course..., Doctor McKeen. And I'm Julia Harrington. This is my son, Manny."

Will said hello again and nodded toward the returning boy. With Julia's help on one arm, he clambered down from the cab. Then he asked if they were both alright.

"Yes," she said. "We had our teeth nearly shaken out, but we weren't hurt. Your nose, though! It must be broken. There's so much blood!"

He examined it gingerly, and decided it was intact. "I think I banged it on the steering wheel. Maybe this straightened it out."

He grinned at Manny, who had returned, but the boy was sullen-looking and silent. Stepping to the front of the truck, Will saw that the right fender was crushed against the bank. The left fender had a paint-scraped dent where it had struck Julia's car.

"Well, I guess it could be worse."

"Our car's worse!" the boy blurted out.

Julia hushed him as Will walked unsteadily toward the small yellow Plymouth, which had crashed into a eucalyptus trunk. Steam was rising from its crumpled hood, soaking the shaggy bark of the tree.

Radiator, he thought, *hood, bumper, grill, and more.*

The car was a late model, probably worth repairing. "This one," he said, watching green coolant trickle over the dirt, "will have to be towed."

As Will checked to make sure the car was far enough off the road, Manny stood by stiffly, waiting. "It was your fault!" he said now. "It wasn't our fault!"

"Manny! *Dejalo! Es un hombre simpatico.*"

"Don't worry, son," Will said, "I know it was my fault." He glanced at the anxious boy's face, sweating now under a shock of black hair. "I'm going to take care of both vehicles, yours and mine.

But first, I think I'd better take you and your mother home—if I can get the truck going."

The boy still gave no blink of surprise or relenting.

Tough kid, Will thought, returning to the truck. He was afraid the right fender might be jammed against the tire. But when he backed the truck out of the bank, he found the fender mashed, but the tire free. While Julia watched for oncoming traffic, Will inched the truck back and forth until he could turn it around.

They were a quiet threesome bouncing back down the Cut-off, with Manny sitting like a disapproving elder between the two who otherwise might have talked. Will was quietly concerned about his condition, still feeling dazed as he sat in the truck that was so new he barely recognized it, heading through greenery still strange to him, packed in closely with a woman and a boy he didn't know.

At the Harringtons' house, Manny ran in the front door. But Julia paused to watch the truck turn back down Arroyo Road. She made a colorful picture in the sunlight, her white slacks and yellow-and-white flowered blouse setting off her Hispanic coloring. Finer-featured than her son, she had eyebrows and lips that were delicately shaped, with a soft crease of dimple in both cheeks.

Turning away, she stepped up the sidewalk after Manny, but before going inside, paused by the potted geraniums to snap off spent blooms. She needed a little time alone to think. Hadn't she always been afraid of that Cut-off? She saw again the curved road and the white truck approaching, swinging wide. It must have been instinct that made her wrench the wheel around fast, even before she could think. Just a hard scrape from the truck, but then the tree had loomed. And though she had practically stood on the brake pedal, she couldn't stop.

Hadn't she practiced this before in her mind, with Manny beside her, as she had known he would be? She let the fright spread out like hot coals, to flash and sparkle and cool itself in the air. Then, taking a deep breath, she felt better.

Well, we've had our wreck. Hopefully, we'll never have another.

"Hey, Mom!" Manny called from inside the house. "What are you doing?"

"Coming!" she said as she stepped inside, carrying her dead flowers to the waste bin.

The boy was rinsing a glass at the sink, a milk mustache on his upper lip. "Well?" he said, watching her face as if for some clue as to how he should feel.

"What would you like for lunch, Babe? Quesadillas? We have such nice, fresh cheese, and my best salsa ever. And the new apples!"

His brown eyes wavered. "I guess so.... Hey, Mom, what about it? What about our car? He's out there driving around, and we're stuck here without any car!"

"We'll get it back as soon as it's fixed, honey. I can ride with you sometimes on the school bus, you know. And Jonas can always help us out." Then, as Manny remained staring, "We're going to come out of this okay. Don't worry, *muchacho*."

"Well, what did you think of the Doc? He sure didn't look like a doctor, did he? He looked like a hippy from up in the communes."

"Yes, he did, didn't he?" She chuckled. "Maybe he's starting a beard. He was nice, I thought. *Muy amable, muy responsable*."

"Responsible? Are you kidding? He almost wiped us out! He drives like a maniac!"

"Oh, now, maniac! You know how many wrecks there are on that Cut-off. He probably doesn't know the road."

Then, in Manny's silence, she suddenly remembered something happy. "Hey! The play-offs are on TV today! The Orioles and the Oakland A's!" Although he remained sullen, she smiled, suddenly feeling shy. "Didn't you think Will was a little bit nice? He laughed with me—wasn't that funny? Sitting there with blood dripping, and he laughed."

"I know! I wondered what was going on. You and him laughing your heads off, with our car all smashed up. You acted like a couple of fools."

"Manny! Watch your sassy mouth!"

As they stared at each other, the boy's eyes filled with tears. Julia had to turn away to hide her own welling eyes. She opened the refrigerator, took out the cheese, and closed it again.

"I'll tell you why I could laugh, Manny. I was just so thankful that neither of us were hurt, I couldn't seem to give a damn about the car. I still can't. What's a car? You and I are alive, and unhurt!"

For a reply, Manny turned his back on her.

"Please, son, try to find a little kindness in your heart. The man isn't well, and he's alone over there. And Jonas says the cabin is a filthy mess."

Manny looked back at the cheese, then blew out a sigh and walked to get the grater.

They ate quietly, saying nothing more about the wreck. Later, in the living room, Julia sat with a bowl of apples on her lap, paring them for a pie, as they watched the A's get trounced by the Orioles, six to nothing.

★ ★ ★

Late that afternoon, a new-looking, dark blue sedan pulled up into Julia's driveway. Looking out her window, she saw that the driver was the doctor. Behind it, Jonas pulled up in the Volkswagen. Smoothing her hair, she hurried out to meet them.

The sedan was a Ford Capri. It was a rental, Will explained. It was hers until the Plymouth was repaired.

"But why?" she asked as he handed her the keys. "It wasn't necessary. We could have ridden in and out on the school bus."

"I tried to tell him that!" Jonas called from the Volkswagen.

Will quietly divulged that it was a stick shift, like Julia's Plymouth, and the gas tank was full. Then he looked toward the house, asking, "Where's the boy?"

"Inside the house."

"Is he still mad at me?"

"Yes, I'm afraid he is."

Will nodded thoughtfully, saying nothing.

"He'll get over it, I'm sure," Julia said, noticing a purple bruise starting across his nose and right cheek. "Thank you for all your help, Doctor. I really didn't expect such… generosity."

"Just call me Will," he said with a thin smile. He glanced about as if making sure he had taken care of everything. Then he walked over and folded his long legs into the Volkswagen.

As Julia watched them leave, she wondered just how old the man really was.

As she entered the house, she caught Manny leaving the window, where he had been watching. "Will asked where you were, Manny. And he asked if you were still mad at him."

"He *did*?"

Julia stared at him, understanding the boy's shocked look: the doctor had asked about *him*? A *kid?*

"He did. And I said yes, you still were."

"Mom! Why the hell did you say that? You got me in trouble with him!"

"I'm afraid you did that yourself, son. And watch your language!"

"Damn it!"

"Manny!"

CHAPTER 5

Daylight was fading in Bill Santone's shack, where Lydia Bird was bent over her drawing board, trying to finish a sketch before dark. Thick black hair crowded her face, causing her to keep pushing it behind her neck. Her border collie, Girlie, lay curled at her feet. With Bill gone all afternoon, probably in some bar, she had enjoyed a long, peaceful time to work.

On her drawing, two mule ear flowers had taken shape, lightly sketched. Now she was applying layers of colored pencil, watching, as she always did, as color started bringing the flowers nearly to life. The plant had large, coarse leaves and two long-stemmed blooms, like big, slightly tattered yellow daisies. She was using their imperfections to portray their character. People who knew her work would see the flowers' strength as they lived out a hot, dry summer.

In local shows, her wildflower paintings found buyers. Though her earnings were less than Bill's disability pay, she knew that as long as she brought money into the house, she could stay, and the rough little lean-to on its north side would be her own.

Suddenly, there was a change in the air: Girlie's head lifted sharply, with her nose pointed toward the door. Bill was somewhere on the narrow road below, coming up the hill. The dog rose up and headed for her usual hiding place, a dark corner by the bed.

By the time Bill was near, Lydia had covered her work and put it away.

"Liddie!" his voice boomed outside. "Liddie, hurry up and open the door!"

When she opened it, Bill came in with a gust of whiskey fumes, carrying two large bags of food. "How's my Liddie, my li'l birdie?"

He was staggering drunk. "Boy, are we gonna eat tonight!"

Bill fried the two steaks himself, while Lydia found places to stow the rest of the groceries. As he charred the meat nearly black, the shack filled with delicious-smelling smoke. The aroma brought Girlie creeping out to take her place beside Lydia's chair.

"Oh, you think you're gonna get some, do you, you little rat?" Bill growled. "You don't do nothin' to deserve it, and you ain't gonna get it."

Lydia looked up sharply and stared at him.

Bill bent his head lower over his meat, grinning. "Don't worry, I'll feed the damn dog."

After they had eaten, and Girlie had gulped down her plate of scraps, Lydia washed the few dishes while Bill sat picking his teeth.

"I learned somethin' strange in town today," he said, speaking carefully. "A guy has gone missin'. I know him. That is, I don't *know* him, but I know *of* him. You ever hear of a guy named Dennis Wheeler?"

"No." She shook her head thoughtfully as she returned to her seat. "Does he have a family? They'll be worried about him."

"I don't know. I think he was reported missin' by some other guy. Bruce Bachman, the paper said. He must've been a friend, I guess."

"Paper? Did you buy a newspaper?" She was always begging him to bring one home for her.

"No, and don't give me those greedy eyes. I ain't buyin' you no paper, so quit askin' for one!" Then he subsided. "I just saw it in the rack, and I could read it standin' there."

She sank lower in her chair. Ever since Bill had stolen her from a mean pimp, when they'd first met in Los Angeles, she had known not to test his anger.

Now she lifted the soft mass of her hair to cool her neck. The hair had no shine, but the deep, dull blackness of kitten fur, or soot. Bill called it witch's hair, and eventually she had begun to see herself as something of a witch. At age thirty-two, and weighing less than a hundred pounds, she had the face and form of a slightly wrinkled young girl.

Growing weary, she sneaked a glance toward the bed. She

wondered if she'd be better off going there now and pretending to sleep, or waiting until after he climbed in first and sank into a stupor. But Bill seemed in no hurry to retire. He was now using his knife to trim and clean his fingernails. So, with her back to him, she slipped out of her daytime dress and crawled into bed.

When he finished with his fingernails, Bill stared vacantly at the darkened window. He realized that his beer had worn off, and he was left with a bleary feeling. But he wasn't ready for bed. Maybe he ought to go out and check around in the valley to see if anything was happening down there. It was growing cold, though. If he went out, he'd need a jacket.

Where was it? He studied the few hooks on the wall across the room. His old army fatigue jacket wasn't there. It must have fallen into the pile of clothes on the floor.

Rising from the table, he paused to scratch his furry chest. Then he trudged over and, grimacing, pawed through the smelly pile. There were pants in there so stiff that they could practically stand by themselves. Here was the jacket. He picked it up and shook the wrinkles out.

Before leaving, he glanced toward Lydia, who was already in bed. Most likely, she was faking sleep, hoping he would leave her alone tonight. The little runt; it was hardly worth bothering to wake her. The scrawny youthfulness about her that had once appealed to him wasn't very interesting anymore.

Then he found a surprise. One coat pocket had something in it. A wallet! He had forgotten about Denny's wallet. He must not have worn this jacket since that night.

Checking the bed again, he saw that Lydia was lying with her back to him and quiet. After tucking the wallet back into the pocket, he put the coat on. Then he stepped outside into the darkening night.

There would be a moon later: the coyotes knew it as they yipped shrilly in the distance. Yes, it was a good night to be out and about.

In tall weeds along the narrow road sat his '62 Ford. It had no front license plate. He had lifted a set from an old wreck in Los Angeles, only to have them both stolen by a friend of his in Santa Cruz. The car now had one plate on the rear end, which he had taken from Will McKeen's truck. Leary of driving it this way, he had let the car sit here, derelict, a constant source of frustration.

After opening the passenger door, he groped on the seat for his flashlight. In its weak beam, he examined the wallet. No cash. The money he had found in here was long gone. But there were credit cards, as he remembered. He studied them now. They included a bank card that he fingered wonderingly.

Then he put the cards back in the wallet. It was not the time to call police attention to himself by doing something stupid, like trying to use a stolen card. Denny would be found one of these days. And here Bill was, less than two miles from that spot. He wished to hell he had hauled the little jerk's body a long way off and buried it.

After stowing the wallet far back in the car's glove compartment, he packed paper trash in front of it. Then he closed the car door softly, so Lydia wouldn't hear it.

He started tramping downhill toward Arroyo Road. If the doc's cabin were dark this early, it would probably mean he wasn't home, which would give Bill a chance to try the door key that he had buried by the redwood stump. He moved quickly on scrubby, dry grass and weeds softened by dew. The coyotes were silent now, and all the night noises were familiar and good: the distant wail of a dog, the creak of a limb, the faint stirring in the brush that likely meant a rat.

From the road above Will's cabin, he saw that it was dark. The window didn't have even the weak glow that he sometimes saw there, probably from a small lamp. With confidence he tramped up the path.

Reaching the clearing, he headed for the old stump to dig up his key.

Then he stopped and stood erect.

Damn it all!

His keen ears had picked up the quiet rumble of Will's truck on the road, coming down from the north. As the sound came closer, Bill started for the path. Then he stopped again. On the road, he could get caught in Will's headlights.

Turning around, he headed straight into the woods, clawing his way through the brush in pitch darkness. When he came around to the road, it was still bright with Will's headlights. He had to wait there, afraid to move, thinking he was probably up to his ass in poison oak.

CHAPTER 6

Several days later at twilight, Will was jogging northward on Arroyo Road. The forest was already deep in shadow with the tops of the redwoods still in sunlight, drawing his eyes upward to their golden glow. But mostly he watched the pavement before him, which was full of dips and slants that showed its inclination to slide into the creek. Breathing hard, he resisted the urge to check his watch.

Three minutes of jogging, three minutes of walking, and another three minutes of jogging—then turning back and continuing the pattern. That was the plan devised by Dr. Garrett. Taking the cardiologist's advice, he'd also had his face x-rayed, and learned that the bones were intact. But his face was still colorful with its earlier reddish-purple fading into a dull yellowish-green.

During the past two weeks there had been workmen in the cabin, starting on Will's planned improvements. He had enjoyed watching them while trying to keep out of the way. The flooring throughout had been replaced with heavier plywood and covered with red, brick-patterned linoleum. In addition to the refrigerator, he had bought a stove, a sink, a mattress and springs set, and an upholstered armchair. He still needed new kitchen cupboards and eventually a whole new bathroom. But he had decided to let those wait a while. He was retired. He could do as he pleased.

Now, as he checked his watch, he slowed to a walk. Hearing a car approach from behind him, he stepped farther off the road. Then came a toot he recognized as Jonas's car horn. He turned to wave as the Volkswagen roared past. Jonas waved but didn't stop. Will knew that his time at home was precious to him.

He had resumed his jogging when he spied a figure on the roadside ahead. Drawing nearer, he saw a lavender dress and blond hair. A girl? On the road? Puzzled, he drew nearer.

The young woman was kneeling at the edge of the pavement with a pale arm reaching into the leaves. She seemed to be working with the roadside plants. When she saw Will coming, she sat up higher, then raised a hand.

"Hello, Doctor McKeen." She had a digging tool and a bucket full of plants—green leaves with small blue flowers. As Will approached her, she rose to her feet.

Breathing hard, he came to a stop and stared at her: pale blond hair lifting now in the breeze, gracefully shaped eyebrows, clear blue eyes.

"I think you're the doctor, aren't you?" she asked. "You already know my husband, Jonas. I'm Amy Schumann."

He opened his mouth to speak, paused, and finally bumbled out a greeting. "Amy, is it? Hello, Amy. Yes, I'm Doc McKeen. Just call me Will." He could hardly get over his surprise. This beautiful girl was Jonas's *wife*?

She was also studying him.

"I guess you're wondering about my rainbow-colored face," he said.

She laughed gently, lovelier still. "Yes, it's really colorful, isn't it? I know about your wreck with Julia's car. She really appreciates your having it repaired and being so nice about it all."

"Well, I was the responsible party. I ran her off the road." Then, as he glanced at the plants around them, he asked, "Are you planting flowers or digging them up?"

"I'm digging them up to transplant in our yard. This is *vinca major*. You might know it as myrtle. It's expensive to buy, but it's naturalized along this road."

As she lifted a leafy spray to show him, he noticed her rings. One was a plain gold band, and the other had a pearl setting.

A pearl for an engagement ring? That's Jonas. He would do something strange.

"How is your heart now, Doctor? I know you've had a heart attack."

"Yes, a myocardial infarction." *Why did I say that? Am I showing off?* "But it's getting stronger now, along with other muscles."

"So you're working at bodybuilding, not just for your heart?"

"Yes, thigh muscles especially. They can help push the blood up and take some of the load off the heart." *Now I'm talking about my thighs!*

"Are you sure it's safe, though, to work as hard as you do? The heart seems such a fragile thing…."

"Actually, it's pretty tough. For an organ, it's fairly simple. Just a pump."

"A pump? What a nice thought. That makes it seem kind of sturdy."

"Well, it's healing now. I'm hoping for good collateral circulation." Then he explained: "New blood vessels, supplying blood to wherever it's needed in the heart."

"Your heart can grow *new* blood vessels? Really? That's not possible!"

He smiled. "Yes, it is. The heart works to heal itself. I've seen it happen many times, but it seems sort of magical to me, too."

"That's amazing! I hope you do grow those new vessels."

"Thanks for that. I think I'm recovering well."

She bent down to pick up her bucket, then, straightening, looked him solemnly in the eyes. "I hope you find a new life here, Will. A whole, new, wonderful life."

He thanked her again, quietly.

"I've got to go. Jonas drove by a few minutes ago and wanted to pick me up, but I needed some more plants. He wants me home before dark. You know about the murders in these mountains, don't you?"

Will, who had become nearly mesmerized by the young woman, came alert again.

"Yes! Jonas is right. It's late for either of us to be out. In fact, maybe I'd better walk you home. I can make it that far…."

But as she protested this, a car pulled up slowly behind them and stopped. It was a friend of Amy's, a woman named Naomi, offering her a ride home. Amy thankfully accepted and loaded her bucket of plants into the car.

As they left, Will lingered, staring after them. In the sudden silence, it seemed to him that he might have dreamed the whole meeting.

How can such a lovely girl be interested enough in an old man like me to want to hear about his heart?

Then he remembered how far he was from home and started out. He stuck to his old pattern, but jogging more than he walked. Alternately he watched the pavement and the narrow strip of sky above the road, which retained some light while his feet tramped along in near darkness. He finally reached home, sweating and chilled, suspecting that he had gone beyond his limits.

At the door, he groped in his pocket for his key. With one hand holding back the meandering tree branch and the other gripping the key, he felt for the dark keyhole. At his touch, the keyhole moved inward.

The door was open.

His heart geared up again.

Calm down. We're okay. We can handle this.

Slowly he pushed the door open and stared into the dark interior. Not a sound. The cabin appeared empty. After reaching in cautiously, he turned on the light and took a good look around. Then he stepped inside. His newspaper had been spread around on the table. His bowl, which had contained two apples, now held only one. His milk carton sat on the counter—probably empty. His clothes, which had been hanging on wall hooks or stacked neatly on the floor, had been rummaged through.

He sat down and gave himself a minute to absorb the shock.

Then he checked for his wallet: yes, it was safely in his pants pocket. Apparently, nothing in the cabin had been stolen but food. How could that be? Should he call the police? He thought a minute. Then he rose unsteadily and walked to the telephone.

Jonas was shaken up by the call. "Are you positive you locked the door, Will? It's so easy to forget! That's probably it. You forgot to lock the door."

"I did not! You know how careful I am. Besides, there's an apple missing from my kitchen table.... Do you still have your key?"

"Of course, I do. It's on my keychain. I'm looking at it right now."

"I wonder if Berryman ever collected Santone's key."

"He said he did, the lying jerk. I'll call him and make sure he changes the lock *fast.* Actually, I'd better change it for you."

"No, no. You're busy. I'll have it changed myself."

"It could be someone else, you know. It doesn't necessarily have to be Santone. Still, who else would have a key?"

"Right. And he resents me mightily for taking over the cabin. The day you brought me here, he gave me a real black look as he started up the road. It must be him. And I'm thinking, since he ate some food but didn't steal anything else, he probably means this as a threat. He wants me to know he can get inside my cabin."

"Yes, that's probably it."

"If he tries it again, maybe breaking a window, I'll call the police."

"Good. You'll need to call the Sheriff's office. Ask for Deputy Alan Hunter—he's our local cop. A nice guy, and we're friends, sort of."

After the phone call, Will lay awake in bed. He had no doubt that Santone was the intruder. He had left his presence in the cabin; Will could sense it. He had moved about touching everything—the food, furniture, clothes. Will's privacy was gone, and so was his peace of mind.

★ ★ ★

As time passed after Will changed the lock, there were no more break-ins. Gradually, the ordeal fell behind him as he resumed something like a normal life. When the brick-patterned floor felt ridgy to his bare feet, he cured the problem with a large, round, braided rug. He bought curtains for the windows, which he could draw at night when his lights were on. He had his truck repaired in Santa Cruz. When he realized he wasn't eating very healthfully, he shopped in Cabot's Mill for fresh foods, and with the help of a couple of cook books, started cooking. He needed kitchen cabinets, but they would have to be custom-built, since he doubted that ready-made ones would fit into his oddly shaped little kitchen.

Then the call came from the auto repair shop: Julia's Plymouth was ready to be picked up.

When he drove her yellow car slowly up Arroyo Road, he took time to enjoy Julia's open meadow, blazing green in the sunlight. It made him think perhaps he lived too much in the shade.

As he got out of the car, Julia emerged from the house. "Oh, my dear old car! It looks brand new!" As she ran her hands over its gleaming yellow hood, Will wondered if she might try to hug him. But she quieted down and thanked him shyly. Probably, he thought, she was too polite to look directly at his bruised face and many-colored stubble of beard.

As he was about to leave in her rental car, Jonas appeared from behind Julia's house.

"Everything still quiet at your place?" he asked.

"Yes, thankfully," Will replied. "No more break-ins."

"Would you like to come back to my place for a bit? I've made a start on my master's project, and you might like to see it."

Amy met them at the door. When she saw Will, her face lit up with a warm, welcoming smile, and he was enchanted all over again.

His smile for her was carefully polite.

What's the matter with me? I'm old enough to be her father. And she's Jonas's wife.

CHAPTER 7

When he entered Jonas's house, Will noticed that the ceiling was a bit low. He felt inclined to stoop, but checked the impulse. With the walls white except for one in redwood paneling, the furniture consisted of a simple wooden sofa and chair with print cushions. They looked to Will like porch furniture, but comfortable enough. The room was bathed in soft, white light from a large window with sheer curtains, and this simple feature cast the room in a beautiful setting. The crowning touch—a delicious food smell wafting in from the kitchen.

"Will, I'm so sorry," Amy said. "We were just planning leftovers tonight, and I don't think we have enough to share."

Jonas looked befuddled. "We mean to invite you for dinner one night soon, Will, but I guess not tonight."

"Don't worry, I didn't expect to stay," Will replied. "Dinner sometime would be great, though. Thanks."

Then he looked around the room with surprise; the wall to his far left was filled with greenery. Potted plants hung from the ceiling and filled several shelves. He stepped closer taking in the variety of leaves, mostly green but with touches of whites and purples—striped, glossy, some as delicate as ferns.

"What a lot of different plants," he said. "And they all look so healthy."

"Amy's indoor garden," said Jonas. "She also works part-time in a plant shop."

"I love plants," Amy explained. "I keep adding to my collection with cuttings that people give me. My dream is to have my own shop someday. Not a regular nursery, just potted plants."

Lifting a leaf here and there, she named a few: piggyback plant, spider plant, elephant foot, prayer plant, creeping Charlie, shrimp plant, and others. "Just their common names," she explained, "not the botanical ones. They do well because of the light Jonas has provided for them." She directed Will's gaze upward to a large skylight.

"Wow, that's impressive, Jonas. Nice woodwork on the frame."

Jonas nodded modestly. "Yeah, well, overhead light is best for indoor plants."

"We've had so much fun decorating this little house," Amy said. "Julia gives us free rein, and even helps pay for supplies. You'd never guess what the house used to be."

"Hey, c'mon, would you?" Jonas interjected, cutting her off. "That's enough of a tour! I asked him in to see my master's project." Taking Will's arm, Jonas steered him away. "Over here, Will. My workbench is in the kitchen."

Barely hiding his surprise at Jonas's rudeness, Will nodded a thank you to Amy and let himself be led away, wondering what the house used to be. *Possibly a garage*, he thought, *or some other outbuilding*.

Then he forgot about it as he saw in the swing of Jonas's young shoulders that he was about to share with Will something of great importance.

Moving from the living room into a combined kitchen and dining area, Jonas led Will to a tucked-away corner that contained a rough wooden workbench. There he turned on a small high-density lamp. Both corner walls above the work area were hung with sets of tools—pliers, mallets, and files. On the bench, a rack held a row of gleaming steel hammers, covered by a leather flap. Will took it all in with an appreciative whistle.

"This is where I work," said Jonas. "Here and in the studio at UC. I do mostly fabricating here—sawing, soldering, hand-finishing. And I do a lot of wax work for casting. Buffing and grinding I do at UC. I can't make a mess like that here. And I use the school's casting equipment."

"Are those nice hammers for forging?"

"Yes. They're expensive as hell, and they're mine. I keep them here because I don't want other guys messing them up." Lifting a hammer, he showed Will its oddly domed head. "See, they're all differently shaped."

Will studied them, nodding.

"When you forge metal over stakes, it's called 'raising,'" Jonas said, flipping a leather cover to reveal three variously shaped steel knobs. "I have three stakes, and there are more at UC. I've raised a couple silver chalices so far, and a copper bowl. I actually sold one of the chalices, and that enabled me to buy a lot of stuff."

As Jonas spoke, Amy slipped into the room to stand by Will. When Jonas paused, she held out her hand for Will to see her gold rings.

He recognized the pearl, having glimpsed it among myrtle leaves. Lifting her hand into the light, he took a closer look. The engagement ring's shank rose with a twist to form a delicately shaped cup that held the pearl.

"It's my favorite of all his rings," she said. "He's sold a few since we were students at UC Berkeley. But none as beautiful as mine."

"I was inspired, I guess," Jonas said."

As the couple exchanged smiles, a look of pure happiness passed between them.

Yes, Will thought, *that's what I need to see. They're happily married, and I'm just a neighbor. I mustn't forget that.*

After Amy returned to the kitchen, Jonas took a sheet of paper from a drawer, showing Will the bold headline: CALIFORNIA CREATES.

"This is a big crafts show in Los Angeles that's coming up in about six months. All kinds of 3-D work: woods, weaving, ceramics, glass, metals…. And here I am, about to start my master's project. How's that for timing? I'm sketching it now. I'd like to get it into this show…, if I'm lucky enough."

"Lucky?" Will asked.

"It's an invitational show. The entries are judged, and only the best are accepted. I brought the announcement home from UC. It wasn't sent to me, by any means."

"And you're drawing your project now?"

"Yep. I'm thinking of one big piece. Something complicated enough to stand alone as my whole master's project. Something sculptural, probably a container of some sort, or it might incorporate a vessel." His eyes brightened as he envisioned his dream. "Know what metals I plan to use? The guys in class think I should stick with silver, but I want it silver, gold, pewter, and bronze. Imagine! How colorful, just with metals! And I want to use every technique I know…, casting, raising, fabricating, enameling, setting stones, everything! I want it to be a sort of culmination of everything I've learned!" His eyes shone now with what he saw, and he stopped with an embarrassed laugh.

Will nodded and smiled along with Jonas, caught up in his excitement.

From the front part of the house, voices were rising. Jonas lifted his head to listen.

"Who'd come here this late?" he said. "Probably it's Julia."

But as the voices came closer, his eyes sharpened. "No! Damn it! Tonight of all nights!" He started furiously straightening up his bench, balling scrap paper and hurling it into a basket, dropping leather flaps, and slamming a drawer shut. "It's my in-laws," he told the startled Will. "The Hainsfords, Amy's parents!"

In sympathy, Will's heart was starting a nervous flurry of its own. "I'd better be going, then," he said. "It's late, anyway."

"No, don't leave!" Jonas said, combing his hair roughly with his fingers. "If they see we have company, they might not stay. Christ, talk about ruining a perfect night! Stick around a little while, would you please, Will?"

Before Will could decide what to do, Amy and her parents entered the kitchen, bringing in a rush of cool evening air and men's cologne.

"Look who's here, honey," Amy said. "Will, I'd like you to meet my parents."

Will stepped forward to shake hands with them, dully aware of his baggy jeans and faded t-shirt. Amy's father was wearing a suit that looked like silk, and her mother had on a short dress that shimmered as she moved. Will wondered where they were going; obviously their plans included more than this stopover at their daughter's home.

Amy completed the introductions: "My father, Robert Hainsford, and my mother, Margaret. This is the new neighbor I told you about, Mom and Dad…, Doctor Will McKeen."

Will shook hands with Margaret, an attractive, gentle-faced woman. Then, turning to Robert, he met steel-gray eyes, slightly higher than his own.

"How do you do, Will? Medical doctor, I believe?"

"Yes. Pleasure to meet you, Robert." Here, Will discovered, were Amy's perfect features, but with silver hair and sharp eyes.

Robert stood stiffly erect. "You're from New York, I believe?" he asked.

"Yes. Queens."

"Did you retire from private practice?"

"No, I was on the staff at Clayton Wheeling. Thoracic surgery."

Robert lifted his brows slightly. Then his eyes swept over Will's small reddish beard, crooked nose, and sunburned arms. "A little young to be retiring, aren't you?"

Will paused, starting to dislike the man. "I had a heart attack a few months back."

"Ah. Ah, yes, I see." Robert nodded, studying Will. "Well, this isn't a bad area for a retirement home. A little far from San Francisco for my liking, but there are some nice redwood lots in these hills, if you put in a decent road. I suppose you've done that?"

"No, I'm just using a rough dirt road. I have a small place there, a cabin. It was on the land when I bought it."

Robert looked confused. "How large a lot?"

"Ten acres," Will said, watching Robert blink. Then he let his eyes stray to Amy, who was taking her mother aside to show her the plants.

"Do you have a wife, a family?" Robert persisted. "You didn't come out here alone, did you?"

"Yes, I'm alone."

"Divorced?" Robert watched him, waiting for more.

Reluctantly, Will replied, "I lost my wife a little while back." He saw Jonas's eyes sharpen; he and Jonas had never gotten into Will's personal history.

"How about children? Any heirs?"

Now genuinely annoyed, Will decided that he would have to answer. "No. No children. We…." He paused, but Robert was waiting for him to finish. "We lost three babies, miscarried."

Jonas inched closer, causing Will to fear that he'd come to Will's defense and make a scene. But the young man calmly interrupted, asking Robert if he'd like to see his workbench.

"Ah, yes! That brings us to the purpose of our visit tonight!" Robert said, ignoring Jonas's offer and brightening so that he seemed to change the mood in the room. "Come join us, ladies! Mother and I have brought you a gift, Amy. That is, it's for you and Jonas."

After the women rejoined the men, Robert drew from his pocket a small black velvet box, which he held up for everyone to see. Then, with a flourish, he handed it to his surprised son-in-law.

Jonas looked at him blankly, then at Amy, and finally opened the box. Inside was a bit of folded tissue paper. As Jonas unfolded it and lifted out a tiny sparkling bit, Robert quietly told him to be careful.

"A diamond?" Jonas said. "Is this a real diamond? Why? I don't get it."

Amy leaned in closer to see it, her lips forming a silent *Oh*.

"I don't get it," Jonas said again, looking at Robert. "Is it for Amy, or me, or what?"

It was an awkward moment; Will winced for his friend.

Jonas's eyes flashed with embarrassment as he tried to explain, "I mean, is it for my jewelry, or is it for Amy? You handed it to me."

"It's for you," Robert said, "to give to Amy."

Silence hung heavily in the room as Jonas rewrapped the gem in its tissue paper, closed the box carefully, and handed it back to Robert.

"What would I do that for?" he asked quietly. "It's from you. *You* give it to her."

Robert's lips curled upward in a smile. "It's for her engagement ring, of course. Don't pretend you don't know what it's for, Jonas."

"Robert," Margaret said gently, "this does seem rather abrupt. They might need a little time to get used to the idea."

"What's to get used to?" Robert said to his wife, his tone

sharpening. "We talked about a diamond at the time of the wedding! Christ, it's been three years!" Then, to Jonas, "You don't expect her to wear that pearl forever, do you?"

"Daddy," Amy said, "I don't remember any talk about a diamond. It's beautiful, but I love my pearl ring. It's special to me and Jonas. I watched him make it. We shopped together for the pearl."

"Amy, you're not thinking." Below Robert's silver hairpiece, his brow glistened. "Look at this diamond!" He opened the box again and fussed with the tissue paper. "Look at it! It's flawless! It's one full carat. Not gaudy, just the perfect size! I could have bought you a car with what I paid for it!"

"Why would I give her a thing like that?" Jonas asked. "I could never afford it."

"You don't seem to understand," Robert said, his face starting to redden. "It's the pearl that's at issue here. It doesn't look like an engagement ring. A diamond is traditional."

"The traditional thing," Jonas said, speaking carefully, "is for the engagement ring to be a gift from the groom, not from the bride's father."

Will decided it was time for him to express a thought. "Does it necessarily have to be a ring, to hold the diamond? Perhaps he could make her some other piece of jewelry."

Jonas looked up. "That's right! With this gem, and plenty of gold, I could make her something beautiful! How would you like your daughter to wear a prize-winning neckpiece?"

Amy brightened at the thought. "Please, Daddy? That's the perfect solution! I'd love a diamond neckpiece!"

After her plea, Robert's face grew blank, as he failed to come up with an argument. He looked at Margaret, who also had no comment. Finally, he conceded quietly that the plan had merit. But he remained grim as he returned the box with the diamond back into his coat pocket.

Minutes later, with the ring debacle behind them, Robert leaned closer to Will, whom he now treated like a cohort.

"You know, raising a child isn't necessarily what it's cracked up to be. Amy's our only child, and look at her. Look how she's living.

Hell, you sweat for them all those years, give them the best education, and right when you think they're set for life and you can quit worrying…."

Jonas lowered his head and started walking away.

With anger rising in him, Will brushed aside concerns for his heart. "Well, she's a lovely girl, and she looks happy. In fact, Jonas and Amy are a fine couple. They're building their future together. Jonas will soon have his master's degree, and Amy is thinking about a business of her own. You should be proud of them."

As the room grew quiet, Will added, "And now I think I'd better say goodnight. Thanks for this evening, Amy, Jonas. I've enjoyed your company, and seeing your lovely home." Then he started for the door.

"That's rich!" Robert barked happily. "Hear that, Margaret? We have nothing to worry about. Our daughter has a lovely home!"

"Robert…," his wife murmured.

"Picture this, Doctor, if you will," Robert continued. "You give your daughter, your only child, a beautiful wedding, all she and her mother could wish for. You foot the bill for the reception, dinner for two hundred…. Price no object, right? Then the happy couple returns from a month in Hawaii and sets up housekeeping. And guess where? In a chicken house! That's right, a goddamned chicken house! It's priceless!"

"Alright! Are you about done?" Jonas confronted his father-in-law. "Have you humiliated me enough for one night?" Amy was in tears, taking his elbow. "No, leave me alone, Amy! I'm going to have my say. This is a damn nice little house, and we've worked hard in here, and it's our home. I don't remember inviting you over tonight. For an uninvited guest, you've got damn shabby manners."

"What would *you* know about manners?" Robert grumbled, his face reddening further.

"Please, Robert," Margaret murmured. "Let's leave."

"He acts like he's slumming when he comes here," Jonas went on. "He can't stand our house, but he keeps coming back."

"Honey, please," Amy said, drying her cheeks with her hands. "Will, I'm so sorry."

"No, no," Will said. "I'm the one who should apologize. I stepped out of line."

"I want you to know," Jonas kept on, "this little house is very well built. For one thing, it has a good foundation."

"And Julia had the house all redone, of course," Amy added. "She added on the whole back half..., the bedroom and the kitchen...."

As Amy continued her defense of the house, Will saw another opportunity to leave. After saying goodnight to the group once again, he headed for the door.

Jonas said that he needed some air, and followed him outside.

In the cool twilight, they walked wordlessly to Will's truck. Will climbed in, opened the window, and sat looking out at Jonas's glum face, searching for something encouraging to say. "You're going to win the battle, Jonas. I think you've already won it."

"No," said Jonas. "No, I haven't."

"What do you mean?"

"You don't know the whole story."

Will gently asked him for an explanation.

But no explanation was forthcoming.

CHAPTER 8

Lydia Bird climbed out of bed without waking Bill and quietly left the shack to look for Girlie. For fear of waking the snoring man, she didn't call to the dog. Seeing no sign of the black-and-white collie, she started down the brush-crowded road, bunching her skirt in front to keep it clear of the coyote bushes, a common habitat for ticks.

Partway down, she met the dog coming up. She knelt for a silent reunion, cupping the collie's soft ears in her hands and letting the dog nose her neck and chin. Her hands swept back over the thick fur, digging in so Girlie could feel it. The dog's fur was free of poison oak oil. Lydia managed to keep her fed, so Girlie had no need to run in the brush.

"Go home now, Girlie. Be quiet."

As the collie stepped out ahead, Lydia watched her obedient, mincing steps, elegant rump, and swaying tail. A beautiful dog. Bill complained that she ate too much, but lately he'd had little to say, since Lydia's paintings had paid for most of their food.

At the door, Girlie paused to look back questioningly. "Go on," Lydia whispered, and the dog nudged the door open. After Lydia followed her inside, she gave her food scraps that she had been saving and fresh water, hoping the dog's loud, slow lapping wouldn't wake Bill. Watching Girlie drink, Lydia decided that if she ever had to leave, there were only two things she would need to take with her, her money and Girlie.

A few steps away, in her painting area, her drawing board waited, with a sheet of paper on which she'd already painted a wash of pale grayish blue. Seating herself, she tested the wash with a finger to make sure it was dry. Showing through its paler center was a faint pencil drawing, a group of three wild irises.

Outside her small window, the sun was high in the sky as she finished the painting. Pointing her brush in her mouth, she made the last fine stroke, sharpening the edge of a leaf. The painting pleased her. On the smooth paper from the pad that Jonas had given her, the blue background had dried with no hard edges, and she had given the cream-colored petals the moist crispness of iris. With each one seeming to cup a secret, they lifted their heads tentatively to the sun.

She quietly washed her brushes at the sink and dried them on her skirt. The clock said 11:20. When Bill rose, he would want lunch. Quickly she took up last night's stew and placed it on the hotplate, setting it on low.

Then she hurried back to her work table, where she carefully packed her paint tubes back into their box. Her fingers brushed the folded bills she had hidden there, a portion of her painting sale money. A thrill of fright ran through her, causing her to jerk her head up. For an instant, she thought Bill had entered the doorway and stood watching, seeing the telltale green at the bottom of the box. But no one was there as she stood with her heart tripping like a bird's. Then she heard him moving, fumbling about for clothing.

By the time he approached to stand over her, she had stowed her paint box under the table, but left the painting out to dry. He had grown fatter overnight, she thought, his pants zipper straining under the bulge of belly, his bare arms heavier, and his drooping shoulders rounder. Glancing blearily toward her painting, then around the room, he spied the stewpot, and smiled with a hint of his old, roguish twinkle.

"How do you feel?" she asked, carefully stepping past him to set the bread on the table.

His smile remained fixed as he watched her move. "With my hands," he replied.

She tried to turn her back, but he caught her by the waist, stopping her. Holding the bread plate, she stood resignedly as he groped upward, feeling her ribs through her thin sweater. Dully thankful for his gentleness, she tried to step away. But his hands tightened. Like a cat teasing a mouse, he let her slip and caught her again, chortling as he held her tighter.

"How come you're so damn skinny?" he asked, pouring his sour breath into her hair.

"Don't," she muttered.

"What's happenin' to you? You're shrinkin'! You got nothin' but little mosquito bites for titties!" He spun her around, sending her bread flying and the plate crashing to the floor.

"You big ape! It's you that's changed, not me! You've gotten fatter!" Shock over the broken plate had added heat to her retort.

"Hee hee," he crowed, grabbing her again and pulling her close as her hands rose up flat against his chest. "What's this? Fightin' me off? You don't think you can stop me, do ya, little Liddie, little birdie? Go ahead, fight me off! Maybe you can. Fight!"

Against her better judgment, she tried to push him away. As he yanked her closer, she pushed against him with all her strength.

"C'mon, little flea weight. Where are ya?"

At last, she gave up and went limp. He hurled her away from him, dashing her ribs against the counter.

Catching herself, she stood holding her side. She glanced toward her drawing board and then quickly away, lest he learn from her eyes the idea of destroying the painting. Looking for Girlie, she located her under the table, where the dog was rolling her eyes toward the door. When Lydia opened it, the dog streaked out.

"Get over here and feed me, woman!"

She filled a plate with stew and set it in front of him with a spoon, ignoring the bread on the floor. He was already guzzling it down as she brought him a glass of water. When she started for the door, he stopped her.

"I want some money out of you, ya hear? How come you ain't brought no money in lately?"

She tried to think. "I'm saving work for the next show. You know I get good sales at the art shows."

"Well, I ain't waitin'. I want ya to get yourself down to the Doc's place, and take your work along. Talk him into buyin' a painting or two. And charge him plenty. He's got it, the old miser."

Lydia glanced away, her heart speeding at the thought of actually walking up the doctor's path and knocking on his door. She looked back at Bill, who was grinning. He knew how hard it was for her to approach strangers.

"Well, I can try, I guess," she said.

"You damn well better do more than try!"

★ ★ ★

Wispy fog had moved in, dulling the sunny day as Lydia Bird stepped outside and crept through the high weeds around Bill's car. Then, sighing as if heading for the dentist, she set forth down the overgrown road. In her arms, she carried four rolled-up paintings in a large plastic bag, the smaller ones inside the larger ones, and each roll tied with string. She held them gingerly, careful not to crush or kink them.

Once, when Jonas had picked her up on the road, he had told her that the Doc was friendly and kind to everyone. She now recalled his words. But she and the Doc had never even seen each other. Now, uninvited, she was just going to show up at his door? And worse, coming like a beggar, peddling her work?

Besides, what if he didn't buy a painting? Even a polite man could say, "No, thank you." She would have to go home to Bill without any money. What would he do then?

She was reaching the bottom of the road too soon, even though she had slowed her steps coming down. Trembling slightly, she forced herself on, up the path to the cabin. After a quick glance toward the redwoods that she had loved when she lived here, she stepped up onto the porch. At the door, she raised her knuckles to knock—just as it suddenly opened inward. She nearly fell forward, clutching her load.

"Whoa, watch out there! Are you alright?" The Doc was reaching out his arms for her and grabbing at the bag of paintings.

"Don't. Please don't hurt these." She lifted them out of his reach.

"Paintings! Oh, you must be Lydia! Come in. I'm happy to see you!"

With her heart pounding, she bobbed her head and took a cautious step into the room.

"I've often thought of you up there," he said, "and hoped you were okay. I should have come up to visit, but, to tell the truth, I didn't want to run into Bill."

He led her over to his table, which he hastily cleared of newspapers.

As she spread out the paintings, he said, "I'm sorry for scaring you out there. Actually, I was a little scared myself. I opened the door, and there you were!" He chuckled, bending to see past her hair to her face. Then he turned to the paintings. "Ah! These are beautiful! Thank you for bringing them down, Lydia!"

"I hoped you would like them," she whispered."

"I love them! They're more real than photographs. Real in a different way. I can tell that the painter really knows these flowers. They're captivating. Look at these—are they orchids?"

"Wild iris," she said softly.

"How in the world do you do this, Lydia?"

Sneaking a look at the man's reddish beard and crooked nose, she just shrugged. Then she laid out the painting of blue violets emerging from grass and turning as if searching for light. It was one of her favorites. Another was a thistle, with soft, hazy lavender blooms and a warning—sharp thorns.

"Scotch Thistle," she told him.

Then wild pea—mostly a tangle of vines, but a pleasing tangle, busy in itself and still ornamental with its delicate pink and amber flowers.

"These would be perfect for my walls," Will said. "I'm trying to brighten up the place."

"It's beautiful now," she said. Pressing her hair back, she dared a good look around at her old home.

"Well, I'm working at it. How much will you charge me for three paintings, that small one and these two large ones?" He had started carefully rerolling the remaining sheet.

"You could just pay me what you think they're worth," she said.

"I have no idea what they're worth. I don't think I've ever bought a painting before. Would a hundred dollars be okay?"

She paused. She had hoped for more, but saw that a hundred would have to do. "Yes, that's enough."

Taking his wallet from the counter, he said, "I've just been to the bank. I have a couple of hundreds in here, and enough twenties to make the third hundred."

As he counted out the bills, she lifted her face to stare at him.

"Is something wrong?" he asked.

"I thought you meant a hundred would pay for them all."

Now he was pressing the money into her paint-stained hands. "Lydia, they're worth three hundred dollars, and one day they'll probably be worth more. I think you have a rare talent. You seem to know the flowers intimately. You almost speak for them."

"Yes," she said, nodding. Then, quickly accepting the bills and thrusting them into a skirt pocket, she retreated again behind her hair. But the man kept ducking his head to see her face.

"Amy Schumann has a lot of beautiful plants in her house," he said. "You ought to get together with her. Can you do that?"

"No," she said. "I don't know her." She glanced toward the door.

Will seemed to be watching her now. "Lydia," he said gently, "are you alright, living up there with Bill Santone?"

She looked toward the door again. "Yes, I'm alright. Thank you for the money, Doc. But I have to go now."

"It's Will," he said. "My name is Will."

"Yes.... Will." She picked up the bag with the single painting in it and started toward the door.

Will opened it for her, then paused, staring at something outside. "I'll be darned," he said. "There's a dog out here. I've never seen it before. I think it's a border collie."

He stepped aside so that Lydia could slip past him.

"That's my dog, Girlie," she said. "She came looking for me."

"What a beautiful dog," Will said. "Yes, she looks like a Girlie."

The dog's tail swayed gently as Lydia hurried across the porch and stepped down to the ground. She petted the dog, and together they turned to leave.

Will spoke up again as if reluctant to let her go. "Lydia, if you should ever need help, you can call on *me*. Do you hear? Any time. Night or day."

Already on the path, she paused a moment to look back at him. Then, with Girlie at her heels, she hurried on toward the road.

CHAPTER 9

On a warm Friday evening, Manny Harrington tramped through low brush near the road, humming to himself. He was filled with the pure joy of an upcoming weekend. There was a summery smell in the air, like sunbaked grass with a hint of smoke—a brush fire somewhere. But summer was long gone. Fall wasn't all that bad, he had been telling himself, in spite of school having started again. The stores were loaded with Halloween stuff already, and the kids were getting in the mood, talking about costumes. And for now, it was buckeye time.

Sweating, he paused to brush his hair back from his forehead. He had decided he looked better with side-swept bangs. Annoyingly, his mom had just given him another of her terrible haircuts, cutting the hair so that it fell forward.

She likes me looking like a little kid.

Through trees ahead, he glimpsed the big house of Sal Marino, a lawyer from San Jose. Slowing down, he planned how he could get into the woods behind the house without being seen. All the land there was probably Marino's, so he would be trespassing. He knew of a dry creekbed back in there, where it was easy to walk. It would lead him to the world's best buckeye tree, with branches so low you could pick the buckeyes. It was late, but there should be lots on the ground. Unless deer and squirrels had taken them. Did deer eat buckeyes? He felt pretty sure that squirrels did.

Last fall, he had taken a bag full of big, perfect specimens home to his mother, and she had been so happy with them that he had decided to do it again this year. She had a round, white bowl that she kept fruit in, and in that bowl the buckeyes just gleamed, almost a true red.

As Manny approached Marino's house, all was quiet, with no one moving about. He stepped quickly, passing over a little footbridge. Then he hurried into the woods, sniffing the air. There it was again, a smell he thought he had recognized a minute ago. Somewhere around here, there was something dead. In fact, as he walked, the smell seemed to be getting stronger.

Bright red poison oak lined part of the creek bed, forcing him to work his way through the woods around it. Farther along, he entered the smooth open trail that the water had made. The smell was becoming so intense that he started to hold his nose. What was it? Whew! It had to be something big—a coyote, or maybe even a deer. Curiosity kept him going. Now he could see the low buckeye tree ahead. Yes, there were still some pods on it, split open, revealing the shiny red nut inside.

Holding his nose as he approached the sprawling branches, he was puzzled over something else he saw there.

Ha! It's a shoe!

Someone had thrown an old shoe into the tree. The sole was facing him, with the toe pointing down. There was a rag of some sort behind the shoe. It looked like…, it was a pant leg. And behind it….

He stopped short. Then he turned and started running. Stumbling, crashing through brush that he normally would have gone around, he headed for home.

★ ★ ★

A couple of hours later, with the forest deep in shadow and golden sunlight high above him, Will jogged along Arroyo Road. Panting steadily and resisting the urge to check his pulse, he raised his eyes to that sunlit splendor and then lowered them again. Today the shade felt good, and he was content in his world beneath the high trees. Just starting to sweat, he swung wide to avoid poison oak that reached like a friendly hand into the road.

He had slowed for his walking stretch, grateful for the respite, when he heard a distant siren. At first, he thought it was over on Highway 17. Then he realized it was closer, approaching from behind him on Arroyo Road. He turned to look back. The sound swelled, and then the vehicle appeared: a black-and-white car with *Sheriff* written on its side.

Will stepped off the road to let the car swing past him, its siren growling, red and blue lights flashing. It took him a few seconds to gather his wits. Then another siren sounded, in eerie harmony with the first. Approaching from farther east, it was coming down the Cut-off. He thought that there must be a terrible wreck. Another car sped by, with *Santa Cruz Coastline, The Daily News* printed on its side.

Will opened up into a careful run.

Ahead, the road straightened near a large house, exposing the first gleam of a car. Then a cluster of cars, parked at odd angles off the road. The *Coastline* car was there, the sheriff's car, and a few others. A deputy stood at the roadside, waving other cars past.

Will reached a group of people who were gathered there, and decided to approach a young man, twenty-something, with wavy blond hair.

"I'm a doctor," he said, "I wonder if they need any help."

"I doubt it," the young man said with a grim smile. "No, they don't need any help." Then he extended a hand. "Terry McCall's the name."

Will took the hand and introduced himself.

Just then, he saw an ambulance up ahead, its rear doors open wide toward the woods. Over a rounded knoll, two deputies appeared, carrying a stretcher. It took Will a few seconds to see that the stretcher held a body, covered with a sheet. The figure appeared to be short. A young person, he guessed, which made the tragedy seem worse. A stillness settled over the crowd.

"Was there an accident?" he asked Terry.

But even as he spoke, he guessed otherwise. Not with the sheriff here, and news reporters.

"They found a body back in the brush," the youth said. "I heard some kid almost tripped over it, walking up a creek bed."

Will nodded. His heart, recently slowed after jogging, started speeding up again. The body must have been there for some time, he told himself. One of the unsolved murders that Jonas had told him about.

While the deputies descended the slope with their burden, one of them slipped, causing the stretcher to wobble. The spectators gasped, but then the stretcher stabilized again.

"Male or female?" Will asked.

Terry said he hadn't heard.

"Male, I think," said a young woman with a backpack. "I heard the sheriff say he had no wallet, no identification."

To Will, mention of a wallet meant the body must be an adult.

"They probably didn't examine the body much," said Terry. "They probably just covered it up quick as they could. That's how we did it in Nam. Just hustled them into their body bags."

His blond hair waved back from his forehead, making him look somehow angelic. Will was struck by his youthful innocence, to have had such an awful experience.

I've been out of touch with the world, worrying about myself while these young kids were fighting the wars.

A man hurried past with a camera on his shoulder. Seconds later, light blazed on the ambulance scene, causing a slight ripple to run through the crowd: they might be on TV.

Then the sheriff started speaking: "The victim's an adult male. It's hard to judge his age at this point…, thirty maybe, or older. He was well-dressed, wearing a light tan suit and a tie. Oddly enough, he was found in some low branches of a buckeye tree, about four feet off the ground. So, obviously, he didn't crawl there. He had to be put there."

A soft question rose from the crowd, to which the sheriff replied: "There were no visible signs of injuries…, at least, none that I saw. You'll have to wait for the coroner's report for that." Then another inaudible question, and the reply: "Again, we can't say at this time. I'd guess it has been there a good two months, maybe more."

Will had been in the cabin a little over two months. When the murder occurred, he might have been in bed asleep, a little over a mile from here. He was learning how to deal with fear, standing straight and calm, letting it ring through him while he took a couple of slow breaths.

Why didn't we know about all these murders, George? Even without knowing, you were right. I never should have come out here.

Will became aware that the forest around him had grown darker, pressing in around the lighted area. The ambulance was starting to leave, the red cross on its side glowing in the lights. Then the *Coastline* car followed closely behind it, leaving only the sheriff's car and two others remaining. One was pulling out now, turning north—the wrong direction for Will. Remembering with a jolt how far he was from home, he approached the other car with an arm raised, but it swept him with its headlights and kept going. He looked after it for a bit, then started out jogging.

The going soon became difficult in the dark, with no light on the ground and that narrow strip of sky between the high trees tops fading. Trudging along, he jogged when he could see well enough. Twice, a car zoomed past him, forcing him to move onto the roadside, hoping he wasn't in poison oak.

Then a car moved up quietly behind him, and didn't stop, but continued slowly beside him. Just as his heart started pounding, a voice called out, "Would you like a ride?"

He saw with relief that it was a sheriff's car. As the officer turned on his inside light, Will could see his uniform. The man reached across the front seat and opened the passenger door. "Climb in," he said. "I'm Sheriff's Deputy Hunter. Alan Hunter."

Will nearly collapsed as he stumbled into the car. His need to get home had buoyed him up to keep jogging, but that energy was gone now. "Sorry," he mumbled. "Been on the road too long."

The officer resumed driving, alternately peering at Will and watching the road. "Could you be the retired doctor who moved in somewhere along here?"

"That's me. My name's Will McKeen. How do you know about me?"

"Jonas Schumann mentioned you to me lately."

Will laughed weakly. "I think that guy knows everybody in these mountains. What did he say, that I'm a basket case?"

"No, he said you were a stubborn old coot who risked his life to live in the redwoods."

"Hmm," Will grumbled. "I guess that's about right."

"Would you mind if I check in on you once in a while? I like to keep tabs on folks on my beat."

"Not a bit. I'd like that. I don't get much company."

At Will's direction, the deputy turned onto Live Oak Lane. He parked at the path and offered to walk Will to his door, but Will said he could make it from there.

Then, looking up the dark path, Hunter asked Will if he had a light outside his door.

"No, I don't. But there's wiring on the inside wall. Maybe I'd better look into it."

"I'd recommend it. You don't want to open your door to someone you don't know, especially at night. You might also consider one of those little peepholes in your door, that you can see out of."

"You're right. Another good idea."

Before leaving, Hunter handed him a card with his phone number on it. "Call me any time," he said. "I mean it. I'm a little concerned about you, living out here by yourself. And, Will, don't do any more running in the dark."

CHAPTER 10

Will's phone rang, startling him. It rang loudly, since he had turned up the volume so he could hear it outside. He had just gotten up; it was 7:00 in the morning. When the phone rang again, he answered it, stirring out a husky, "Good morning."

"Will! Is that you? You don't sound very good!"

"Ah, George! I should have known it was you, calling so early."

"Blast, I keep forgetting! It's ten o'clock here. I'm sorry, Willie."

"It's okay, I'm up. I like to run early. How's everything there, George?"

"Everything's busy, as usual. Listen, Willie, I need to know how you're doing with the murders. Tell me the truth. Do you feel safe there?"

Will paused. "Perfectly safe. I've even made friends with the local deputy sheriff."

"Well, what about the murders? Have there been any more lately?"

Another pause. "Not since I've been here. I guess they're still working on a couple old ones that aren't solved yet."

"Will, don't give me any of your BS. There's a new murder, and you know it!"

"George. Oh, sh—. Damn it, George, you trapped me! You did that deliberately!"

"Right near you, too! Cabot's Mill, the paper said! And now you're trying to hide it! Damn it, Will, you don't confide in me! You know I worry about you, and you only make it worse!"

"Let's calm down a little, George." Will took a deep breath to compose himself. "This man was probably killed somewhere else, with the body dumped here in the mountains."

"Dumped conveniently right where you live! And you with a heart still on the mend. Tell me, how's your health through all this?"

"Actually, I feel good, George. I think my general health is better than it's been for a long time. The cardiologist here put me on an exercise program. I jog every day."

"Yes. And, knowing you, you're probably overdoing it. If you dropped over on the road without help, you'd be dead in ten minutes. And another thing, have you bought yourself a gun?"

"George, for God's sake!"

"You needn't be so contemptuous of the idea. I'd feel better about your safety."

"Well, I'll think about it. How about you, George? How's your weight? Are you watching the fats and sugars and salts?"

"I'm fine, and don't try to change the subject. You're the one who had the heart attack, not me. But I have to go now. I have a young girl brought in from a car wreck, and she's losing a leg. It's good you're not here to see her."

"So long, George. Stop worrying about me. You've got enough worries there."

"Think of me once in a while. Don't try to hide things from me. And don't forget to get that gun!"

"Alright. I promise."

They said goodbye. Will hung up the phone and sat staring down at his scrawny bare ankles and feet. The skin was so thin, covering blue veins just below the surface, it looked translucent.

He's probably right about a gun.

★ ★ ★

Jonas Schumann considered himself an extremely responsible young man. He recognized that he was more so than most people around him. That realization had helped to shape his character—sharp-witted, prudent, and hardworking, if a little lacking in humor. Occasionally, he became impatient with people who were less responsible than himself—a group that included nearly everyone he knew.

Jonas was responsible not only for himself and his wife, but also for his landlady and her son. He saw to the repairs and maintenance of Julia's car as well as his own. He advised Julia how to vote, particularly on environmental issues. And it was he who kept an inside wall of her garage stacked with firewood, and had set up a recycling center for paper and cardboard, plastics, metals, and glass. He had also done his best to promote Lydia's art, supplying her with good paper that he bought from the university bookstore and arranging an occasional sale of her paintings. In a circle of pot-smoking friends, he scorned the use of it and tried to convince others that life was better without it.

With a murder occurring near his home, Jonas had assessed the danger to his little community of four persons and decided they were relatively safe. They didn't use drugs, they kept pretty much to themselves, and they didn't travel at night, except for his own trips to and from Santa Cruz, and driving a cab.

When he learned that Doc McKeen was coming out from New York, he had decided to meet his bus, partly out of curiosity, but mostly from genuine concern that the guy be given safe and easy transport to his wreck of a cabin. When he had found the doctor in frail health, that had seemed too great a burden at first. However, like other burdens, once he had grown accustomed to it, it became lighter.

But Will McKeen was alone in his cabin, and so foolishly welcoming to people he didn't know that he continued to be a problem. The fact that Deputy Hunter was keeping an eye on him—as Jonas had requested—did provide some help.

Then came a new dilemma. The Doc phoned him one morning, saying he was considering a climb to the high meadow. Jonas was strongly against it. That would be a dangerous trip for a man recovering from a heart attack. What if he had another one up on the hill? Could he get back down by himself?

But Will explained that he had climbed up there twelve years ago, when he had first seen his land, and the amazing view from up there, looking down over the redwoods, was largely the reason he had bought the land. He wanted to get up there again. Besides, he said, he felt ready for more strenuous exercise.

In the end, Jonas took the responsibility on himself, as usual, insisting that if Will went about the risky plan, at least he should come along.

When the chosen Sunday arrived, they tramped up the road, later than Will had planned. He had hoped to climb in the cool of early morning, but Jonas had appeared just before 10:00. As they walked, Will gazed upward at the dim, hazy sky. From a treetop came a raucous *Crack! Cr-racker!* Then he watched a flutter of black-and-white, a woodpecker's windmilling flight.

"It's a beautiful day," he said.

"It's gonna be a scorcher," Jonas said. The keys on his belt clinked against a metal canteen.

The climb meant more to Will than he had admitted, and he would rather have come alone. He needed to get up there again, where his California plan had begun. Contemplating his life lately, he wondered if his California dream had dissolved away in all his worries and fears, with the local murder the crowning blow. From up on top, he might see things more clearly, and discover whether or not his dream was still there.

After turning off the road, they started up the hillside meadow rising before them. Jonas silently took the lead, causing Will to think that if the boy were watching out for him, he probably should have stayed to the rear.

"Shoot, it's getting hot already," Jonas said, glancing back at Will. "You doing okay so far?"

Will spoke shortly, "Yes. I'm fine."

"How do you feel about the neighborhood murder? Pretty worried?"

"A little worried." Then Will resigned himself to having to talk. "No, worse than that. I'm worried. And I'm amazed that the murders out here came to me as a surprise. I should have done a little research before planning to come."

"My guess is that you just didn't read the papers a lot, Will, as sick as you were with your heart attack."

"True."

Will glanced ahead to Jonas. Pushy and aggravating as the boy sometimes was, he was very perceptive. And it dawned on Will that, through thick and thin, Jonas was always on his side.

Then Jonas had a new idea. "Say, didn't you mention something about new kitchen cupboards for the cabin?"

"Yes, I did. I'm tired of my kitchen stuff all crammed onto a few rickety shelves."

"A woodworker friend of mine, Terry McCall, does all kinds of construction…, porches and things. I bet he could build cupboards for you, and do a nice job."

"I've met Terry! He was one of the people watching when the dead body was carried out of the woods, and we spoke a little. Nice guy." This required a big expenditure of breath for Will as he plodded on.

"*Damn* nice. And honest. He wouldn't overcharge you. We were in a crafts class together at UC. That's how I know him. I'll have him give you a call."

"Good. Thanks for that."

Checking his heart rate, which was faster but steady, Will was cautiously pleased. But he still suggested a short rest.

Jonas offered Will a drink from his canteen, which he refused. While Jonas drank, Will gazed at the hillside above and around him, which from below had looked smooth and golden, but from up here was parched grass covering bumpy, rock-hard ground.

"Something else," Jonas began again. "I've been thinking about how you heat the cabin with those two little electric heaters. We get a lot of power outages in the winter. Tree limbs fall, you know. If you lost electricity, you'd freeze in there."

"Winters are that much colder?"

"Yes, they are. You oughta get one of those little potbellied stoves, flat on top for cooking. You have room in the cabin. You'd have to put it off to the right, to keep the flue away from the madrone tree."

"Hmmm. I'll think about that. I'd like better heat. But I'd need firewood."

"Just small stuff, from downed wood. Get yourself an axe."

"Right. Like Paul Bunyan."

"See there?" Jonas said, "I've given you *two* good ideas!"

"That you have. Thanks again."

Jonas was so pleased with himself that Will chuckled along with him. But then he fell quiet, struggling to catch up with the boy.

As Will climbed, he watched Jonas's legs below his shorts, the calf muscles tightening and swelling. Never, not even at Jonas's age, had he had legs like that. Jonas was leaning slightly forward now and bouncing on the balls of his feet. Will tried the bounce, but it made his calves ache. Also, he was growing annoyed because Jonas was speeding up again.

"There are some huge live oak trees up here," Jonas said. "I don't know if you've noticed. See that big sprawling one over there? It has a couple heavy limbs resting on the ground. You don't have to climb a tree like that. You can walk right up it." He chuckled. "A beauty like that would be two, three hundred years old. It would've been here when the padres were hassling the Indians."

"Hey!" Will shouted.

He had fallen behind again and finally stopped. His heart's pounding was jarring his chest, worsened now by aggravation.

"Oh, damn, I'm sorry! Jeez, what's the matter with me? I keep forgetting." With anxious eyes, Jonas scrambled down to join Will. "You gonna be alright?"

Will nodded, with his head lowered and wet hair hanging around his face.

"If you can make it to the shade over there," Jonas said, "we can sit down and rest for a spell."

Will looked over, nodded, and didn't speak. Under leafy tree limbs they found places to sit, with Will stiffly perching and Jonas sprawling in the dry grass. Will took a few deep breaths and felt better. He wanted to glance downhill, but was carefully saving that for the big moment at the top.

"Feel that?" Jonas asked as a cool breeze wafted by. "That's fog."

"Where? I don't see any. The sky's clear."

"Trust me, it's coming," Jonas said, uncapping his canteen again. After Will drank a few conservative swallows this time, Jonas drank loudly and long.

They rested a while, until Will struck up a conversation.

"How's Amy these days?"

"Good. She's clothes-shopping with her mom today, buying a warm winter coat. I don't think she needs it…, *I* don't have one. A jacket is enough. They've bought her so many clothes. I think they're secretly inferring that I'm too poor to dress her right."

"That's too bad. It's a shame they can't be more accepting of your lifestyle. You and Amy have it pretty nice, so far as I can see."

"They were so impressed with me, at the start. I had a big one-man show at UC Berkeley…. Amy and I were students there…, and she brought her parents to it. Hainsford commissioned me to make a brooch for his wife. I made a gorgeous one, which she loved. I was flattered by all that attention. It was like the rich patrons and the young protégé, you know? But it was degrading, too. Phony as hell."

"Why phony? Just keep working. Keep on impressing them."

Jonas fell glumly silent, finally murmuring, "That's the problem. I can't. One of these days, it's just gonna fall apart."

"What do you mean? They have faith in you to develop your art and complete your master's degree. And you're doing that, aren't you?"

Jonas remained silent, which made Will wonder if he had said something wrong. He suddenly recalled the young man once telling him that he didn't know the whole story.

"C'mon, let's get going," Jonas grumbled, rising to his feet. "This is gonna take all day!"

The climb had gotten harder, the hillside steeper. Jonas had finally dropped back to let Will take the lead. Soon he started calling ahead to him. "Easy now. Watch the gopher holes!"

Will kept stumbling and having to catch himself. The pace had become step-pause-step-pause-step. For Jonas, it was an easy uphill saunter; for Will, an engrossing job. He kept looking uphill, marking their course by trees—a red-barked madrone on the left, and live oaks sloping down to the right. Perhaps he could just glance to the side.

"Don't look back yet!" Jonas shouted behind him.

"I won't. Not yet," Will said, panting.

They were very close now.

Finally, Will reached the spot. "This is it," he declared weakly.

"Okay. Turn around when you want to. I'll see you later, I gotta pee."

Jonas walked off to the side, disappearing from Will's view.

Facing uphill, Will was worn out. With a deep, steadying breath, he turned around.

Yes! What a shock! Yes, of course! It was still here, his whole wonderful dream! With the amazing panorama stretching wide and far below him, he could almost fall off the mountain and drop into that beautiful world—ranges of amber hills and dark green forests, with a slight glow behind the last ridge suggesting light from the ocean. He should never have doubted it. He had made friends here! Jonas, who confided in him about his in-law problem and his planned master's project. And Julia—who would have thought? A pretty Mexican woman and her son. He had made a comfortable home from the run-down cabin he had found here, with more improvements planned. He not only had a life here, he had a future!

Jonas returned. "Well, old man, what do you say? Do you like what you see?"

"Yes." Will laughed. "It's still wonderful. It's even better than before."

He smiled happily at Jonas. Yes, with his boyish grin and straggly hair blowing past his face, Jonas was a large part of the dream.

The young man climbed to stand beside him in the rising breeze and gaze downhill. "You know," he said, "I envy you, having this big, brave goal, and making it come true."

"You have an admirable goal yourself, Jonas. Your master's project. I think it'll live beyond you, like other great works of art."

"That's what I'd like to create, something to be remembered by."

"You and Amy ought to have children. Don't end up like me,

alone and with no family to live beyond you. Children are the best immortality."

Glancing across at Jonas, he discovered that the boy's eyes were shining with tears.

"Jonas?"

"I've got to hand it to you, old man. You put your finger right on it. Maybe you guessed, I don't know." He sniffed as his eyes welled. "Sometimes, I think it shows on my face..., weak-kneed, dumbshit, good-for-nothing, useless! *That's* how I justify the Hainsfords' faith in me! I'm sterile!"

Turning away, he sat down on the grass and snuffled loudly, staring dully downhill.

Will stood watching him, thinking. Finally, he walked over and sat down beside the boy. They rested a short while, with Jonas still sniffing and occasionally wiping at his nose. Below them, they watched a hawk float by, its wingtips lifting in the breeze.

"Sterility," Will said quietly, "is a matter of degree."

Jonas spoke more normally. "Not always, it isn't. Sometimes it's absolute and final. In my case, it's final. I was told not to get my hopes up."

"What is it, low sperm count? Your general health seems so good."

"I've got sperms enough, but they don't move. They're supposed to whip their little tails around."

Will nodded. "Low motility. How much have you got, thirty percent, forty?"

"Less than ten, I think. They hardly move at all. It isn't even feasible to concentrate them." He sniffed again and turned away to spit. "There's nothing left for us but to adopt a kid, I guess. We haggle over it, from time to time. Either that or a sperm donor, but I can't stand the thought of that. Amy doesn't want it either, thank goodness. She wants kids, though, all the more because we can't have any. We're just dragging along, waiting for her parents to start asking questions."

In Will's silence, Jonas went on.

"Remember that night at my place, when you said not to worry about Amy's father because I was gonna win the battle?"

"Yes."

"Well, what do you think now? Still think I'm gonna win? Hainsford's holding all the cards, isn't he? He's got all the aces. And he doesn't know it yet, but I'm void in trump! Ha! Get it, Will? I'm void in trump!"

With his arms around his knees, Jonas started rocking back and forth, laughing at his own irony.

They remained there for a while, watching as over the farthest ridge a row of small puffs appeared, fog starting inland.

CHAPTER 11

The next day, Will walked the streets of Cabot's Mill while his laundry whirled and spun in the machines at the laundromat. He had planned to learn more about the small town, especially where the hardware store was. While he felt certain that he had seen it once, today it was nowhere to be found. He couldn't fully concentrate on the passing storefronts, as Jonas's problems were still on his mind.

He wondered if he would ever have a chance to talk with Jonas again about his sterility. Certainly, he would not be the one to bring up the subject. But adoption could be the solution to the boy's problem. He would like to tell Jonas to take a good look at his own situation. He could have had grown children by now, to help fill his solitary life, if his wife, Gloria, after the three miscarriages, hadn't turned down the idea of adoption. She had said that she and Will would have each other, and that would be enough. Then she had died.

Finally, Will found the hardware store, practically outside of town. He entered and walked around, finding it wonderfully stocked compared to the ones he had known in Queens. He bought himself a welcome mat for outside his door, and, remembering how dry the cabin's air had become, a teakettle. Then he gathered his dry laundry and drove home, with Jonas still on his mind.

He was barely settled in the cabin when a knock came at the door and he opened it to Deputy Hunter. His spirits were lifting as he greeted his friend.

"Alan! It's good to see you! Come on in!"

After Will made coffee, they sat down at his table. The deputy said he had come with news about the local murder.

First, he divulged that the corpse had been identified by using dental records, and that Will would likely read of it in tomorrow's newpaper. "His name was Dennis Wheeler. He was thirty-six years old, and he lived on Tunnel Road, a short distance south of where his body was found. You most likely wouldn't have known him."

"Never heard of him."

"The coroner now sets August first as the approximate date of the murder."

"Good Lord!" Will said. "So the sheriff was right. He guessed that it occurred about two months ago. I moved in on July twenty-eighth, so I would've been here at the time." His first days in the cabin came sharply to mind. "Right about then, I was shut in here like a hermit through scorching hot weather."

"I remember that heat wave," the deputy said, and took another sip of his coffee. The plump-faced young man shaved so closely that his skin shone. "Will, is there any chance you heard music one of your first nights here? Hard rock music, with loud guitars and drums? You're probably too far south. I'm just asking because a bunch of people did hear it."

"No, I've never heard anything like that here."

"We think it came from Sal Marino's place, close by where the body was found. Julia Harrington lives near there, and she remembers the music. Marino works in San Jose, but he has a rock band that plays at his house sometimes. Julia also remembers a lot of traffic on the road, the night of the music. So we figure Marino was having some kind of party. And, get this, Wheeler had small plastic bags of drugs in his coat pockets, probably for sale. So that would have given him a reason for going to the party."

"Well! That all fits, doesn't it?"

"Maybe. It depends on the timing of things. We don't know the date of the party."

"Have you talked to Marino about it?"

"Not yet. He's in Hawaii, at a lawyers' convention, wouldn't you know? He's expected home in a couple days, and I'll find him, either here or at his office in San Jose."

"It sounds like you're on top of things, Deputy."

"Yes, well, we hope for good information from Marino. And there's something else we've found out. Manny Harrington said that on the night of the music, he saw someone he knew on the road near Marino's. Terry McCall. I know him remotely, and I'll look him up today."

"Terry McCall? I've met him. He was one of the people gathered at Marino's when the body was discovered."

"Really? So he was in that area the night of the party, and came back later to watch when the body was found. That's interesting." Hunter took out a small notebook and started writing.

"I liked Terry," Will said. "I thought he was a heck of a nice young man. A Viet Nam veteran, he said."

"Hmm. Did he say anything to you about the body when they brought it out?"

"He did say something. He said they probably hurried it into the body bag, the way they did in Viet Nam. Honestly, I can't believe he'd have been involved in the murder."

"Well…, we'll be looking into it."

"I heard talk in Cabot's Mill about the victim being part of a drug ring in San Jose," Will went on. "Any credence to that?"

"Possibly. We're starting to check out his dealings in San Jose and Santa Cruz. We do know he was manufacturing PCP and growing marijuana. A truckload of plants has been hauled out from his property on Tunnel Road." Hunter paused, staring about the cabin's interior. "I've been meaning to ask you, have you got a gun?"

"No. I've never owned a gun."

"Well, I won't tell you not to get one. But if you do, I'd like to give you some pointers on how to use it safely. By the way, I saw your new porch light. You still should have a peephole in your door. And there are other things to consider. When you're in town, I wouldn't flash a lot of money around. No use making a target of yourself. And don't be too quick to tell people where you live."

"Right," Will said, more subdued. "Good advice, all of it."

Together they moved out onto the porch. "I've been meaning to ask you, Alan. When the body was found, the sheriff said something about it being above the ground, in a buckeye tree. Manny also said that he found it in a tree. Do you have any explanation for how it got there?"

"That's odd, isn't it?" The deputy laughed. "Yes, there's talk of Wheeler having climbed into the tree to hide, maybe, or to pick buckeyes. But nothing like that happened. He was killed by a blow to the back of his neck, crushing the base of his skull. So he didn't climb there. He was found at the bottom of a hill, and Mount Timothy Road crosses the hill right above that spot. With the body in the tree like that, it had to have been tossed down there from Mount Timothy Road."

Will waited silently as the deputy stepped down from the porch and then turned back to speak further. "Something else about Terry McCall..., he lives on Mount Timothy Road." Alan gave Will a meaningful glance.

"That right?" Will asked. "I'd like to ask a favor, Alan. Would it be possible for me to see the place where the body was found? Manny Harrington could probably take me there, but I imagine the area's being protected."

"Yes, well, it's still cordoned off. But we didn't learn much from the site. Too much time had passed, and anyway, we don't think he was killed there. Why do you want to see it?"

"Just curious, I guess. I'd like to see the spot, with a tree that a body could land in."

The deputy thought a bit. "Well, I guess you could go back in there, if I took you."

"If we did it in the morning, we could have breakfast here first. How does that sound? I make a mean omelet, with vegetables and a little bacon."

"Oh, man, that sounds good. I usually just grab a danish and coffee at the office."

"When would you like to do this? I'll have to shop for fresh vegetables."

"How about tomorrow?"

Will laughed. "Really?"

Hunter just shrugged.

"Okay," Will said, "tomorrow it is."

CHAPTER 12

The following morning, fog hung thick and motionless as Will and Hunter stood in front of Marino's house, staring at its dim shape in the trees. Since Marino was still in Hawaii and had no family here, they didn't go to the door, but crossed a small footbridge and then turned into the woods. Hunter took out a pack of gum and offered Will a stick. Will first refused it, then changed his mind, took the stick, and said thanks.

While they chewed the stiffness out of their gum, Will gazed here and there, as if listening. When Hunter raised questioning brows, Will said softly, "I can't get over the silence in the woods today."

"Right," Hunter murmured in reply. "The fog seems to quiet everything. I like the woods this way. Very peaceful."

They started into the gloom, tramping around bay trees and rotting redwood stumps, avoiding red patches of poison oak. At one point, they saw the shape of two pointed ears making a dim V in the fog. Hunter pointed toward it with his chin, but neither man spoke, as one ear twitched, and the doe faded silently into the woods.

Then, in an opening, they stared across a flat creek bed to the buckeye trees, whose tan, crumpled leaves made lighter spots in the fog.

"There probably won't be any buckeyes left," Hunter said. "They disappear. Critters carry them off." He took a long step across the dry creek, landing on the far side.

Will shuffled through leaves, finding no buckeyes, and then followed the deputy. The tree nearest them was low, with sprawling branches. "This is it, I bet," he said.

"Yep. The body was right in there. See where the branches are sort of crushed? He was spread out, face down, his head pointing upstream, and his feet down this way. I saw him there, just before they carried him out."

"Humph," Will grunted. He glanced across the creek, to the side from which they had come. "He lay spread-eagled, you say?"

"Yes. Just like he'd been tossed down from above."

Will gazed up the hill, a steep, rounded hump receding back into the fog. "I think I see a cut across the hill, like a ridge."

"That's Mount Timothy Road. You can't see the road itself, even on a clear day. You just see the edge."

"Judas Priest, that's a long way for a body to have fallen."

Hunter was slightly taken aback. "Yes, but it's steep, with nothing on it to stop him from rolling. He might have bounced a bit. I've been up there, and when you look down here, it's a pretty straight shot."

Will took two steps back over the creekbed. From there he looked sharply across to the low buckeye tree. Then he returned his gaze to the ground at his feet.

"What's up?" Hunter asked.

Will didn't answer. Bending down, he spread his arms slightly, pretending he was picking something up. Then he straightened, swung his spread arms to the right, then swung them sharply leftward toward the low tree.

"What the heck are you doing?" Hunter asked, chuckling.

"I was just thinking," Will said, staring at the tree. "The body could possibly have been thrown into the tree from here, instead of being dumped from the road."

"No, no. No way, Will. A body isn't that easy to toss."

"If you swung it like that, though? He was a small man, I understand, not very heavy. Have you seen any wrestling matches? The real muscle men practically toss each other around like dolls."

"Yeah," the deputy admitted reluctantly. "But to actually pick up a person, and throw him? And he was thrown a few feet off the ground. It would have taken a big, strong man." Then, shaking his head, he checked his watch. "I've gotta get going, Will," he said, turning to start back through the leaves and brush.

Will followed him, lost in thought, until they reached the patrol car. "Say, Alan, I've thought of someone you might have skipped over, when you questioned people around here. Unless you talked to him without me knowing."

"Who's that?"

"Bill Santone. He lives on the hill above my place. Up where the road narrows almost to a trail."

"Santone? I don't think I know him."

"He's a big, powerfully built man with a pot belly and a thick black beard. You've probably seen him in town."

Hunter frowned and shook his head.

"He seems like a buffoon," Will said. "I can't quite imagine him as a murderer. But he's a heavy drinker, and I think he's pretty rough on the little woman he lives with."

"Well, these domestic things, you know, if people don't report it, there's not much we can do about it. But I'll check on Santone, see if he has a record. Does he have a phone?"

"I doubt it."

"To tell the truth," Hunter said as they climbed into the car, "I'm very interested in Terry McCall as a suspect. He was seen on the road the night of Marino's music, and now you say he was there when the body was found. You like him, I know. But he was prowling around on the road by foot. And..., you know, Will..., he lives on Mount Timothy Road."

"How important is it that he lives there? That nice young man can't be a murderer, Alan! That's not possible!"

The deputy replied grimly, "It *is* possible. You'd better believe it."

The disagreement seemed nearly to be causing a rift between them. Rather than let that happen, Will thanked him for letting him see the murder site and invited him back for breakfast, any day he liked.

★ ★ ★

In the shack on the hill above Will's home, Bill Santone sat at the table, slowly drinking from a bottle of bourbon. He had poured a small glass for Lydia, too, which she was sipping while she washed dishes, waiting for a time when she could throw it out.

Bill was staring bleary-eyed into space, and occasionally blowing out a sigh through his lips. Lydia recognized a dangerous mood in him, and tried to keep her distance.

She had been out of the house recently, walking around the hillside meadow, where she had found a few late, pink checker blooms clinging to dry stalks, and prickly, rust-colored teasel. Taking her time and enjoying her freedom, she had made small sketches to be copied later onto good paper.

Today, while Bill slouched over his bottle, she took up her sketchbook and two pencils, as she had before. He watched through slit eyes as she moved toward the door, but he made no sound. Quietly she slipped outside.

Instead of heading toward the meadow, she rushed down the road. She knew Jonas's schedule roughly; he had an afternoon class. As she had hoped, while she waited on Arroyo Road, he spied her there, picked her up, and dropped her off in Cabot's Mill, where she could buy new pencils.

On the way, Jonas told her about the murder and the dead body that had been thrown down from Mt. Timothy Road into a gully, where Manny had found it. It meant little to her. She had never felt threatened when she heard about murders in the mountains. She had enough to dread at home.

In Cabot's Mill, she found and purchased the pencils she needed. Then she left the store and stood in the shadows by the laundromat, where Jonas would look for her on his way home from the university. But she soon spied Naomi, a woman she knew and trusted.

Naomi gave her a ride to Will's road, where Lydia thanked her and stepped out of the car. She hurried up the hill. Entering the cabin with trepidation, she found that Bill's drunken stupor had turned venomous.

"You bitch! You were down there with Jonas, weren't you? Shootin' off your hateful mouth about me!"

Mystified, she admitted that she had spoken with Jonas.

"What about?" Bill shouted.

"What does it matter?" she dared to ask.

He gave her a slap that sent her flying back against the table. "Speak up!"

"He told me…he told me there's been a murder somewhere around here," she cried, covering her red cheek with her hand. "He said it was one of the crazy murderers. He killed the man and threw his body down over a hill, so it landed in a tree. Honest, in a tree. That's what he said."

Bill grew silent, staring at her for long seconds. Then he straightened, and stepped to the table, where he sat down. All the tension seemed to have gone out of him. With his shoulders relaxed, he sat looking dazed.

When Lydia started moving about again, she watched him secretly. He was brightening. Something about her description of the murder had made him happy.

"Grab me a beer, Liddie!" he finally called out. "And get one for yourself!"

CHAPTER 13

High on the hill above Will's cabin, Bill Santone stood working on his car. In the autumn warmth, which folks were calling an Indian Summer, he had stripped to his waist. That was a mistake, he saw now, because he was drawing bugs. He kept having to slap himself and chase a swarm of gnats that hovered around his face. His white shoulders and belly shone with sweat and greasy black handprints.

Here it sat, his most prized possession. Although he started it frequently, he hadn't driven it off the hill for over a year and a half, allowing two summers' growth of grass and brush to accumulate around it. Worse, part of the brush was poison oak, to which he was highly allergic. He didn't dare try to clear it. Since the road was overgrown, his car was marooned. Groaning at the thought of it, he checked the dipstick and then wiped it on his pants.

Now he had picked up dirt on the dipstick! In frustration, he balled a fist to pound the hell out of the fender. But he paused with his fist raised, hearing a faint rustle from the trail below.

He listened sharply. Dog, coyote, or deer, taking an unaccustomed trail? No, it was two-footed, and not bothering to be quiet. He decided to bring his fist down on the fender after all, just to watch the effect. BAM!

Silence. The intruder hadn't run away. He had to be waiting below, behind tall brush, listening.

Then the footsteps resumed, closer.

"Hello, up there!" a man's voice called. "I don't want to startle anyone. It's Deputy Hunter. I'm coming up to talk a little, that's all."

Bill's thoughts roiled, shooting here and there with fright. The cops! Then he found that his anger was saving him from being really afraid. "Over here, Deputy. Over here beside the car."

"Are you Bill Santone?" Hunter asked.

"That I am."

"I'm Deputy Alan Hunter…, uh, from the Sheriff's Department."

Bill perceived that the sight of his half-naked body had made the deputy stammer. The man was pale and sweating. Could he be scared himself? A happy thought. Bill saw that Hunter didn't want to extend a hand, but he was so steeped in good manners that the hand came out anyway. Bill gave it a hard, lingering squeeze.

"What can I do for you, Deputy?"

"Well, whew, hot, isn't it?" Hunter looked at his own greasy hand, then hiked up his pants. The gesture led Bill's eyes to the holstered gun on the deputy's belt. "I was wondering if you could shed any light on events around here last July twenty-eighth. I'm investigating the murder of Dennis Wheeler. I've talked with most of the local residents, but I missed you somehow."

Still holding the dipstick, Bill cleaned it with his fingers and thrust it back into its slot. "Who put you onto my trail?"

Hunter paused to think, and then answered. "Nobody, actually. I've seen you in Cabot's Mill, and someone told me who you were. Now, if you could answer a few questions…. Do you remember where you were and what you were doing on that evening? July twenty-eighth?"

The fool said it again. As if it mattered.

Bill had turned his attention to the fraying tape around his radiator hose. "Yeah, I ate my dinner and took a crap. Like always. How the hell do *I* know? Do you know what you did on July twenty-eighth?"

Hunter's face stiffened. "Yes, I do. I took my mother to dinner. I know it's a long time back, but I'd appreciate it if you'd be more helpful. Do you remember hearing Sal Marino's band playing at his house any night this summer?"

A twinge of fright, but Bill kept busy, brushing acid corrosion off the battery with his fingers. "I mighta. I've heard his music three, four different times this year."

Hunter paused. "Not way up here. You can't have heard it this far away."

"The hell I can't. I can stand up here and hear voices down on the road. They come floatin' up on the breeze. I hear traffic right now over on Highway Seventeen. Do you?"

The deputy lifted his chin, listening, his face blank.

"*I* can," Bill said. "I got real good ears." He pointed to his left ear and leaned closer to Hunter, lifting his thick hair so the deputy could see it. "Damn right, I can hear Marino's band from up here. Even *you* might be able to, if they was playin' now, blastin' the woods with their racket."

Hunter looked slightly confused. "Did you know Dennis Wheeler at all?"

Bill's courage held. "Sure, I knew the little jerk. Anybody around here who says they didn't is lyin'."

"Did you ever purchase drugs from him…, say, a little grass? Did he ever give you a joint?"

"Naw, I got no use for any of that shit. I know what's good. I got a bottle of it inside the house right now…, bourbon. Do you like bourbon, Deputy? How 'bout you and me goin' inside and havin' a little snifter?" He grinned, watching Hunter flinch.

"No, no. I'm on duty. Just answer my questions, please. About the music, can you remember ever walking up Arroyo toward Marino's at night, and hearing his band playing?"

Bill heard his mouth start off on its own, skirting the danger. "Are you kiddin'? I avoid that damn music! I can't even stand it from up here! It's ugly as sin, to begin with, and they pump it up so with their damn speakers. You oughta get on them for disturbin' the peace, 'stead of comin' up here to badger me!"

"Have you ever been to Wheeler's house?" Hunter asked, more quietly. "Do you know where he lived?"

"Sure, I know where he lived. Everybody did. I never *been* to his house, though, and he ain't never been to mine."

The deputy's next question was very important. Bill could see this in the sneaky, careful way he asked it. "How long is it since you've been on Mount Timothy Road?"

Bill gave it its due importance, standing upright and looking Hunter in the face. "It's been a while. I used to have a friend over in Big Tree, but he died, two, three years ago. So I got no reason to go back in there."

"And the name of the friend?"

"Jack Thompson, poor soul. Rotted his liver with booze." Bill was so happy to have a true statement for the deputy to check on that he had trouble looking sorrowful.

Hunter took out a little notebook, wrote Jack's name in it, and put it away again. Bill saw that he looked discouraged, having come all the way up here for practically nothing.

Then Hunter glanced at the grass and weeds around their legs, and frowned. "Say, you've got a regular fire hazard here, you know that? You'd better clear a good-sized space around the house. Do you always park your car in this stuff? A hot exhaust pipe can touch it off, you know, especially when it's dry like this."

Bill looked around obligingly. "You're right. I guess I better do something."

Then Hunter started parting the weeds to locate the car's front bumper. He was searching for a license plate where there was none. Bill's sweat broke out anew.

"No license plate?" In Bill's silence, Hunter waded through the weeds to the car's tail end, and pushed grass away from the plate that was there. "Ah, here it is. Good. Just checking." Hunter pulled out his notebook again and wrote the number down.

The plate was from Will's truck, and that smart-ass deputy was going to trace it!

Bill was so frozen with shock that he almost jumped to get out of the way as Hunter brushed past him.

"I thank you for your time, Mister Santone."

The deputy headed for the trail, notebook in his hip pocket, where Bill could have slipped it out if he didn't know better.

"I'll probably be seeing you again before long," Hunter called back. "Let me know if you hear anything more about Wheeler, would you? I'd appreciate it. And...," he paused to glance back at Bill, "get this brush cleared up. I'm not kidding. I have to report it to the fire department."

As the deputy started down the hill, Bill lifted a hand to give him a sissy-like wave.

★ ★ ★

As Bill turned the ignition key and pumped the gas, he had his bottle of courage in his left hand. The engine sputtered a bit, and caught. She was rarin' to go, the pity of it all. It was a sorry day as Bill dried his eyes with his hand and tilted the bottle up for another swig. As he stowed the bottle beside his seat, the engine faltered and died. He turned the key again, pumping the gas harder this time. She was running now. He rammed the stiff gears into reverse and let out the clutch. The car leaped backward into the weeds and died again.

There were gas fumes now. She was flooded. Bill paused for another two gulps and pressed the key, flooring the gas pedal and keeping it there. The car coughed and roared, clearing herself out. Then she spun back to the right as he yanked the steering wheel down. When he shifted into low, she shot forward like a hay mower through the weeds, now swinging left as he aimed her eastward toward Highway 17.

"Ride, you sorry bitch!"

The crunching of weeds made him laugh and scared him at the same time. No car could plow through this, but she was doing it, her wheels spinning now, then lurching on again. As he reached for his bottle, the car plunged into an overgrown dip that he had forgotten was there, nosing down so steeply that he banged his forehead on the steering wheel. Then the car reared up the other side, throwing him backward, and his lap was soaked with booze.

Heading for the trees, he turned the wheel to avoid a looming oak, and hoisted what was left in the bottle for a last hasty swig. As he picked up speed, the car backfired. Then it careened off a redwood stump and plunged into poison oak. There was a hot engine smell now, and the temperature gauge was climbing so fast that he could see the needle rise. A puff of steam rose from under the hood.

The car lurched through a dense wall of leaves and crashed at last into a eucalyptus trunk. BANG!

With a cricking sound, the windshield had shattered into a spider web held together by plastic. The hood was crunched back nearly to the windshield, blinding Bill. But he couldn't have seen what he had hit anyway, with steam and smoke pouring out as the car died for good.

"Woo hoo!" Bill laughed softly, with blood in his nose and mouth.

Then he cried.

CHAPTER 14

Will's first rain in California arrived at night. As he listened to it in bed, the light, steady patter on his roof was soothing. A rich, evergreen smell filled the cabin, and the air seemed softer as he lay peacefully in the dark.

Gazing up at the ceiling, he thought of the tree right above his roof. It had a Spanish name, Jonas had told him—*madrona* or madrone. Tonight its big, glossy leaves were freshly washed and dripping. He could imagine their relief, finally losing their coat of summer grime that until now had been only speckled by mist. Occasional gusts of wind brought a small torrent on his roof as the branches shook. He had gotten over his annoyance with the limb that had invaded his porch and partially blocked the door. He still meant to cut it back, but less drastically. Jonas had said the tree produced fragrant, white blossoms in the spring, and soon, at winter's approach, red berries that could actually be eaten. A jewel of a tree, Jonas had called it, the gem of the forest. Will felt richer, adding to his collection of prized trees this colorful madrone practically wrapping itself around the cabin.

He was about to drop off into sleep, when he was jolted awake. There was a noise outside. Someone was scurrying up his path! He sat up, and when the footsteps sounded on his porch, he was on his feet with his heart pounding.

Then a small voice spoke outside the door: "Don't be scared, Doc. It's just me, Lydia. Please let me in, I'm freezing!"

Will unlocked and opened the door to the small, dark figure that rushed past him so fast that she wet him with her streaming clothes.

"My God, Lydia, you're soaked! You don't even have a coat!"

"I know," she sobbed. "I'm so cold. I have to keep going, though. I think he's coming after me! I'm sorry to put you in danger, but I have to beg a little money." She stood hunched, hugging herself and trembling.

Will grabbed the comforter from his bed, wrapped it around her, and held her in his arms. They stood locked together while Lydia grew quiet.

"Are you running away from Bill?"

"Yes, he wants to kill me with his knife. I had a little money I was hiding, and he found it. He started after me, but then he turned around to grab his coat. I think he's still coming."

"You can stay here for a few days, till you get your bearings."

"No! He mustn't find out you helped me! He'd come after *you*, I know he would. And he's got Girlie! I had to run out without her." She cried softly, pulling the comforter tighter around herself as Will searched for his wallet in the dark.

"I think letting you go is a mistake," he said, dazed. Then, locating his flashlight, he turned it on.

"No!" she begged. "He'll see the light in the window."

Will held the flashlight closer to the wallet to cut off the beam.

"Two hundred forty-five dollars, that's all I've got."

"A hundred is plenty, Will. I'll be earning more. You're saving my life."

He folded it all and pressed it into her hand.

"Lydia!" He had caught sight of her in the dim light. Vivid colors, red and orange, were smeared in her wet hair and running down her face. "What happened to you? You look terrible!"

"Bill squeezed my paint tubes over my head. Then the rain.... Oh, I'm dripping on your good floor!"

"My God!" he exclaimed. "How you look! You can't leave like this. Go step in the shower! I'll find you some dry clothes."

"I don't have time!"

"You *do* have time," Will insisted. "Bill doesn't know you're here. And you'll be safe in my truck. I'm taking you to town."

"No! No, I'll meet Jonas on... on Arroyo Road. At ten-thirty. He drives the night shift at eleven, and he'll stop for me."

"Jonas is picking you up? Why didn't you tell me? Thank goodness for that."

Checking his watch, he saw that it was ten-twenty. In the near darkness, he scribbled his phone number on a piece of paper. Reaching to the wall hooks, he took down his new raincoat. He thrust the paper into a deep pocket, and they added the money to it.

"Take off the bed cover now," he said, "and I'll give you my warm robe. You can put the raincoat on over it."

Without protest, she worked her arms into the robe, then into the raincoat, which fit her like a waterproof tent that reached nearly to her ankles.

"That'll do, I guess," Will said. "Damn it, I knew I should have bought an umbrella!"

"Will, please, could you try to help Girlie? He'll hurt her. He won't feed her."

"I'll try."

"You mustn't ask him for her, though. You can't even know that I'm gone! But if you see her somewhere down here, maybe on the road—"

"Absolutely. I'll watch for her," Will said. "Where will you be? Call me. You've got my number in your pocket. Can you support yourself, Lydia?"

"I have friends. I'll be alright. Watch out for yourself, Doc! I'm afraid Bill will come after you!" Will buttoned the top of the coat, drawing the robe collar higher around her neck, and they turned to the door.

On the porch, they stared into the darkness. There was no sign of Bill. In the faint light, Will saw that this side of Lydia's hair was streaked ghoulishly with yellow and green. With slitted eyes she looked toward the hill muttering, "Damn him! I hope someday all the misery he caused me comes back on his own hide!"

With a whispered goodbye, she left, vanishing almost instantly into the rain.

Back in bed, under a dry blanket, Will lay sharply awake. Where would she spend the night? Probably no bus would be leaving Santa Cruz until morning. Why hadn't he written her a check for more money? Should he contact Hunter about Santone having driven Lydia out of the house in fear for her life? The deputy hadn't seemed much concerned about domestic issues. And although Lydia was terrified, she didn't seem hurt.

Then Will remembered Jonas, and found some relief. The very thought of his picking her up restored some sanity to Lydia's plan. Fixing his thoughts on Jonas, he finally found peace and fell asleep.

The next morning, Will was up at six o'clock, but waited until seven-thirty to call Jonas, thinking he would have returned by then from driving his night shift.

Jonas answered sleepily. At Will's question, he fell silent, then became quickly alert.

"Lydia? On the road? What are you talking about, Will? I didn't even drive last night! I haven't seen her in over a week!"

CHAPTER 15

On the evening after Lydia's escape, Will had dinner with Jonas and Amy, seated at their kitchen table. He picked worriedly at his food as he related to them the events of the previous night, then gave up and laid down his fork.

"Jonas, where did Lydia come up with the idea that you would pick her up on the road?"

"She didn't exactly make that up," Jonas said. "I *have* picked her up occasionally." Jonas paused to swallow a bite of Amy's delicious meatloaf. "Mostly she went to the laundromat in Cabot's Mill with Bill's filthy clothes. When I drive down your way, I actually slow a little at your road, in case she's waiting there. But I didn't drive last night."

"I was a fool to believe her." Will shook his head at his own gullibility. "When she mentioned your name, it was a such a relief. It seemed like the perfect solution for you to drive her into Santa Cruz."

"Don't browbeat yourself over it," Jonas said. "You gave her money and warm clothes. You probably saved her from pneumonia."

"I wish she had come here to us," Amy said. "She could have made it this far."

"That's right," Jonas said. "I wonder why she didn't."

"Probably she was protecting you," Will said. "The same as she protected me. She was certain Bill would come after me if he found out I had helped her. She wouldn't let me drive her away in the truck. She wouldn't even let me turn on a light in the cabin."

"Poor Lydia," Amy said. "She must have been terrified."

"She thought Bill was still coming after her," Will said glumly.

"Imagine! Then, just before she left, she told me not to worry about her, because she has friends. I think she was just placating me, so she could get out and run."

"There's some truth in her having friends," Jonas said. "The artists around here know her, and there are a lot of them. She might be with some of them right now. And another thought…, Bill brought her here from somewhere near Los Angeles. If she can make it that far, she might find old friends down there. She's got money, so she can take a bus."

Amy lifted her head with a new question. "Will, what if Bill finds out you helped her escape? What will you do if he *does* come after you?"

Will shook his head. "I don't know. Try to bluff my way out of it, I guess. What I ought to do is tell him what I think of him."

Jonas stopped eating and straightened to look at him. "I don't think I'd advise that."

After dinner, while Amy tended to the dishes, the two men stepped into the studio corner of the kitchen, where Jonas turned on the small high-intensity light over his workbench.

A card table beside the bench was covered with drawings of his planned master's project—a large, complicated urn.

Will whistled in admiration as he studied the drawings. "This looks to me like some kind of spaceship, or a rocket."

"You're right! That's exactly what I intend it to be," Jonas said, brushing back his long hair and seating himself at the workbench. "I plan to have a smaller vessel hanging inside it, maybe of pewter, that holds the person's ashes. It's a canopic urn. The ancient Egyptians used them to hold the entrails of a dead person. I'd plan for ashes, of course."

Will leaned closer over the largest drawing. "What are these sloping sides made of? You've drawn them with a sort of rippled surface."

"Yes, they're actually like that. Here, I'll show you one. I've got them all here." Jonas leaned down to take a rectangular bronze slab out of a drawer. It was nine inches by three, tapering a little at one end. "I have six of these babies. I poured a big sheet of molten wax outside on a windy day, and it took on this beautiful texture. Talk about serendipity! I was really happy with that. Then I cast it in bronze, cut the bronze into these six pieces, and made them all uniformly concave. These will be bay doors, like on a rocket, hinged at the bottom so they open outward to reveal the pewter vessel inside."

By now, Amy had quietly joined them, and was standing by Will to peer over Jonas's shoulder. "I'd like to see that, Jonas. Please? I know about your bronzes, but I haven't seen them…."

"Amy…, not now." With an irritated look, Jonas turned away from her. "You wouldn't understand this stuff."

Will gave him a sharp look. "She knows at least as much about it as I do."

Jonas sighed as he lifted the piece higher between him and Will. "Okay, Amy, here it is. Take a look."

She leaned forward to peer closely at the piece, reaching a tentative finger to touch the rippled surface. Then she turned away, and left them without another word.

Will frowned. "What was that all about, Jonas? You should be glad she's interested in your work."

Jonas sagged, leaning back in his chair. "I don't know. I'm just so engrossed in the project right now. I'll show it to her later. Now, do you want to hear about my plans, or not?"

"Yes, you know I do."

"Well, anyway…, I intend the rocket to carry the person's ashes. And not only the ashes, but also the spirit. I need an idea, though, for a nose cone that can house the spirit. The rocket will carry the person's remains to an other-worldly place, like a second life."

Will pondered for a few seconds. Then, nodding, he said, "That *is* impressive. But you mentioned having several metals. You've got pewter and bronze…."

"I want silver and gold in the nose cone, and a gemstone or two. It should be beautiful. Let me know if you get any ideas for the nose cone, Will. I'm drawing a blank on that so far."

Will considered it briefly. "I'll give it some thought," he said.

Later, after thanking Amy for the dinner, Will said he was weary and left for home. When he was in bed and nearly asleep, an idea for the nose cone crept into his brain. At first, he thought it was idiotic. Then, more awake, he decided that maybe the idea did have some merit.

Rising quickly, he telephoned Jonas, hoping to catch him before he left to drive his night shift.

"I'm glad I caught you home, Jonas."

"Will? Is that you?" His voice sharpened. "What's up? Is something wrong?"

"No, no, everything's fine here. I've just been thinking about what you said…, that I should call you if I had any ideas for the nose cone. Did you mean that? Because I have an idea."

"Yes, of course, I meant it."

"You're thinking about the afterlife, right? About carrying the person's remains to a new life." Jonas murmured his agreement. "What's more symbolic of new life than an egg? How about an egg shape for the nose cone?"

After a pause, Jonas replied in a hushed, excited tone. "You're right! I can see it! A silver egg that opens, maybe with a top section that's either hinged or lifts off. It should have gold in it, and some kind of gem. I could enamel the inside for color. There are all kinds of things I could do with an egg! Thanks, Will. That's a fantastic idea!"

"I'm glad you like it, Jonas. I feel honored, if I can actually contribute something."

Jonas grew silent, causing Will to wonder if he had hung up. Then he spoke: "I want to apologize for that little scene with Amy. You probably don't realize what my life is like now."

"What do you mean, Jonas?"

"It feels like I'm caught in a trap. My in-laws detest me, and they don't even know I'm sterile. Not yet! What's gonna happen when they find out? Amy just goes along willy-nilly, but I'm suffering, because I'm the one at fault."

"Never! Never think that, Jonas! A good percentage of men are born sterile. Or they become sterile, due to injury or disease. It's not your fault, and it doesn't diminish you as a man." Without realizing it, Will had become loud.

After another pause, Jonas thanked him for the encouragement, but in a dull voice. Then they said goodnight and hung up.

Will lay awake in the dark, thinking about Jonas's situation and becoming furious with the Hainsfords, who were so lucky to have a young man like him for a son-in-law, and were too arrogant and stupid to realize it.

CHAPTER 16

Julia and Manny sat together on their back porch steps while hamburgers sizzled on a nearby grill. They were watching the western sun's late glow sweep up the hills east of the valley. The shadow of the western horizon first cut its dark edge across the bottom trees. Then, as the sun dropped and the shadow rose, the light above it seemed to compress, turning the dry grass and chaparral a deepening amber color, and finally a rich reddish gold.

Julia was happy just to sit and watch the glowing celebration of the day. Manny, seated beside her in cut-off jeans with his arms around his knees, kept claiming to hear the sonar song of a bat. "Hear that? Did you hear that now?"

Julia replied that she hadn't heard a thing yet aside from the squawking jays. Finally, she glimpsed a darting movement, scarcely more than the memory of a tiny shape against the sky.

"There now! I hope you saw *that*, at least!" Manny said.

"Yes," she said, laughing. "I saw it." She glanced over at him, and then away again. Since Manny had found the corpse in the woods, Julia had watched him for any sign of fear or mental unrest. They had talked often about his discovery and the murder itself. He seemed to have taken it in stride.

He's tough for a twelve-year-old, she thought. *He's smart, and he's tough.*

Smiling in contentment, she returned her gaze to the glowing hills.

With a new, grownup stillness about him tonight, Manny sat thinking. He was working, Julia knew, to get Will McKeen invited to their house for dinner. He had started by stating bluntly that Will's truck had been parked outside the Schumanns' for so long the other night that Amy must have cooked him a huge meal.

"She probably realizes the poor guy needs to be fed," Manny said. "Have you ever noticed how thin he is? I've seen him in shorts, and his legs are skinny."

"Oh, now…, skinny! I like to see a man tall and thin. It's healthier than being fat."

"Mom, have you even looked at him? He's too thin. It's no wonder, alone like he is. I bet he eats out of cans."

"Maybe," she conceded. "I wouldn't be surprised." Although she looked serious, on the inside she was smiling. The boy was trying so hard not to be obvious, not to press.

"What he needs," Manny explained, "is some good home-cooked food. Something like your *chili verde*. Everybody likes pork, and you make it so good. Yum, I can taste it now."

"How do you know he even likes Mexican food? Living in New York, maybe he's never eaten it. He might find it too *picante*."

Manny sat unfazed, and soon came up with another strategy. "Well, the trouble is, the poor guy needs to be educated in Mexican food. He's in California now. We could feed him something good, but not too hot. Something like *chilis rellenos*, and use the mild chilies."

"You have a point there. Maybe we could carry a good, big batch of it over to him, along with my special rice."

"Mommm! He came to eat with the Schumanns! Why wouldn't he come here? I want to invite him to our *house*!"

"But what if he doesn't *want* to come, Manny? I think he's kind of shy."

"Not half as shy as you are! You're a real chicken!"

"Oops! The burgers are done. They're probably well done!"

While Julia hurried over to the grill, Manny thought of another argument. "I hope you're not forgetting all he did for us when our car was wrecked. Remember? You were plenty grateful to him then."

"That's true." She rescued the burgers, laying them on a plate. "I'm still grateful."

Back inside, they prepared their burgers with canned chilies, mustard, mayonnaise, and lettuce, then added refried beans to their plates.

"Maybe Mexican food is too much work," Manny said. "We could just have hamburgers like this, and beans. I don't think we'd have to get fancy with him. He's not like that."

"*Muchacho*," she said, starting to see sadness in the situation, "I'm sorry to tell you this, but I don't think I want to invite him here. I'm afraid that if I did, it would just embarrass him."

"What do you mean? He'd come. I know he would!"

"Yes, he'd probably come. He'd feel he had to, to be polite. It would be a stiff, awkward evening, and I'd hate that."

"What are you talking about? Will isn't one of those stiff, snooty people! He's just a nice, easygoing guy!"

"The awkwardness I'm talking about would be between Will and me."

Manny's dark eyes grew anxious. "Well, then, you need to get better acquainted with him! You'd like him, Mom. And he'd like you. I *know* he would!"

She sighed. "The truth is, Manny, he's not a bit interested in me. I've spoken with him a few times, and a woman knows these things. It just isn't there, between Will and me."

"How do you know what he feels? You have to give him a little encouragement! Men are like that! I know how *I* am around girls. If they didn't make the first move, I'd never even work up the nerve to talk to them."

"C'mon, lover boy, don't start telling me about your moves. Let's just eat now, okay? The burgers are getting cold."

The boy kept his eyes on his food as he ate, remaining silent for so long that Julia started to regret having crushed all his careful efforts.

"Manny," she said quietly, "I'm sorry for being so strongly against your wishes. If you really want to invite Will over, I guess I can consider it."

★ ★ ★

That evening after her shower, Julia closed her bedroom window, shutting out the chilly night air. Then she turned on the light at her dressing table and sat down to brush her hair.

Watching her image in the mirror, she decided that she looked ten years younger with her hair down around her shoulders. Still damp, it had a tendency to curl. But as it dried, it would smooth out nearly straight. Not a trace yet of gray. Lifting it above her head with both hands, she fastened it with a clip. Then she applied face cream, followed by a thin layer of makeup. Finally, with a spot of rouge on a brush, she traced the precise shape of her lips.

Staring at her softly lit face, she decided it was not bad for a mature woman; she had recently turned thirty-eight. Her dimpled cheeks didn't sag, and there was no double chin, although the skin was a little less smooth than it had been at age thirty. Or twenty-four….

A memory crept into her mind. A starry summer night on a patio outside a large home, with red bougainvillea spilling over a stucco wall. She had worn a red *roseta* over her ear, with a green and red ruffled skirt and a lacy white blouse. She and Michael, her girlhood sweetheart, were dancing the *jarabe*, a classic dance that she had learned from an old *señora.*

Michael's brother Raymond's mariachi band was playing at a wedding fiesta in San Jose, with Julia and Michael performing the dances. A large Mexican family and their guests were seated at tables around the wide patio. The *jarabe*, a spirited dance of courtship, was performed with rapid steps like the prancing of horses' hooves. Laughing with the gaiety of the dance, Julia had swooped low to lift her circular ruffled skirt and swirl it high in the air. Glancing up, she spied a young man dressed in white, who was standing at a nearby wall. For an electric moment, their eyes met.

Startled, she had continued dancing, now having to concentrate on the steps that previously had come as naturally as breathing.

During the applause at the end of the set, she had retired inside the house with Michael and the band for their break.

When they all returned, she had changed into a long, low-cut, yellow gown, fitted over her hips and flaring below her knees. She had looked for the man in white, but had seen with disappointment that he was no longer at the wall. Soon she located him again, seated now at a table with two male companions. The three young men were wearing what appeared to be white uniforms. Raising her arms over her head, she had arched backward under her clicking castanets, and as she whirled, caught glimpses of that same steady gaze. He had thin, handsome features and sober eyes.

After the performance, she had dressed hurriedly and stepped outside. He was waiting for her in the shadows. She had seen the pinpoint glow of his cigarette, and watched it drop to the ground as he put it out. Then he had moved forward into the light and introduced himself in a shy, formal voice that was unmistakably English—Thomas Harrington, with the British Merchant Marine, on shore leave from a freighter docked in Oakland.

The bedroom had grown dimmer as Julia turned away from the mirror. Outside the window it was dark. She rose sighing, turned out her light, and walked into the living room, where Manny was watching television.

He was sitting on the couch with his arms crossed behind his head, engrossed in a basketball game. Taking a seat beside him, she pretended to watch the game. But her thoughts were traveling out into the night and down Arroyo Road. Without telling Manny, she was making a decision.

Her heart quickened at the thought of actually walking up Will's path and knocking on his door to invite him to dinner. She realized that it might be easier if Manny went with her, but, considering the boy's overblown enthusiasm, she decided that she had better go alone.

Finally, on a morning while Manny was in school, she found her courage. While she drove down Arroyo Road, she practiced what she would say. When she reached Live Oak Lane, Will's private road, she encountered a parking problem. Three trucks were taking up the parking area—Will's own and two others—one of which nearly blocked the path. With some difficulty, she drove past the trucks and parked farther up the road.

After squeezing by the obstructing truck, she walked up the path to find the cabin in turmoil. Two men were on the roof, measuring, while from inside the open door came the noise of heavy thumps and men's jovial voices.

When she reached the door, Will came to meet her, stepping over boxes and trash.

"*Julia!* Is that you?"

"I'm…, I'm afraid I came at a bad time, Will."

"No, no. It's a good time! I'm having my new stove installed! Come in and join the melee. Did you come to visit me?"

Surprised by the warmth of his welcome, she gathered her wits to speak. "Well, no, not exactly…."

Will stood facing her, with his head leaning slightly toward her.

From staring at his shirtfront, Julia lifted her eyes to his, which were bright blue and fixed intently on her. She was stymied again.

"I've been wanting to know you and Manny better," he said. "Has he forgiven me yet for running you off the road?"

"Oh, yes." She nearly laughed. "He's come completely around. He's been asking me to invite you to dinner."

"Really? Is that what you're here for?"

"Yes. We'd like you to come over and have dinner with us."

"Wonderful! Thank you! When shall I come?"

After they settled on Saturday, Will asked what he could bring.

"Just bring yourself, Will." Her dimpled smile was more relaxed, and less shy. "And a good, big appetite."

★ ★ ★

The next morning, Will shopped in Cabot's Mill's good hardware store for a hatchet, an axe, matches, and a bundle of firewood. Later that day, another workman arrived, who built a brick hearth for the stove, setting the bricks without concrete and encasing them in a snug redwood frame.

The following evening, while early fog promised a chilly night, Will built a fire. First, he made a bed of crumpled newspaper and dry kindling. Then he touched a match to the paper, gratified to see the first glow spring up into flame.

Why didn't I do this months ago?

He carefully built up a larger fire, watching the needle rise on the heat gauge that had been attached to his stovepipe. When the fire was burning steadily, he hurried outside to see the miracle of smoke rising from his flu into the foggy air. Back inside, he chose his "over-nighter," the heaviest log, and positioned it carefully on the burning wood.

Next came a delight that he hadn't known of late—a genuinely warm evening in the cabin. But the best part came while he lay in bed, listening to the wood's gentle snapping and popping until he fell asleep.

★ ★ ★

Two days later, in the morning, Will had just eaten his breakfast eggs and toast when a knock came on the cabin door. He opened it to a young man with a shy smile and wavy blond hair.

"Hello, Doctor McKeen. I don't know if you still remember me...."

"Terry! Of course, I do! We met on the night Wheeler's body was brought out of the woods. It's good to see you! C'mon in."

Terry bobbed his head politely as he stepped inside. While Will poured him a cup of coffee, he spoke in a slow, gentle voice. "I've heard you're making improvements in the cabin, Doc. I hope they don't include new cupboards. Jonas said I should stop by and see if I can build them for you. I do all kinds of woodwork."

"Good! I've spoken with Jonas, too, and I've been planning to contact you. How've you been, Terry?"

"Not too good." He was unsmiling. "I mean, I'm okay, but I'm getting worried. I'm being questioned by the cops about Wheeler's murder."

"Really?! Deputy Hunter mentioned your name. Are you connected with the murder in any way?"

"I'm afraid I am connected," Terry said. "I went to Marino's party that night. Wheeler wasn't even there. Actually, I was there to drum up business. I do that sometimes, at parties and get-togethers. I did pick up one small job, replacing some rotted window sills."

"And for just being at the party, you're considered a suspect?"

"Well, yeah." He shifted his work boots uncomfortably. "I was so darn truthful, I admitted once buying a little pot from Wheeler. My wife used it for a neck sprain. It eased the pain and stiffness. I guess you would frown at that, being a doctor."

"Not necessarily. I know it can be helpful. Is that all the sheriff's office has on you?"

Terry took a long breath. "No, it's worse than that. I built a small deck for Dennis over a year ago, and he never paid me in full. I billed him for the materials first, then for my labor, and he only paid me for the materials. When he was killed, I was still trying to collect the rest from him."

"So at the time Wheeler was murdered, he owed you money."

"Right. I hoped to find him at Marino's party. I wanted my money from him, and that's a motive. As if I'd kill a guy over eight hundred bucks. Or kill anyone, ever."

"Surely the truth will come out, Terry. I don't think the cops could get a conviction for a motive as thin as that. And there's your reputation to be considered. Deputy Hunter thinks well of you. But he has to look into all their leads."

"Thanks for that, Doc. That's good to hear." Staring at the walls, he gave a low whistle of appreciation. "Lydia Bird's paintings! Wow, these are good. I've never seen any of these, but I recognize her work."

"You know her, then?"

"Sure. I see her at the art shows all the time. She sells her work, and I sell wooden bowls and such."

Will paused. He was about to ask Terry if he knew where Lydia was, but decided it might be safer for her to keep her disappearance secret. Instead, he led Terry to his small kitchen sink and counter, where the shelves below were cluttered with canned food, cereals, dishes, and cookware.

Terry raised his blond eyebrows as he took it all in. "This is your whole kitchen?"

"This is it…, plus my stove and refrigerator." Will motioned with his chin toward the new appliances. "I hope you can make nice cupboards in this small space. I'll need them clear up to the ceiling too, of course."

"Don't worry, Doc, I have enough room here to make you something beautiful." With that, Terry took out a tape measure, pencil, and notebook, and began measuring.

When he was finished and about to leave, the two men stepped out onto the porch. Will had already given Terry a check for a down payment. Now the young man offered his hand, and Will shook it.

Looking into Terry's eyes, blue and boyishly honest below his light-colored hair, Will decided to trust him about Lydia.

"Do you know anything about Lydia Bird? Do you happen to know where she is right now?"

Terry looked surprised. "No. All I know is, she lives somewhere around here with a big, ugly guy named Bill Santone."

"Not anymore, she doesn't. She used to live with him. But she left him recently, and I don't know where she went. I thought her artist friends might know something about her."

Terry shook his head. "*I* sure don't. You say she just took off?"

"Yes. She ran away on that rainy night last week and disappeared."

Terry looked perplexed. "By herself? How in the world could she make it alone? Unless she has friends to take her in."

"That's been my concern, exactly." They stood together gazing up into Will's redwoods.

"We have our big Christmas Art Show soon," Terry said, "down in that open space below the Santa Cruz courthouse. I'll try to find out if any of the guys know what happened to her."

"Let me know if you learn anything, will you? In fact, I'll try and make it to the show myself. I'd like to see the art work, anyway."

"Great! You can watch for the date in the *Coastline*. When you go, just park in the courthouse lot. We'll be spread out down along the river. We generally serve coffee and hot chocolate, if you're interested. You have to pay for it, though…" He looked regretful.

"That's fine. Hot chocolate would be a treat."

CHAPTER 17

On a chilly afternoon three days later, Will stepped outside the warm cabin with his axe in hand, aiming to replenish his small supply of firewood. Inhaling deeply, he enjoyed the smell of wood smoke in the air—from his own chimney now, although there were many other wood stoves in the mountains.

He had just walked off the porch when he heard shuffling footsteps on the path.

When he looked toward the sound, he froze.

A bearlike man stepped into the clearing, heavy shouldered and large headed, his thick black hair merging with his beard. It was Bill Santone.

A thought flashed through Will's mind: *Amy warned me about this, and here I am, totally unprepared.*

When Bill saw him, his small black eyes darted between Will and the axe.

"You gonna come at me with that?"

"Of course not," Will answered calmly. "I'm about to chop firewood for my stove." He laid the axe down on the porch. "What can I do for you, Bill?"

"I wanna talk to you. I wanna ask you a question."

"Go ahead."

Bill thrust his beard forward, in the stance of a belligerent child.

"I wanna know if you helped Liddie the other night. Did you take her someplace in your truck, that night she ran down here in the rain?"

Aware of his racing heart, Will frowned as if puzzled.

"No, I've never taken her anywhere in my truck."

"But you helped her get away, didn't you? Dammit, did you give her money?"

"Money? I've given her money for paintings, partly to help her, but mostly because I wanted the paintings for my walls. What do you mean, she got away?"

Santone came a step closer. "You know damn well she ran away."

"She ran away from *you?* Why?"

Santone's heavy black brows furrowed, but he had no reply.

Will asked again, "Why would she do that? Why would she run away from you, Bill?"

Santone looked down, scratched the back of his neck, and came up angrier.

"I wanna ask you a question, Doc," he shouted, nearly spitting out the words. "And I want a good, clear answer outta you!"

"Ask it, then."

"I wanna find Lydia Bird! Do you know where she is?"

"I have no idea where Lydia is. And if I did know, I wouldn't tell you. You know why? Because of how you treated her. You've been a mean son-of-a-bitch to her, haven't you, Bill?"

Stunned, Santone wet his fat pink lips. Then he burst out. "Damn you! I oughta bash your head in!"

"That's just like you. But you're forgetting something, Bill. You're known around here. People know what kind of guy you are. If something happened to me, where do you think Deputy Hunter would look first?"

"You're the guy that sent him up the hill to badger me, ain't ya? You couldn't let me live in peace...."

"I asked Hunter if he had spoken with you, that's all. Now *I* have a question, Bill, and I want a good clear answer from *you*! Did you know Dennis Wheeler?"

At the name, Bill's little eyes widened. "You, you..., you don't ask me about that. You just talk to the deputy about it! He'll tell ya! I'm innocent! I ain't done nothin' to that smartass little jerk! I don't have no use for his pot and other junk, and I don't have no use for him, neither! You stop sendin' the deputy up to me, and don't send anybody else, either! You got your nerve down here, big bucks and all, fancy stove! A rich guy like you oughta have a little pity for guys like me, who don't have hardly nothin'."

"Alright, Bill, that's enough. It's time for you to leave."

But Bill couldn't stop. "I just want to live up there and mind my own business, and I want you"—he pointed a finger—"to stay down here and mind yours!" He bobbed his head to accentuate the point, then turned angrily and started down the path, shaking and nodding his head before he disappeared from Will's sight.

After that, Will sat down on the porch, blowing out a few deep breaths. Waiting for his heart to settle down, he gazed long and thoughtfully at his redwoods, noticing that their sucker growth needed to be cut back.

He finally decided that he had done the best he could with Bill. Taking up the axe again, he resumed his search for firewood.

★ ★ ★

Late that evening, before the time Jonas would be leaving for his night shift, Will telephoned him and described in detail his visit from Santone.

Jonas was shaken by the news. He wondered if he would also be visited, and if he was, how he would handle it.

Will advised him to just tell Bill what he recalled of that rainy night, since, unlike Will, he had nothing to hide.

"We did learn one good thing today," Jonas said. "Bill doesn't know where she is. So, whatever her situation is, she's free of him."

"I hope you're right about that. But I learned something else that bothers me. Bill is angry enough, and wants her back badly enough, that he threatened me. He could become a danger to others as well."

"Yeah. Well, consider yourself lucky." Then Jonas started a new topic, which mildly annoyed Will, who was ready for bed. "Say, Will, I know you have a dinner at Julia's coming up soon. You'd better watch yourself around Julia, if you're not interested in her. She's got her eye set on you."

"Jonas, that's not true! Damn it, you have nothing to base that on!"

"Don't worry, you'll have a good time, and you'll love the food. Julia's a great cook. And, incidentally, she's also a beautiful woman."

"I think somebody should mind his own business," Will said.

Jonas laughed.

★ ★ ★

When Saturday arrived, Will geared up for the event, and when the time came to leave that evening, he was prepared. Recalling Jonas's words, he had decided to be cordial with Julia, but not over-friendly. Hopefully, he could eat and then leave as soon as politely possible.

After parking his truck, he walked through the arched entryway of her house, noticing that the red geraniums were gone, and their ceramic pots were empty and clean. Having assumed earlier that Julia liked red, he had brought her a bouquet of long-stemmed red roses. Also, thinking he should have something for Manny, he was carrying a box of chocolates.

As he waited at the door, it struck him that he had come like a suitor, with candy and flowers. He wished he had time to return them to the truck. But from inside, he heard running footsteps and Manny's voice calling, "He's here!"

The boy swung the door open with a wide grin, followed by Julia, who was still wearing her apron. She looked flushed and slightly rattled as she invited Will to come in.

"I never know what to bring the hostess," he said, handing her the candy and flowers.

"Will! You didn't have to bring us gifts! But these roses are so lovely. And chocolates! You spoil us. I'll dole the candy out to Manny one piece at a time."

"Yeah, while you eat two pieces!" the boy said.

"Manny!" she scolded in mock exasperation as she led Will to the kitchen. "With just three of us, I don't like the big dining room table. We can visit better in here."

Will took the seat she offered him.

While Julia arranged the roses in a vase, Manny poured Will a fruity drink made of orange juice, strawberries, and red wine.

Using potholders, Julia lifted a large baking dish from the oven and set it down on the counter.

To Will, who had little experience with Mexican food, the aroma was tantalizing.

"*Chilis rellenos*," Manny told him. "Stuffed chilies. It's one of my favorites. Know something funny about it? Sometimes people who don't speak Spanish go to a Mexican restaurant and just order 'rellenos.' They don't know it, but they're ordering 'stuffed'!"

The boy laughed, and Will laughed with him.

"Whatever it is, it smells wonderful," he said, trying to spoon a strawberry from his drink. It occurred to him that the chilies might be hot as blazes.

While dinner cooled slightly, they sipped their sangria.

"Jonas told us that you confronted Bill Santone the other day," Julia said.

"I'd say Bill confronted *me*," Will said. "He just showed up in my yard. It was a shock, but it was kind of funny. I was carrying my axe to chop firewood, and he asked if I was going to come after him with it."

"I bet *that* surprised him!" Manny said. "Wasn't it lucky you had the axe?"

Will studied the bright-eyed boy, trying to recall what it was like to be twelve.

"Well, no," he said, "I just laid it on the porch because I didn't want any trouble."

Julia said quietly, "Discretion, Manny…, the better part of valor."

"I know," the boy said. "But laying it down like that was really brave."

"Oh? How so?" Will asked.

"You showed him you didn't need to defend yourself. You weren't afraid of him."

Will adjusted his appraisal. This twelve-year-old was more complicated than he had thought. "To tell the truth, son, I *was* afraid of him. I don't even like him living on the hill right above me."

"Well, then it took even more cour—"

Julia stopped the boy with a pointed look, which struck Will as comical. He had to subdue a chuckle.

Then she changed the subject. "I don't suppose you've heard anything yet about Lydia?"

"No, not a thing. She just disappeared that night. I'm very concerned about her."

"What was she wearing, to run out in the rain like that?" Julia asked.

"She didn't have a coat, just a long dress and whatever she wore under it, all soaking wet. I gave her a warm robe and a big raincoat, but we put them on over her wet clothes. That seems miserable to me now, but I had no choice. She refused to take the wet things off. And I had no umbrella to give her, which I really regret."

Julia stared at him a moment, then spoke gently. "I don't think you have a thing to regret, Will. You did your best for her. Warm clothes and money, Jonas said. Just what she needed."

Will nodded. "Well…, thanks for that."

Then Manny interrupted them, asking his mom when they were going to eat, and Will said he seconded the question.

Julia brought over a large leafy salad from her refrigerator and served it into three bowls. Will noticed the black wisps of hair that had escaped her braid and curved around her face, and as they spoke, he watched her dimples come and go. He recalled what Jonas had said about her being beautiful. *Jonas was right.*

In the baking dish, the tops of long green chilies emerged slightly above molten cheese and tomatoey sauce. Julia spooned out a generous portion on each plate.

Will took a careful bite, thinking it might burn his mouth. It was spicy, but so delicious that he decided he could stand the heat. Glancing up at Julia, he smiled.

"Is it too hot for you, Will? You seem to be enjoying it."

"It's perfect," he answered. "I love this. I've never tasted anything like it."

"I knew it!" Manny said. "See, Mom? You used the Anaheim chilies, didn't you? They're almost too mild." As he spoke, the boy rose from the table and brought back a glass jar of red sauce.

"Yes, I did," she replied, taking the jar of salsa from Manny. "Don't forget my special rice, Will, and try this, too. My own homemade salsa. You can put it on the rice, or on a corn tortilla. But be careful, it's hot."

Will took up a thin, round tortilla, spooned the red salsa liberally onto it, folded it gently as he saw Manny do, and took a big bite. Fire exploded in his mouth as he fell back suddenly into his chair, nearly choking. He grabbed a napkin and pressed it to his mouth, glancing toward the kitchen sink.

"Get him some water!" Julia ordered, and Manny ran to fill a glass and rush it to Will, who sat teary-eyed and desperate.

"He's a real gringo!" Manny said as he thrust a finger into the salsa, stuck it in his mouth, and grinned.

"I'm so sorry, Will!" Julia exclaimed. "It's *picante*, but I thought you could handle it!"

She poured more sangria into his glass. "Here, take something sweet. That's the cure. The heat will soon fade away."

As Will took a few gulps of his drink, then mopped at his eyes, the heat in his mouth did subside. Soon he was able to laugh at himself, although he made no further attempt at the salsa.

As they ate, Julia gradually steered the conversation toward Will's cabin and land.

"You're so lucky to have those beautiful redwoods, Will. I saw them years ago, when I walked back in there with my husband, Thomas. Are they as wonderful as you remembered?"

"Even more so. I had forgotten how massive they are. I can't see their tops, of course, but I know they've grown. Sometimes I just stand against one of those trunks and feel the tree's strength at my back."

"Really?" asked Manny, enchanted by the idea. "I'd like to try that."

"Well, come over. Come and see the cabin. I'm kind of proud of it now. I've decorated it with Lydia's paintings and Amy's hanging plants. And Terry McCall is building me kitchen cupboards. I'll have a custom-made kitchen."

"I'd like to see your little stove," Julia said. "When I came over to talk with you, it was being installed." Then she chuckled. "You had men on the roof and men in the cabin, and the whole place was a mess."

Will laughed. "You're right. My improvements always make a grand mess. The worst time was when the brick hearth was built. You should have seen that. But I sort of enjoy cleaning up. It always looks so good afterward."

Later, when Will was leaving, he leaned toward Julia, paused, and what might have been a peck on the cheek became just a pat on the shoulder.

He drove home with a dish containing the two leftover *chilis rellenos* beside him on the seat, tucked in with dish towels. Smiling in the dark, he steered the winding road carefully to keep the dish from sliding. Why hadn't he just gone ahead and kissed her on the cheek? Something told him she would have liked it. And the boy had called him a gringo, whatever that meant. He would have to look it up in his dictionary.

Meanwhile, in Julia's bright kitchen, Manny was carrying dinner dishes to the sink.

"Mom, Will called me 'son'! Did you hear him?"

"Manny, stop that! Stop scheming! You don't know how embarrassing that is for me."

But as she rinsed the plates, she bent her head to hide the hint of a smile.

CHAPTER 18

On a cloudy day, Amy Schumann walked southward on Arroyo Road. Earlier, she had been crying, but she had gotten over it. Lifting her head, she caught a glimpse of Will McKeen's high meadow, becoming visible through the trees. It was her planned destination, and she knew the way, having been up there a few times with Jonas on wildflower expeditions. On their most recent trip, in the Spring, they had worn waist packs, hers carrying sandwiches, and his, paper cups and wine. She recalled that day as one of the happiest she had known with Jonas.

On the top of the hill, there was a large patch of teasel that grew with heads on stems three or four feet tall. Since it was November, the heads would be reddish brown and covered with tiny barbs in an even pattern that made them attractive in dry floral arrangements. Amy was carrying a large burlap bag to bring home as many stems as she could for Christmas arrangements to sell in Naomi's shop.

Jonas had told her, in that recently authoritative manner of his, never to go up there alone. With every step, she acted out an unhappy rebellion. The thought of him brought tears to the surface again, and once more she wiped them away. Reaching Will's road, she walked quietly around his parked truck, avoiding an encounter that ordinarily she would have welcomed.

During the past few months, Jonas had become increasingly absorbed in his metalwork, leaving Amy feeling left out. Married couples, she had tried to tell him, should share their joys and sorrows, and their projects. But the two of them seemed to communicate less and less. She found it impossible to confess the problem to her mother, knowing that any complaints about Jonas would only bolster her parents' dislike of him.

Then there was the financial problem: Jonas's project was starting to cost them a lot of money. In addition to a proposed base for the urn in bronze, he was considering an egg-shaped silver nose cone that would involve gold plating. Amy had increased her work in the plant shop from two days a week to three, the limit that Naomi could afford to pay her.

Most recently, there had been a new problem, having to do with her engagement ring. After telling her that it hurt him even to look at it, Jonas had suggested that they invest in a small diamond, after all. A diamond! Not only was the idea too expensive, it had come to Amy as a personal blow. She had defended Jonas and his pearl! Stood up to her parents on his behalf! Besides, she loved the pearl ring and didn't want it changed.

As she walked up Will's road, she lifted her left hand to look at the ring, its sculpted shank nestled against the plain wedding band. She had never thought of the rings as cheap. Jonas had used an expensive gold, 18 karat, making for a bright, rich color. She thought back to a happy day when they had sat in a coffeehouse as he made early sketches for the ring on a paper napkin. Tucked away in their large, expensive wedding book, she still had that napkin.

As she stepped off the dwindling road onto the beginning of meadow, she had to watch her step on rough, rock-hard ground. Sparse grass, dun-colored. Any trace of golden hillside was long gone.

Her thoughts flew to the teasel. Would it still be its beautiful reddish brown? Over winter, the rains would turn it a dull gray, but so far there had been only one good rainy night.

From a nearby oak, a crow called harshly, causing her to look up. Then she climbed again, step by step, watching her feet. A rustling sound nearby caused her to lift her head again to listen.

A towhee, she thought, *scratching for seeds or bugs in the underbrush. Even a lizard can make such a rattling in dry leaves that you'd think it was a larger animal.*

Then came a shock—the snap of a dry branch. A thrashing in the brush to her left, and she saw him. He was some forty feet away, peering at her from the bushes on his overgrown road. She stared back. Not actually frightened, she was aware of a problem—he was between her and home.

He's a neighbor, she thought. But her heart started tripping.

Holding a large paper bag in his arms, he stood motionless, his small black eyes fastened on her.

Amy was unable to smile, but managed a nod. "Good morning, Mister Santone."

He didn't reply, but cautiously looked around, his bearded head turning left and right, as if checking the lay of the land. Then his eyes returned to hers, and he started slowly lowering his paper sack to the ground.

Seeing how stealthily he lowered the bag, Amy could feel her heart racing.

She took a step downhill, and then another.

Suddenly, he let the bag drop, which landed with a crash of breaking glass.

The sound startled a cry from her. She watched unbelieving, thinking this couldn't be happening. It was her disbelief that held her motionless, while he was free of his burden and moving.

At last, she came unfrozen and ran, weightless with fright, downhill toward the joining of their trails. He was ahead, disappearing behind trees. He would get there first. Cut off, she paused as he reappeared at the foot of her path.

"What are you doing?" she cried.

Trapped, she turned around and sprinted away. The wrong direction, away from home and uphill. In desperation, she plunged on regardless, buying time to think. But she wore out quickly, and heard his footsteps pounding behind her. After a few horrified seconds, she glanced back and saw his grasping hand.

"No!"

Turning around, she struck out at him with her fists and landed one kick with the toe of her shoe on his knee. As he fell back, she headed for the brush, trying to get around him and head back downhill.

Reaching with one long arm, he caught her blouse.

She screamed, thinking dazedly of Will McKeen, who was too far below to hear. As she wrenched away, the blouse hurt her before it tore, freeing her to run. But after she had labored uphill, the land dropped suddenly, and she couldn't adjust to the change. Getting ahead of her feet, she reached out to catch herself as she plunged forward.

He laughed behind her as she hit the ground.

On hands and knees, she was skidding now, flesh grating, and still she kept falling.

When he overtook her, he forced her down onto her back and pinned down her flailing arms.

★ ★ ★

After Bill was finished with her, he released her to scratch himself.

As he kept on scratching, she struggled away from him. She made it to her hands and knees, and then, shakily, to her feet.

He ignored her, resting with his pants gaping around his dough-like flesh.

She made it away from him, tripping and stumbling as she ran. Then she dashed through brush to the road, hearing no sound behind her. With the narrow road dropping under her, she struggled to keep from falling again.

Jonas! Tears came now. It had taken the thought of Jonas to make her cry. How would he feel when she told him about this? He would be as hurt and angry as she was. He'd be furious, filled with fierce, fiery rage! His eyes would burn with it!

Finally, she slowed down, gasping for breath and hurting now from Bill's roughness. A last look back showed no sign of him.

First of all, she and Jonas would call the police. Moving steadily now, she made her plans. She would testify against Bill, and Jonas would stand with her. Together they would brave the whole miserable ordeal, to see Bill punished.

Below her, Will's truck had come into view. Will would help her, with a fury of his own. Then he would drive her home.

But as she drew nearer to Will's path, she imagined facing him and telling him what had happened. The thought of describing her personal ordeal to him now brought a trace of doubt. She slowed down to think.

Should she even *tell* him about this? Or keep it private, between herself and Jonas? Couldn't the two of them together manage to see it through?

But Jonas had warned her never to come up this hill. She had deliberately disobeyed him. If only she had listened to him! She had brought this on herself!

Gradually, she came to a complete stop.

The thought of her parents had arisen. How would they take this? Could they face a hospital scene and, perhaps, a courtroom trial that dragged their daughter through scandal and humiliation?

Finally, it came to her with a shock that she was actually alone. She couldn't bear to tell her parents. She couldn't even count on Jonas. In his anger toward Bill, he would fight for her at first, but what about a month from now, a year? Would he still see her as his lovely girl? Even now, the two of them seemed to be drifting apart.

And worst of all—she knew that Jonas wished to be free of her meddling parents. Could he secretly wish to be free of her, as well?

On the road below her, she saw a figure turning off Arroyo onto Will's private road. Wearing bright blue, it was Will in his jogging suit. He had seen her and was lifting an arm to wave.

She got moving again. *Think fast!*

As Will slowly approached, she watched the expression on his face change. "Amy! What's happened to you?"

When he stood before her, the decision reached her tongue before her mind was even sure. "Hello, Will. I fell, up on the hill. Look at me, I'm in terrible shape."

She found that her stiff face could perform a wry, shaky grin, and the matter was sealed.

"Fell? How? Where?"

"Don't be alarmed, Will. I'm alright. Really. Except my hands are starting to burn."

As she examined her palms, she saw that the left one was bleeding, while her elbow and one knee were scraped raw.

"How did this happen, Amy? How could you fall so hard? Your blouse is all torn! This is serious! C'mon, let's go inside. Let me help you!"

"No, Will, please. I just want to go home. Could you drive me in your truck? I fell on that rough meadow. Just lost my footing and fell. It was downhill, and I couldn't stop falling. You should have seen me!"

She laughed—a mistake, because it turned into a sob. As she tried to control it, she burst out crying.

His arms came around her, holding her up, gathering her in closely as she buried her face in his jacket.

"Amy!" He tensed as he held her away to see her face. "Was someone chasing you when you fell? Did you see anyone up there?"

She stared at him, dazed by his sharpness.

"Did you see Bill Santone up there? Tell me!"

"No. No, I didn't see anyone."

"What were you doing on that hill? Didn't Jonas warn you not to go up there alone?"

"He did. But I didn't go anywhere near Bill's place. I was just heading for the top of the hill to get some teasel for the shop. I lost my burlap bag up there." She tried to grin.

He stared at her intently for long seconds, then took her in his arms again, pressing her head into the hollow of his shoulder. The comfort was pure indulgence to her, as they slowly rocked back and forth.

He was thinking it over, she sensed, weighing everything she had told him and deciding cautiously to believe.

Then, releasing her, he drew her toward the path. "Let's go inside first, and let me tend the worst of your hurts. I have a good spray. It's antiseptic and anesthetic. It'll take away much of the pain."

"No, Will, I want to leave right now. Jonas won't be home yet, but Julia has a cabinet full of medicines. She'll have everything I need. We'll clean me up well, don't worry, and we'll guard against infection."

In mentioning that Julia would help her, she had found the best argument.

Will reluctantly gave in.

Riding beside him in the truck, holding up her torn blouse at the shoulder, Amy made the final decision. "Will, I don't think I'll tell Jonas about this. And I don't want you to tell him, either."

"What? Of course, you'll tell him! How would you hide all those scrapes? And why would you *want* to hide them?"

"I mean…, I think I'll just tell him I fell down the bank behind our house. It goes clear down into a gully. I don't want him to know I went up the hill."

"But Jonas is your husband! You don't have to hide things from him!"

"It would just cause a big fight, Will. He told me not to go up there, and I ignored his warning. We haven't been getting along very well lately. Nothing serious, you know. Mostly about the diamond from my father, and all…."

"I don't understand this, Amy. Jonas loves you! There isn't a thing in the world you can't tell him."

But finally, grudgingly, he agreed not to tell Jonas that he had seen her today.

When they drove into Julia's driveway, they saw that the garage door was open, with Julia's yellow Plymouth parked inside.

"Oh, good," Amy said with relief. "Julia's home."

While she climbed out of the truck, Julia emerged from her entranceway, apparently having heard Will drive up.

He watched the two women meet and speak briefly.

Julia shook her head, examining Amy's scratches and scrapes. Then she held the girl in an embrace.

With one arm still around Amy, Julia waved to Will, who waved back.

Then Will backed up the truck and pulled slowly back out onto Arroyo Road.

CHAPTER 19

The next morning, Will padded morosely about the cabin as he made himself a late breakfast and then didn't feel like eating it. The previous day's events were still harshly bright in his mind. Realizing that he was helping Amy lie to her husband, he was seeing with increasing clarity that this was wrong. Why had he agreed to her ill-conceived plan?

Because she had pleaded with him, of course. She had been hurting, bleeding. How could he have refused her? If only he could have treated her wounds. Never before had he wanted so badly to give medical help and had it refused.

While he mulled over his own situation, his phone rang.

It had to be George, he thought, and instantly scolded himself for not calling him. He picked up the phone. "Hello."

"Hello, Will. It's me, Julia. Good morning."

"Julia! This is a real pleasure! It's nice to hear your voice over the phone! I think you and I need to talk."

"Yes, Will. I'm still a little shaken up today, mainly because I'm lying to Jonas about Amy's fall. We need to compare notes, don't we? I think Amy told you about climbing the hill for teasel…."

"Yes. And her fall downhill. She was really dinged up, wasn't she? I wanted to treat her hurts, but she was in a hurry to get home. I think she wanted to get cleaned up before Jonas got there."

"Yes!" Julia replied. "He had given her *strict orders* not to go up that hill—he's been like that, lately. I think she was actually defying him, and I don't blame her."

"He does get bossy with her, I've seen it. It's pretty recent, and I think it has to do with his getting the urn finished on time…."

"And now she has to hide her hurts from him. She told him she was working in her myrtle and fell into the deep gully behind their house."

"Okay," Will said. "That's what I need to know. She had mentioned that plan to me. So that's what we're telling Jonas."

"Yes," Julia replied. "She told him last night, and he believes it. I treated her cuts and scrapes the best I could, Will. You'll be glad to know that I cleaned them well and used antiseptic ointment. And I had a sterile bandage for her hand."

"That sounds excellent, Julia. I probably couldn't have done better, myself. And how about Manny? Are you telling him about Amy's being on the hill?"

"No! Please don't mention it to him. I'm afraid he'd say something about it to Jonas. Manny believes that she fell there behind their house. So the lying is *done*, I hope! All this deception, Will, it's hard to live with!"

"I don't like it either. We're corroborating a lie. But I think it's a pretty small lie, and we really don't have a choice."

"Right. You have a way of seeing the truth, Will."

★ ★ ★

The next afternoon, a Saturday, Will was working on the path with his pruning shears when Manny surprised him, coming in from the road. He was carrying an axe. Will ruffled his hair, then smoothed it again, and they headed for the cabin. "I hope you didn't have to walk over here."

"No, Mom dropped me off. She has to go in to the school for a couple hours."

In the clearing, Will showed him two long oak limbs that he had dragged there to be chopped up for firewood.

"You knew I was coming," Manny said, eyeing the limbs.

"No, I didn't. I swear. I meant to chop up these babies myself."

Manny grinned at him, flashing his big, bright front teeth. "Okay, go ahead. I'll watch. Maybe I can learn a trick or two."

"The best way to learn, my friend, is by doing." Will chuckled and started up the porch. "Which will it be, cocoa or lemonade?"

Manny chose cocoa, and Will went inside to make two cocoas. When he came back outside with the drinks, he found Manny examining Will's old axe that he had left on the porch.

"Is this the weapon that scared Bill Santone?" Manny asked.

"That's it. Looks pretty lethal, doesn't it?"

Manny ran a careful finger over the blade. "It does! It's really sharp."

When they had finished their drinks, Will helped the boy position one tree limb so that it rested on two smaller pieces of wood and wouldn't roll. Then he watched closely as Manny started cutting into the limb with his own axe. After some preliminary hacks, he surprised Will with his ability.

"I'm good at this," Manny said.

Will nodded. "I see that. I've had to sort of relearn it myself. I did some woodcutting years back, when I had a fireplace. I used both an axe and a chainsaw."

"That's what *I* want to try!" Manny said, looking up, bright-eyed. "A chainsaw!'

Will grew thoughtful. "I don't know about that. I'd probably say okay, but I'm not sure your mom would. You can really hurt yourself with a chain saw."

"She'd probably allow it if you would. You know me, Will. You know I'd be careful."

He continued chopping the wood into stove lengths, with Will spelling him once, until the limb was finished. While they stacked the wood, they heard Julia's car coming up Will's road.

When Julia reached the clearing, Will invited her to come inside the cabin while Manny stowed his axe in her car. On the porch, with Manny gone, Will broached the subject of a chainsaw. Julia's face became serious, but she said she'd think about it.

When Manny returned, he was delighted to find her inside the cabin.

"Hey, Mom! Look what Will's done in here! It's super neat!"

"Feel free to look around," Will said. "I have quite a bit of new stuff, all the appliances. In fact, everything's new. Even the kitchen cupboards. Terry McCall just built them for me. As you can see, he still has to put on the handles."

"I love this colorful rug!" Julia said, looking down at its braided blue and green. "And the wood stove! I'd like to have one of those. Our fireplace doesn't give us much warmth. It sends a lot of heat right up the flue."

She turned a smiling, dimpled face to him. "Manny was right, your home is beautiful, Will. It's warm, and inviting, and…beautiful."

★ ★ ★

Later the same afternoon, Will heard another vehicle drive up his road and park. As he walked down the path, he found Terry McCall bending low beside Will's truck, examining the tires.

"You've got a great vehicle here, Will. With the tread on these tires, you can probably haul people out of the mud this winter. Are you getting good use out of the truck?"

"Hi, Terry. Not a lot. I thought I'd need it, living here in the mountains, but so far, I haven't. I've bought things and brought them home in it a few times, my big rug, a couple chairs—stuff I could carry."

"Don't worry, you'll find plenty of use for it when the weather gets bad and your neighbors come begging for help."

"I wish somebody *would*," Will said.

As Terry gave him a quizzical look, it struck Will that he was not his usual pleasant self today.

Stepping to his own truck, Terry drew a sturdy paper sack from the cab and held it up to show Will. "I brought the drawer pulls and handles for your cupboards, hoping you'd be home."

"Good. I've been looking forward to those," Will said.

As they passed Will's truck, Terry stopped by the front end. "Hey, Will, did you know you don't have a license plate here?"

Will leaned down to see for himself. "Damn! Somebody stole my front plate!"

"Maybe it was that big ape on the hill above you. Santone."

"It could have been him. In fact, it probably was."

"Do you think you'll go up and ask him about it?"

"Are you kidding? I have no desire to meet up with Santone again. I think I'll just report it stolen and get another one from the DMV." Stepping to the truck's back end, he said, "Fortunately, I do have the rear plate."

Inside the cabin, Terry set his paper bag on the counter and paused, turning to Will. "I've been wanting to talk to you again, Doc, about my situation."

"I thought you might, and I'd like to hear it."

"Things aren't getting any better for me. The truth is, they're getting worse. I seem to be in deeper trouble, without doing anything. I've been questioned several times, always more or less the same questions. This week, two deputies searched my house."

"No! Really?" Will's jaw dropped. "They searched your house? I can't believe it! Did they have a search warrant?"

"Yes. That's how serious it is. They showed it to Sheila, my wife. Scared the wits out of her and the girls."

"What's changed? Why are they badgering you?"

"I don't know. I'm just going about my business, same as usual. They seem to think they have a lot on me. You know, about the money Wheeler owed me, and all that. And they're making a big deal out of the fact that I live on Mount Timothy Road."

"That should have no bearing on anything."

"I know. I keep telling myself not to worry, 'cause I'm innocent, and they're not gonna arrest an innocent man for murder." He looked to Will for validation of this hopeful view.

"You're right, Terry. Try not to worry so much. I'm going to get hold of Deputy Hunter again and try to find out what's going on. I'll let you know as soon as I learn anything."

"Would you, Doc? That's what I was hoping for. Thanks a lot."

CHAPTER 20

A week passed during which Will tried and failed to contact Deputy Hunter, who was out of the area on another murder case, and Terry's worries continued unabated.

Then the day of the Christmas Art Fair dawned. Will stepped outside the cabin in early fog and studied the overcast sky, glad to see faint beginnings of its clearing. Terry had been concerned about possible rain, which had been mentioned in the weather forecast and would have been the ruination of the fair.

Lying awake in bed before arising, he had renewed his memories of the night he had bundled up Lydia and let her out into the storm. He'd had a little reassurance lately in the fact that she appeared free of Santone.

But where is she? Is she okay? Can she support herself?

He planned to question every artist who would talk with him about the girl. Hopefully he would learn something of her whereabouts.

After he drove down Highway 17 to Santa Cruz, he pulled into the parking lot at the County Courthouse, as Terry had instructed him.

Then he walked down a grassy slope toward the river, near a group of other fair-goers heading that way. Among them were a few children, some holding their parents' hands, some running free and shouting back and forth.

The pervading happy mood started to affect him and he grinned, watching their antics. *I don't get to see little children anymore. Well, there's Manny…, but he's too grown up.*

At the bottom of the hill he entered what appeared a small city of canopies. On green grass, he walked parallel with the river with open canopies and booths on both sides of him, displaying various arts and crafts.

The air was delightful, smelling of coffee and filled with talk, laughter, and music—a mingling of guitars, drums, and some kind of fife, or whistle. Another, more distant strain, haunting and sweet, occasionally wafted by. At first, he thought it was a harmonica, but soon decided it had to be a musical saw. Hoping it was the real thing and not a recording, he promised himself that he would find it.

Glancing left and right, he was surrounded by color: paintings on easels or hung from canopy frames; racks of woven shawls; piles of knitted caps and sweaters; glazed ceramics; wooden crafts; silver and enameled jewelry; tie-dyed t-shirts and dresses; and more. He planned to visit every display.

As he smelled coffee again, he remembered Terry mentioning hot chocolate and headed toward the beverage booth.

This is like a carnival. Only better.

He was carefully sipping hot chocolate from a paper cup when he heard the strange music again and started in that direction. Presently he found a small, elderly man in a derby hat who was sitting bent over a curved saw, playing on it with a violin bow. Holding the saw between his knees, he curved the saw blade with his right hand to vary the pitch, while his left hand worked the bow. Eerily sweet music ensued. Sliding smoothly higher and lower, it soared, then sighed, holding a group of passersby entranced.

"That's amazing," Will murmured to himself, and the old man nodded, but didn't look up. "Thanks for this rare, beautiful music," Will said, dropping a dollar into the man's ceramic bowl.

Then he pulled himself away and glanced over the artists he could see, searching for one who looked approachable and could possibly have news about Lydia.

He finally settled on a young woman who was selling watercolor paintings, with framed landscapes hanging from the railings of her canopy. A sign proclaimed, "Marty's Art."

Approaching the plump, smiling girl with a knitted cap pulled over her blond head, he said hello and introduced himself. "I'm looking for anyone who might know Lydia Bird," he said.

Marty looked up and studied him intently. "Will, did you say? And you're looking for Lydia Bird?" she asked, then frowned sharply.

Will wondered why she gave him such a cross look. "Yes. I'm trying to find her. I thought she might even be staying with one of the artists here."

By then, Marty's glance was darting to the canopy beside hers. "Benjamin, come out here, will you?" she called.

A tall, sharp-eyed young man was already on his way over, scrutinizing Will as he approached. "Did I hear right? You're looking for Lydia Bird?"

"My God, he's back," a passerby said.

Marty spoke up. "We don't like men coming around here looking for Lydia. Why don't you just move along?"

"Or better yet," Benjamin added, "get the hell out of here."

"Why?" Will asked, stepping back as the young man came up close to him. "What have I done?"

A small crowd was gathering around them now.

Voices called out:

"Is that Bill?"

"What's he doing here?"

"He was here when we were setting up, wasn't he?"

"I thought we'd kicked him out."

Will answered them loudly enough to be heard. "My name's *Will*, not Bill! I'm not Bill Santone! I'm Doctor Will McKeen, and I'm a friend of Lydia Bird's."

Murmurs rose again from the artists:

"I don't think that is Bill."

"He doesn't look anything like him."

"But he's looking for Lydia!"

At last, Will heard a voice that he recognized. "What's happening, guys?" Terry McCall was making his way through the crowd. "Great! It's Doc! I see you made it to the fair."

"Terry! Finally, someone who knows me."

"Hey, Terry," Benjamin said, "are we wrong about this guy? Bill

Santone was here early this morning. I didn't see him, but the others—"

"This is Doctor McKeen," Terry said. "He had a heart attack back east and came out here to retire. He's a good, honest man, and a friend of mine. And a friend of Lydia's. He's bought paintings from her. And I just finished building new cupboards in his cabin."

By now, quiet had settled over the crowd. A few artists hurried away to man their booths.

"Jeez, man," Benjamin said to Will, "I'm sorry about this. I owe you an apology." He reached out to shake Will's hand. "You can tell we're a little touchy about Lydia. I didn't see Bill when he was here. But Marty says that he seemed to think we were hiding the girl, who I guess has left him. Apparently, Bill was getting mean about it. Marty had to threaten to call the sheriff."

"And then he took off like a shot," said Marty.

"He didn't want anything to do with the sheriff!" someone said, laughing.

Benjamin remained sober. "If you don't mind, Will, why are you looking for her?"

"I just want to know that she's alright," Will said. "She ran away from Bill because she was afraid of him, and I've been worried about her. I'm her neighbor. I was hoping to hear from her friends where she is."

Benjamin still wasn't smiling. "Why do you have to know where she is?"

Will paused, reluctant to answer, but seeing that it was necessary, he spoke with a quieter voice. "Wherever she is, she may not be able to sell her work right away. I'd like to give her some money."

Talk tapered off to silence in the crowd, with all eyes now on Will.

Suddenly, everyone wanted to help. Voices arose as people compared notes and bits of information about Lydia. A girl said she was in Los Angeles. Then a man said he would run and fetch Gabe Malloy, who made frequent trips to L.A. to sell his ceramics in a department store.

A minute later, Gabe, a short young man with carrot-colored hair and a wide grin, arrived. "Actually," he said to Will, "I've been in

L.A. for a few days, and just got back in time for the show. Yes, you bet…I saw Lydia down there."

Will spoke up quickly: "You *saw* her?"

"I did. An old woman she knew years back gave her a room in her home. I think Lydia helps around the house, or something."

"Is she able to paint there?" someone asked.

"Yep! She has some fantastic new stuff, her usual crazy wildflowers. But she isn't selling yet. The artists there had a Christmas show, but she couldn't get in. They didn't welcome artists from outside."

"She needs to find a gallery," Benjamin said. "Her work is plenty good enough."

"What I need is an address," Will said, "so I can mail her a check."

Gabe shook his red head. "Sorry, but I don't know the address. The guy I stay with down there took me to her place, but I didn't notice what street it was on."

Will was stymied. He glanced back at Terry, who gave him a short, slow nod. It occurred to Will that the young man was sending him a message.

Turning back to Gabe, he said, "Are you going down to L.A. anytime soon?"

"As a matter of fact, I'm taking a load of artichoke bowls down next week. Do you want me to give her the check? You can trust me. I'm honest."

"Well, I guess that's…the thing to do," Will said, pulling out his checkbook and pen from his coat pocket. "Can I just make it out to Lydia Bird?"

"Yes, I think Bird's her last name," Gabe said. "I'll see to it that she gets it cashed."

Will quietly wrote the check for a thousand dollars.

Gabe read the check and raised his eyebrows before folding it carefully into his wallet. "I'll help her open a checking account," he said quietly, "and deposit this in it. By the way, stop by my booth, Will. I want to gift you with a nice bowl. Oh, heck, I'll go bring it myself."

"Thanks, I'd appreciate that!" said Will. Relief and joy were washing over him as he shook several hands that reached out to him.

Marty's wide smile lit up her face as she handed him a small framed landscape with redwood trees.

While Will awkwardly accepted it, Terry reached out to him with a thick cutting board made of checkerboard squares. “End grain oak,” he said, tapping it with a wood-stained fingernail. “You can sand it down, and it’ll last forever.”

Will was starting up the hill to leave when Gabe Malloy caught up with him, bringing a ceramic bowl shaped like an artichoke. Next two girls came running, one with a ceramic mug, the other with a colorful, handwoven tablecloth that she hung over his free arm. Then a young man handed him a small, clever animal sculpture made from bicycle parts.

From partway up the slope, Will turned to thank them all for their help and their handmade gifts. Calls of “Merry Christmas” rang in his ears as he headed for the parking lot, his arms nearly overflowing with gifts, which now also included a wind chime and a knitted red wool cap.

CHAPTER 21

Early on the morning of December 24th, Will stood on his porch with coffee in his new mug. It was a beauty, with a blue-green batik glaze parting to reveal a few oak leaves. He was filled with contentment.

The day before Christmas, and there's no snow.

He missed it—for about two seconds. The colorful gifts from the artists had made the cabin bright and cheerful. Even outdoors, the woods were decorated. His madrone tree showed clusters of red berries among its glossy green leaves, while the coyote bushes were thick and white with fuzzy tufts of seed.

My first Christmas in California, he thought. *And I've been given a terrific gift—Lydia's safe now and set for a happier life. I think I can quit worrying about her.*

A little later, he gathered up a large fruitcake and a bottle of Black Muscat that he had bought and carried them out to the truck. The Schumanns were having a tree-decorating party. No one had mentioned an arrival time, but Jonas was home, which probably meant that they would start early. Will drove happily up Arroyo Road—the bearer of dessert and good news.

When he arrived, Jonas was setting up a Monterey pine in the living room, where its tip touched the low ceiling. When Will commended his efforts, Jonas replied, "Thanks, Will, I could've used your help a half-hour ago."

"I didn't know I was late."

Then he greeted Julia, who was sitting on the floor making a wreath of redwood and cedar boughs.

Manny, on his hands and knees, was trying to untangle strings of tree lights.

"I'll help you with those," Will said, "after I take this food out to the kitchen."

Amy was making party sandwiches, looking housewifely in a ruffled apron over jeans. Seeing her face brought Will a moment of pure joy. But it was slightly painful, like bumping an old bruise. Her shining blue eyes said nothing to him about either her fall on the hillside or the story she had invented for Jonas. Evidently, she had managed to put that ordeal behind her and move on.

Will smiled happily, keeping back his news until he had handed Amy the wine and fruitcake. Then, with great pleasure, he told her that he had found Lydia Bird.

"*Really!*" She gave a happy little shriek. "Where is she! Is she alright?"

"Apparently she's fine."

"What a relief, Will! I've thought about her so many times, running at night in the cold rain. Let's go tell the others! This will make everyone's Christmas."

In the living room, the two of them announced the news. Lydia was safe, living in Los Angeles, and even painting again.

A burst of joy filled the room. Jonas brought glasses from the kitchen, along with the bottle of Black Muscat. Will had intended it to be served with the fruitcake, but as they raised their glasses to Lydia and to each other, he decided this was better.

Will regaled them about having nearly gotten thrown out of the Fair. But as he continued on, his story became more serious. "Bill is still searching for her and he's aggressive about it. The artists said he had harassed them before, but this time, he got so mean about it, they threatened to call the police."

The group grew quiet as they digested the news.

"We'd better take a warning from this," Jonas said. "Now that we know where she is, we'll have to keep our mouths shut about her. If Bill hears of it, he'll go down there looking for her. He and Lydia used to live in L.A., so he'd likely know just where to look."

Jonas added, "I hope the artists themselves can keep quiet about it."

"They're very protective of her," Will said, "as I can attest."

"That's good, Jonas said. "They're aware of the danger from Bill. I guess you'll send Lydia money.... Or did you already? Did you get her address from the guy who found her?"

"Actually, he didn't know the street name," Will said. "But he goes down there all the time, so I sent a check with him."

"Oh?" Jonas said, frowning. "Who was it, Terry McCall?"

"No, Gabe Malloy," Will replied.

"Gabe? That little goofball?" Jonas looked incredulous. "You didn't trust *him*, surely? I had a ceramics class with him, and he wasn't there half the time! I don't even know if he made a passing grade!"

Will was taken aback, but just briefly. "Did you know he sells his ceramics to a department store down there? He looked pretty responsible to me. And Terry sort of okayed my sending the check with him."

"Terry recommended Gabe to you?"

"Well, he gave me a nod."

"Gave you a *nod*?" Jonas said.

After that Will quit talking, hoping Jonas wouldn't ask him the size of the check.

★ ★ ★

Standing on a stepladder, Jonas started decorating the tree. As joy lingered among the others over the good news about Lydia, only Jonas seemed less than happy.

"Somebody hand me a bulb up here! This one's broken."

Manny, still working with the light cords, scurried for a bulb and handed it up to Jonas. "Red okay?" he asked.

"I don't care about the color! Oh, hell, the old one broke off, and I can't get it out. Go get my needle-nose pliers from the workbench, would you?"

Manny glanced up at him, then turned to run, stumbled, and fell over his cords.

"Never mind, I'll get them myself!" Jonas muttered as he stepped off the ladder and headed for his studio, leaving Manny to gaze after him.

Will, watching Jonas, was reminded of his sterility and imagined that it colored every exasperated move the youth made. After stepping carefully past the ladder, Will knelt down beside Manny to help him separate the strings.

When Jonas returned, he seemed to be in a better humor, or at least making an effort. "Buck up, folks, we'll soon be done with the lights. Then comes the easy stuff, the glass balls and Julia's tin ornaments. We have lots of both."

"Can I help with them?" Julia asked.

"Yes! Please! Everybody pitch in!"

"Hey, Jonas, could I ask you something?" Manny said timidly, evidently counting on Jonas's improved state of mind.

Leaning far out to hang a light, Jonas grunted and then said, "Go ahead."

"You know that old chainsaw of Dad's? Mom said she'd pay me ten bucks if I'd stack the back wall of the garage with firewood. I'll never get it all done with the axe. Could you show me how to use the saw…, mainly just help me get it started?"

Jonas was already shaking his head. "No way, kid. You'd cut your arm off. I'm afraid of that damn thing myself."

Julia, who was hanging a red-and-blue tin angel, spoke up gently: "I would have agreed with you, Jonas, until just lately. But now I'm thinking maybe twelve isn't too young. He seems to have grown so much this past year, and he's pretty capable."

"Forget it," Jonas said. "I'm not gonna be responsible for him hurting himself. I'll cut the lengths, and he can split them if he likes. That's dangerous enough."

After that, the room grew quiet again.

"Coffee's hot, everyone!" Amy suddenly called from the kitchen. "And the food's ready. Come help yourselves…. Hey, I think we need some music! I'll go put on the Christmas records." She hurried off to the stereo set in the bedroom.

After filling his plate, Will carried it to a chair near the tree, while

Manny and Julia settled themselves near him. Will appreciated their closeness and could now tell them about an idea that he had recently concocted concerning a chainsaw.

"I plan to buy one for myself, to cut my firewood. I'll get a fairly small one, I think sixteen inches. That would provide wood for my stove, and still cut larger pieces for your fireplace, Julia. What would you think of Manny learning to use it?"

Manny grew wide-eyed, but remained silent.

Julia slowly nodded. "Our old saw is large and heavy. Yours sounds lighter. And if you would help him…." She tapered off.

"When I get it, Manny," Will said, "why don't you come over, and we'll figure it out together? We'll go through the instructions carefully. There might be some assembly, I'm not sure. You could use it at my place, and bring it here too…, if Jonas doesn't object."

While they were talking, Jonas came in from the kitchen, carrying a plate with nothing on it but fruitcake. His eyes were somber and staring straight ahead.

Knowing that the couple were traveling to Oakland the next morning to spend Christmas with Amy's parents, Will wondered if this fact looming over him was putting a cloud over Jonas's day.

"You know," Jonas said, stopping by to talk to Will and Julia, "I've been having second thoughts about Manny using a chainsaw. I think I was a little hasty about it. He *is* a smart kid, and he's pretty careful."

"And he's almost thirteen," Julia added.

"I know. February, isn't it?"

Red-cheeked and raising his head high above his shoulders, Manny looked as if he might explode.

"Hurrayyy!" he yelled, drawing everyone's attention, and then laughter. "Finally! I'll get to use a chainsaw! Thanks, Jonas! Thanks, everybody!"

Will reached around the boy's shoulder, giving him a squeeze, and Manny returned it, as far as his arm could reach.

★ ★ ★

A group of dogs traveled regularly up and down Arroyo Road. Not small dogs, they included two retrievers, a German shepherd, a hound, and one or two that Will couldn't identify, so he classified them as mutts.

Early in his running days, Will had been wary of them. But eventually he jogged alongside the dogs, or among them, sometimes allowing noses to sniff his hand.

Driving his truck home after the Christmas party, he spied the pack on a straight stretch of road some distance ahead. Coming closer, he saw that they had collected a newcomer—a black-and-white border collie.

With his heart pounding, he slowed down, not wanting to get past them and lose sight of the collie.

Driving closer, he pulled to the side of the road and parked the truck. Then he had to run a few steps to keep them in sight.

"Girlie!" he called. "Girr-leee!"

Drawing nearer, he called again. Finally, the entire pack paused and looked back at him. As he called once more, "Girlie, come! Come, Girlie," they turned and ran on—all but the collie, who lingered, staring at him.

Then she, too, turned and ran away.

CHAPTER 22

The air in the shack was dank and sour-smelling, but Bill didn't notice it until he opened the door to a bright day, sweet with grass and dew. It was Sunday, and his sharp ears picked up the sound of traffic zooming down Highway 17.

Stupid Valleys, headin' for the beach, where it's probably freezin' cold.

Squinting in the sunlight, he unzipped his fly and managed to clear his pants before letting loose a yellow stream that arched out over coyote bushes to spatter on the poison oak. Yawning, he shuddered and woke up a pain that had been sleeping behind his eyes.

Holding his head level, he stepped inside and left the door open behind him. The floor was littered with trash, and the table nearly covered with empty cans and soiled paper plates. Girlie was lying under the table with her nose on her paws. He knew she was trying to be invisible, watching his bare feet go by. Probably in the night she had helped herself to the pizza scraps he and Jeanette had left on the table. The dog's ears drooped as Bill's eyes fell on her. She needed to go out and do her business, he knew, but first waited to see if there might be any breakfast she could steal.

He stepped back into the bedroom, which was darker, its dim clutter still softened with sleep. On the bed lay Jeanette, his new girlfriend, quietly snoring. He kicked a few scraps of her clothing together and walked them on his toe to her pile in the corner. One of the few good traits he remembered about Liddie was her tidiness.

Then came a sour thought. *That girl's opening her mouth about me somewhere.*

With the sheriff searching for Wheeler's killer, Bill had never been sure how much Liddie knew. He used to think she was stupid, but her actually making money with her paintings had recently made him wonder about that. The sharp little eyes behind all that hair might have seen more than he ever guessed.

And yet, although he tried to stifle the thought, he missed the girl. Thinking of her brought a feeling something like homesickness. The shack was messier now, with no one to pick up trash and wash the dishes. And there was no pleasure in coming up the hill, knowing she wouldn't be there.

He wished to God he could remember everything he had said to her that night, before she ran out the door. But it was just a blur, with an occasional glint of remembering. He knew he had accused her earlier of blabbing about him to Jonas, and of poking around in the car. Then he discovered that she was hiding her money. Did he use the knife on her, or just threaten her with it? The way she went tearing out of here, he may have cut her a little.

Then he remembered the smeary paint in her hair, all those bright colors running together, and it made him feel queasy.

With his head pulsing harder, he hurried back to the open door to breathe in the fresh air outside.

Soon he felt a little better.

He started to make coffee, and while waiting for it to perk, busied himself scratching the thick, rough rolls of skin on his neck. Jeanette had told him that he had poison oak, but he had loudly denied it. He knew the plant, he said, and he kept well away from it. Jeanette insisted that she knew the rash, and he had it. Now he thought, if she was right, so be it. It felt so good to scratch.

Hearing a sound behind him, he turned to watch the woman come creeping out of the bedroom, wrapped in the ragged quilt and dragging it with her.

"I see you're up," he said, being a gentleman about it, even though she disgusted him in the morning, with her fleshy face drooping in its smudges of yesterday's makeup. Unlike Liddie's hair, which was the soft color of soot, Jeanette's glossy hair was so heavily dyed that it stained the yellow pillow black.

"Just wait," he said, reaching out to pat her goosebumpy arm, "some hot coffee in your gullet, and you'll feel like dancin'."

He had made the brew using Liddie's old trick—one spoonful of new coffee and one of old grounds. The can was almost empty now. They were pretty much out of food.

When Jeanette was sober enough to talk sensibly, Bill needed to bring up the subject of money. She had a welfare check about due, and he intended to get hold of the cash before she blew it on magazines or the hairdresser. She ate as much food as he did and gulped down so much bourbon that he could hardly keep it in the house. And she talked back to him sometimes, which confused him

As he padded away into the bedroom for clothes, he decided he would get that money if he had to slap it out of her.

There was a hump in the bed, under the sheet. Girlie was in there already. She slept in the bed every chance she got, probably still finding a trace of Liddie's scent there, as well as his and Jeanette's.

The dumb dog actually thinks she's hidden by the sheet, with her tail stickin' out.

Bill sneaked over and struck her such a blow on the hipbone that it hurt his hand.

CHAPTER 23

In January, it rained steadily for nearly two weeks. Mudslides became a serious problem as the mountain soil absorbed all the water it could, and then slid. Roads became blocked with mud and fallen trees. As the maintenance crews were overwhelmed, the residents labored with shovels, axes and chainsaws to clear their own roads.

One night, a black oak tree fell across the road behind Will's parked truck, blocking his access to Arroyo Road. The next morning, Jonas dropped Manny off at Will's road, and in the cabin, Will and the boy unpacked the new chainsaw. Together they read the brief instructions and did the bit of assembly required. Then they oiled and fueled the saw, made a few practice starts, and went out to tackle the fallen tree.

In a light drizzle, they started by sawing off the branches. Then, since they couldn't turn the twelve-inch trunk, Will cut it by turning the saw this way and that. Finally, Manny took his turn, working under Will's watchful eye. Becoming more skillful as they worked, they cut the trunk into lengths for Will's stove, with longer pieces for Julia's fireplace. These sections, Will explained, would have to be split.

After a while, the drizzle stopped and golden rays of sunlight came slanting down through the surrounding redwoods, turning their steaming trunks a brighter red. Will straightened from his work to breathe in the smell of freshly cut wood, and saw Manny doing the same. They shared a smile, with no words necessary. Then Will wiped his brow and said, "How about we take a rest?"

Will lay down the saw, and together they stepped through the branchy mess on the road into a patch of sunlight.

"Look at that hanging limb," Manny said, pointing up to a heavy oak branch that had broken off and stayed caught in the tree.

"I know," Will said. "I've been watching that limb ever since I moved in here. It's been up there for a while. Maybe years."

"I bet Jonas could lasso it and pull it down," said the boy.

Will nodded, thinking, *Yes, that's how it is. The hard jobs we leave for Jonas, and he does them without expecting thanks.*

"If I could get his stepladder out here," Will said, "I might be able to pull it down myself."

Manny shook his head. "The ground isn't level enough, and those whips below it are poison oak. See the little red buds?"

"You're right. It's a dumb idea," Will admitted. "There's nothing dumber than an old man with young ideas."

Manny gave him a quick look. "Don't talk like that. You're not old." When Will didn't reply, he continued, "You're young for your age. And your age isn't all that great, anyway."

"Come on, don't flatter me," Will said. "If I tried to climb a ladder out here, I'd break my fool neck."

"So would I! And I'm not old, am I? Just the other day, I heard someone say how young you looked. Can you guess who?"

"*What?*" Will asked sharply, realizing that his thoughts had drifted away.

Manny paused, embarrassed. Then he repeated in a lower voice, "Can you guess who thinks you look young for your age?"

"No. I'm sorry, Manny. Who is it?"

Bending down to pick up a branch, the boy said, "My mother…. Oh, forget it."

Will made no reply. And when they returned to work, he did forget it.

Carrying the heavy wet rounds of tree trunk in their arms, they lined them up along the road and placed several in the back of the truck for Julia. They also stacked a large pile of smaller branches that could later be cut into firewood. Then, worn out but in good spirits, they headed for the cabin, where they left their muddy boots on the porch.

Inside, Will built a fire in the stove, while Manny took a shower. With the water running, the boy kept laughing, which puzzled Will. Looking up from his burger patties, he called, "What's so funny?"

"I can't even turn around in here!" the boy called back.

"Sure you can. *I* manage it," Will replied. "Suck in your gut.... Oh, that's right, you don't have one. Then, you should have no trouble."

Later, as Will scooped ice cream for milkshakes, Manny, wearing the fresh clothes Julia had sent with him, resumed his story. "By the way, I meant that about my mom. She *does* think you're young for your age. Nice-looking, even. She said so, just lately."

Will sighed, thinking, *here we go.*

"Well, you can return the compliment for me," he said. "She's very attractive herself, and young-looking. Of course, she *is* young." As he spoke, he looked Manny directly in the eye.

Manny blinked, but pressed on. "Do you know how old she is? Older than you think, I bet."

Will mumbled a guess, "In her early thirties?"

"Ha! She's almost forty! Soon she'll be thirty-nine!" With no response to that, Manny continued, "She used to be a dancer. I've seen pictures of her in her costumes. Those long dresses with lots of ruffles. And flowers in her hair. She was really pretty. In fact, I think she still is."

"I'd like to see those pictures," Will said. "You're right, she *is* still pretty. However, Manny, do you know how old *I* am? I'm fifty-seven now. Old enough to be your grandfather."

"So?" Manny finished chewing his bite of hamburger and swallowed it. "I *like* grandfathers. One of mine's in England, and died last year. I never met him. The other one's in Mexico, and died a while back. I did meet him years ago, when we visited down there."

After that, they ate in awkward silence, until Manny swung into another subject.

"What was school like for you, Will? Were you good at sports?"

"No, not very. I played a little baseball, and went out for track a couple years in college, but I was never what you would call athletic."

"Me neither. Actually, volleyball isn't bad. I can serve real well, without sending it out of bounds. I like it when it's my turn to serve. What all did you like in school?"

"Everything, practically. I joined a few clubs…, the Science Club, the Men's Chorus, the school newspaper, the yearbook staff…. I liked most of my classes and made good grades."

"How about math?"

"Yep. I was good in math. Algebra, geometry, trigonometry…."

"Me, too! I'm one of the best math students in the whole school!" The boy's voice had taken on a bright edge. "Guess what my grade average was last quarter?"

"Ninety percent." *Oops*, he thought, *too high.*

"Ha! A hundred and eight!"

"That's not possible."

"Yes, it is! Every test, Mr. Cassler gives two extra-credit questions you can do if you have time. They're worth nine points each. I get a hundred and eighteen percent sometimes. And I never get below a ninety. So it averaged out this time to a hundred and eight!"

"I'll be darned. "Will chuckled. "Kids are smarter today than they were when I was your age."

As Will got ready to leave for Julia's, Manny gathered up his dirty clothes and carried them out onto the sunny porch.

When Will went out, he found the boy seated on the step, playing with a small lizard. While he watched, the lizard ran up the boy's arm and disappeared inside the sleeve of his t-shirt. Startled, Will said nothing as Manny groped around inside his shirt to dig it out, then placed it gently on the ground.

"Don't those things bite?" Will asked.

"No. It's a blue belly. And anyway, this one's just a baby. Don't you have lizards in New York?"

"Not that I know of."

"Hmmm." Manny looked surprised. "I like them. Except for alligator lizards. They get pretty big…. Once I saw one a foot long. They've got teeth, and they do bite. They actually look like alligators, too. Long heads, you know. I hardly ever see one, but sometimes I find the dry skins that they shed."

"Really? I'd like to see an alligator lizard." Will picked up Manny's boots and started for the path." Let's get going."

"Could you wait just one more minute?" Manny asked.

Will stopped and looked back to see the boy step over to the nearest redwood tree. When he reached it, he turned and inched his feet into place with his back pressed solidly against the rough, massive trunk. As he stood there, he closed his eyes.

Will watched and waited a little while, then asked, "Feel anything? Do you feel the strength of the tree?"

Manny gazed into the distance and slowly, slowly, nodded his head.

CHAPTER 24

On a rainy afternoon at the Schumanns' house, Will sat with Jonas in his studio in the light of the high-intensity lamp. Having earlier sanded the silver egg, Will now sanded the pewter bottle that was to hang inside the urn's skeletal frame. Using sandpaper wrapped around a wooden block, he was smoothing out the hammered planishing marks that Jonas had made in shaping the round-bottomed vessel.

After Will wiped his perspiring forehead with his arm to avoid smudging himself with his pewter-glazed hands, he looked over to see how his friend was doing.

Jonas was sitting hunched over one of the six rocket-like bay doors. On its bottom end, two small bronze hinges were wired in place and ready to be soldered. When finished, the hinges would allow the door to open outward from the bottom.

From behind them came the sound of cups clinking on a tray. Then Amy appeared.

"Would you hardworking gentlemen like some hot chocolate?" she asked.

Will sighed gratefully as he reached for his cup. "Yes, thanks. I really like this stuff."

"Don't shake," Jonas murmured as he lifted his torch, then lit it with his striker in the other hand, producing a hiss and a spurt of fire.

Amy stepped quietly behind him to watch.

Slowly Jonas played the flame over the bronze, carefully heating the whole piece. Then he adjusted the fire to a fine blue taper, focusing it on the tiny pieces of solder that he had placed along the seams.

The solder suddenly sparkled and flowed, molten. "Ahhh!" he said triumphantly, turning off the torch with a pop. Then, using tongs, he lowered the whole piece into a large crock filled with a mild acid solution. With a sputtering hiss, steam arose, along with sulfur fumes and the smell of hot metal.

Behind them, Amy sighed and held her nose. But she remained there, watching.

"Aren't you having any cocoa?" Will asked her, stirring his cup.

After she said no, he had an opportunity to study her.

This cold, damp weather is hard on her. She looks pale.

Amy's hair was drawn back with a carelessness that also seemed unlike her. As she held the tray against her chest, he could see one elbow scrape, now faded to pink. His memory of holding her in his arms was not so much of her softness as of her tough young bones. As he had felt her ribs through her thin blouse, she had seemed almost childlike.

"Did they solder well?" Amy asked Jonas.

"That's the last pair," he said, examining the seams under the lamp, "and they're perfect! Twelve of these devils, and the last two are the best!" Laughing loudly, he tossed the piece onto the bench with a flourish.

Will scowled as he returned to his sanding. Since Jonas had received his coveted invitation to the *California Creates* crafts show, Will had thought several times that his personality was being made obnoxious by success.

"Tomorrow," Jonas announced, "I'll solder the bolt into the bottom half of the egg. Then the disk can be screwed in there like a little floor, where I'll attach the stone. Look at this, Will."

From a shelf, Jonas took a small box and opened it. "It's citrine. I found a chunk of it once, lying out in a field. I didn't even know what it was till I had it cut and polished."

He handed Will a gumdrop-shaped, translucent stone, nearly an inch wide at its base. "I'll make an elaborate bezel to hold it, like a little crown."

Will studied it, then handed it to Amy, who examined it and handed it back to Jonas.

"Almost colorless, isn't it," Will asked, "except for a faint tinge of—what, amber? It looks like a big drop of water."

"Hey! Why not? The earth is a water planet. The egg will contain a little cosmos, with this stone a crystal to guide the spirit on its journey. I want to have the egg gold-plated. And I think I'll enamel inside the top half, a bright sky blue."

"Good," Will said. "I'd like to see color in there."

"It needs to be beautiful," Jonas said, "if it houses the spirit. The concept of the whole thing is hopeful. Man's hope for life after death. *La Vida Segunda,* Julia called it the other day, the second life. I think I'll keep that for the urn's title. I like Spanish words, don't you, Will? They have a nice sound."

"Yes, I agree. Much nicer than our blunt Anglo-Saxon. Of course, we also use many words from other languages."

By now, Amy had moved in closer. "I wish I could help with the urn in some way."

"I was thinking," Will said, "the heavy sanding is about done, isn't it, Jonas? Couldn't she do some of the last finishing with fine paper?"

"No. Sorry, Amy," Jonas replied. "It still takes muscle. Will has strong hands, and he's done so much sanding, he's very good at it."

"I could give her some help," Will suggested.

But Jonas shook his head, brushing the offer aside. "Right now," he said, "I'm trying to figure out something for the urn's base. I've actually considered bird feet."

"Bird feet?" Will asked.

"You know, something that relates to the egg." Jonas absently scratched his cheek with his fingers, leaving black streaks. "I'd carve the original foot in wax, and then cast copies in bronze. They'd have claws, and I'd make neat scales, like on a real bird's foot. How many feet, though? Maybe three…, or four. It's gonna be heavier'n hell."

"How about six, if it's hexagonal?" Will asked. "One for each bay door."

"Six! Yes, there *should* be six!" Jonas agreed. "That'll be a lot of work." But then his eyes sharpened. "They could flare out in a big circle at the bottom! I could make them jointed and hinged, so they'd dangle when you pick up the urn, just like real bird legs! Hot damn!"

"What kind of bird?" Will asked.

"I don't know..., hawk maybe, or eagle. The museum in Santa Cruz has stuffed birds. I'll have to go down there and study their feet."

Behind them, Amy carried her tray quietly over to the sink, and then went into the bedroom.

"I'll have to start the first foot right away," Jonas said, more soberly. "I have one month. And now I have to write my damned thesis report."

"Well, there you are!" Will said. "Maybe Amy could help you with *that.* My wife typed all my papers over the years, and sometimes she practically wrote them."

"Are you kidding? Come off it. What does Amy know about a thesis? This has to be in regular thesis form. Do you have any idea what that means?"

Will held back a sharp response, then said calmly, "I was writing theses and treatises before you were born. They aren't that difficult, and you'll probably be given instructions. I wish you'd let Amy help you with it, Jonas, or with something. *Anything.*"

As Will spoke, Jonas's mouth was setting in contempt, a look that struck anger in Will.

"Damn it, Jonas, she needs to spend time with you! You're making this master's project your whole life!"

Jonas straightened in his chair. "Now, hold on, Will! Aren't you the guy who told me to work hard and develop my art? Show the Hainsfords they were right to be impressed, you said. Justify their faith in me! Well, that's what I'm trying to do..., trying my damnedest! And I'm working under pressures you can't imagine!"

Will slowly rose from his seat and walked a few steps for his coat, giving himself time to think. "I know that, Jonas. I'm sorry. I know how hard you've worked. And the urn is turning out so well."

On his way out, he paused at the door.

"I know I shouldn't have opened my mouth about you and Amy. What's between the two of you is none of my business."

When Jonas made no reply Will left, stepping dismally out into the cold evening air.

CHAPTER 25

A few days later, Will drove to Cabot's Mill and pulled into the parking lot at the supermarket. Nearby, he saw Terry McCall loading groceries into his truck. Will called out cheerfully, "Hi there, Terry!"

The young man gave Will a preoccupied look and then turned his attention back to his grocery bags. Sensing that Terry's news was not encouraging, he grew even more concerned as he walked over. "How are things with you now, Terry? I haven't seen you since the Art Fair."

"Oh, hello, Will. Not good. Things are not good with me." He carefully pushed the last bag into place. "They might as well put me in jail right now and get it over with."

"No! You don't mean that, Terry! What's happened?"

"I'm hamstrung. I can hardly find work. My neighbors are suspicious of me. Besides, I've been warned to stay in the immediate area. There are a couple good jobs further out, one clear over in Watsonville."

Studying Terry's face, Will found him pale and hollow-eyed. "So the sheriff's afraid you might run away?"

"It's so stupid. How could I run, with my wife and the girls here?"

"Have they found something more they can use against you?"

"Yes, they searched the house again…, really tore it up this time. I think they were looking for drugs. Guess what they found? My high-school baseball bat."

"Oh, for Pete's sake. The murder weapon?"

"Yes. They tested it at a lab, then sent it to another lab and tested it again. Trying real hard to find something on it…, blood or skin or whatever."

"They must be getting desperate."

"They had two other suspects, musicians in Marino's band. But they got off somehow. I guess it's easier to pin things on me." Turning his head away, Terry took a moment to close the gate on his pickup. "People are looking at me funny now. Even our friends. I guess I don't blame them. This has gone on so long."

Will had been thinking hard. "Even if you're charged, Terry, I don't think it would stick. You'd likely have a pro bono lawyer, and any decent one would get you off."

"Is there anything more you can do for me with Deputy Hunter?"

"I've tried several times. I think I'll invite him to breakfast again. He likes that. He occasionally listens to me, and I have some good points I can bring up about the murder."

That night, lying awake in the dark, Will planned his arguments for defending Terry.

In the morning, he telephoned Hunter and caught him at his desk on the first try. But when he invited the deputy to breakfast, he heard the man sigh.

"Will, I'll have to say no thanks this time. I'd like to come, heaven knows. But I don't think I can accept your hospitality when I know I'm going to shoot down your arguments about Terry. That's what you want to see me about, isn't it?"

Thrown off-balance, Will had to gather his wits before he could speak. "Yes, of course, Alan. The man *needs* defending! His life is pure hell right now…, he's having trouble finding work. And I'm still convinced that he's innocent. How can you convict a man on nothing but circumstantial evidence?"

"Will, even if our evidence is circumstantial, we have so *much* of it! It's overwhelming! Everything we know about him, in his past and on that night, points directly to him."

"There are some pretty good arguments for his innocence, too, Alan. To begin with, why did he tell the police he had bought marijuana from Wheeler? He's like that. He tells everything because he has nothing to hide. Would he have said it if he were guilty?"

"Well, but that's just a small point. Don't forget, in addition to all the evidence we have on him, we also have motive."

"Yes, I know about the eight hundred dollars. I don't think it's a very impressive motive, do you? When Terry told me about it, he scoffed at it. As if he'd kill a man over eight hundred dollars, he said."

"People have been murdered for less, Will."

"And I know about the baseball bat, Alan. The guys at the labs must have scraped deep into bare wood, trying to find blood or skin on it."

"Just standard procedure."

"Testing it twice? Two different labs? That doesn't sound very standard to me."

After a brief silence, Hunter asked, "Are you saying we're manufacturing evidence against Terry?"

"No, no. Not that. I just think you're trying extra hard to *find* evidence. You've searched his house twice…, really tore it apart this last time, Terry said. Do you know if they found drugs?"

"They didn't find drugs. Just the baseball bat."

"And all the time, Alan, there's a powerful bully of a man living on the hill right above me, whom you seem to forget about. Have you checked on Santone since that visit you made?"

Hunter cleared his throat. "No. When I question someone and am convinced that he's not the killer, I don't feel a need to examine him again." Hunter sounded slightly offended.

In Will's silence, he went on. "Why should we even suspect Santone? Because of his size? He wasn't at the party. He had no reason to be up on Mount Timothy Road. He used to have a friend up there, but the man died a while back. That's true; I checked it out. So I'm not wasting time on him."

Will nodded and backed down. "Okay, Alan. I'm sorry. I didn't mean to press you like this. I just…. I'm sorry."

Sounding mollified, Hunter changed the subject. "Let's get back to the case we have against Terry. Starting with Dennis Wheeler. Did you ever even *see* the man?"

"Not alive, but I watched his corpse being carried out of the woods on a stretcher. The body was covered, but it was so short, I thought it could have been a child until the sheriff said it was a young man. I believe a powerful man could have picked up that body by an arm and a leg and swung it forward so that it landed in that low tree. Remember me showing you that, the day you took me to where the body was found?"

Hunter paused, then spoke deliberately. "All the evidence we have painstakingly collected tells us that wherever Wheeler was killed, his body was thrown down from Mount Timothy Road, from a spot right above that buckeye tree. Try as you might, you can't refute that."

"Yes, I can. I don't think that could have happened, Alan. The distance downhill was just too great, and the slope isn't a straight slant—it's slightly rounded. Since the body was pretty lightweight, it would have gotten stuck someplace. The ground itself isn't smooth. I've looked at it from above and below. It's rough and bumpy, with a few scrubby bushes that could have snagged the body."

Then a new thought struck Will. "Have the sheriff's men tried throwing something like his body down over the hill, to see where it would land?"

Now the deputy blew out through his lips. "I *knew* I didn't want to talk with you. You're too good at muddying the water. And that we don't need!"

"The case *is* muddy, Alan. I didn't make it that way. I think you'd better look hard for another suspect. You don't want to arrest the wrong man."

"Damn it, Will, this case is dragging on! People who live around here are scared, and they want arrests."

"But you're not going to rush your search to please them, are you? You'd be throwing justice out the window."

Hunter fell silent again, and when he spoke he sounded weary. "I'm just a deputy, you know. There are teams of men, higher deputies and detectives, working on these murders. They're working extended hours, and even with a lot of new hires, we feel understaffed."

"Are you on one of the teams?" Will asked.

"Yes, I am. But I don't carry a lot of weight. I answer to my captain."

"You have a voice, though. Please, Alan. I'm convinced that the real killer is out there somewhere. He may have killed more than once. He may kill again."

After a brief silence, Hunter made what became the concluding statement. "Well, you've made a few strong points, especially concerning that damned hillside. I'll bring them up with Captain Baird and the detectives. But, frankly, I don't think it will do much good. The crux of the whole matter is your idea of someone having picked up Wheeler's body and thrown it into a tree. Nobody at the station can believe that."

CHAPTER 26

On a warm evening suggesting an early Spring, Will and Jonas sat on the Schumanns' small front stoop, working on the urn. With darkness around them, they worked in the small area of light from Jonas's high-intensity lamp, which was clamped onto a wooden box. On the ground by Jonas's feet sat his alcohol lamp, and near that a bowl of cold water.

Oak moths were fluttering weakly around the porch light behind them, while a few more bobbed in the air at the edge of darkness. They could become a real scourge, Will had learned. In sufficient numbers, they could strip the live oaks of their leaves.

Jonas was finishing a bird's leg made of blue wax, while Will worked with steel wool on the pewter bottle, which was now finished to a smooth, gleaming satin.

Wondering why the house was so quiet, Will lifted his head and looked back through the dark screen door.

"Amy went to bed," Jonas said, answering the unasked question. After flopping his hair back from his face, he reached down with his tool, a tiny pointed scoop. He held it briefly to the flame of the lamp, then touched it to the wax leg. "Oh, no," he muttered. "I mushed over a scale. I'm losing detail, damn it! And I need this finished by tomorrow, so I can cast it in bronze. Then I'll have the master."

"Master?" Will asked.

"The original metal leg. I'll make a rubber mold from that, and from the rubber mold I'll cast the other five waxes. Then each of those will be cast in bronze."

"It sounds like a complicated process."

"It is, but it's a lot easier than carving each leg in wax."

Will looked up to watch the oak moths gently bumping the wall near the light. Higher, in the corner of the doorframe, two tiger moths were spreading and closing their wings.

"How come Amy's in bed so early?" Will asked. The question came out as naturally as the opening of the moths' wings.

"Beats me." Jonas completed a tense stroke with the tool, then relaxed, blowing out a sigh. "Maybe she's still watching television. She hasn't felt too good today."

"Does she take iron? She looks like she might be a little anemic."

"Yeah. I don't know. She used to. Some iron and vitamin compound."

Will nodded and grew thoughtful. "Do you and Amy have a family doctor?"

"We do," Jonas replied without looking up.

"Do you both get regular checkups?"

"No, we only go to the doctor when we're sick."

Speaking cautiously, Will said, "The way Amy looks lately, I think this might be a good time for her to have a checkup." He knew he was going out on a limb with this.

Jonas grunted something unintelligible. Then, with Will waiting, he murmured, "I'll give her a little time yet, to see if she doesn't get better by herself."

Will stared uneasily out into the darkness, restraining himself from saying anything more.

"She's backed off lately," Jonas said. "She doesn't care much about anything. She's taking a few days' break from the shop, and hardly lifts a finger here." Turning brusquely aside, he thrust the wax leg into the bowl of cold water. "Damn it, my hands keep softening the wax!"

"What do you think is the matter with her?"

"Who knows? Maybe she's getting sick of living in the mountains…or sick of living with me. I think she misses her old life."

Will looked up to see an oak moth that seemed to have lost its bearings, bobbing feebly away from the light. On the ground, he discovered dozens of the worn-out insects with their wings frayed and tattered, some still faintly moving.

"All I know is," Jonas said, intent again on the scales that marched shingle-like up the wax leg, "I can't worry about it now."

"If I were you," Will said quietly, "I'd be worried."

"You're *not* me."

An owl hooted softly from the forest as Will lay the bottle in his lap and studied his blackened hands.

"Damn these scales!" Jonas yelled, dropping his tool and accidentally kicking the bowl, which spilled out much of the water. "They're too much work, and there's enough texture without them. The bay doors are ripply. The only thing not textured is the egg."

And the pewter bottle, Will thought, but he didn't say it. He rearranged his steel wool, now worn to a stringy knot. Somewhere inside his right thumb, a bit of steel was painfully imbedded.

★ ★ ★

After Will's truck rolled away in the dark, with Jonas still working out front, Amy stood at the open bedroom window, staring out through the screen. With no fog tonight, there were just a few stars, silently sparkling. The sky had a hushed stillness, she thought, waiting for the moon to appear above the eastern hills.

Turning back into the darkened house, she thought of ice, which had a peculiar appeal to her these days. She yearned for its hard coldness in her mouth. Earlier, she had poured herself a glass of iced tea, but left it on the counter. Even tea was upsetting to her now.

Stepping into the kitchen, she took an ice cube from the freezer and placed it on her tongue. But it was too big for her mouth. She removed it and cupped it in her hand. Then, taking up a table knife, she used its heavy handle to give the cube a hard smack. Shattered ice flew everywhere, leaving little in her hand.

As she stared at her wet palm, Jonas, who had just come in the front door, said, "That was smart."

Amy reached silently for a hand towel. She had heard Will asking Jonas if she might be anemic, and Jonas's nonchalant response. Then Will had suggested that she should see a doctor, which had shaken her. Jonas's lack of interest in that had actually come as a relief. The last thing she wanted was to see a doctor.

When Amy kneeled to pick up the bits of ice, her stomach suddenly became roiled. As she rose carefully, it was all she could do to walk smoothly, not running or holding her mouth, as she rushed to the bathroom. Inside, with the door closed, she bent over the toilet, quietly gagging. Finally a little came up, mostly water, as she stood there, perspiring. She had been nauseated every morning that week.

After washing at the sink, she pressed a cold washcloth to her face and throat. Her thoughts strayed to Julia as a possible source of help. Also Naomi Cook, who thought she had a stomach flu and had given her time off from work. Then, of course, there was her mother.

Staring into the mirror, Amy puzzled over the barrier that had risen between herself and her parents. Perhaps it was time to put aside all the problems and entanglements over her marrying Jonas. Time to remember the happier old days and perhaps, possibly, confide in her mother.

Practicing a face with which to greet her, Amy curved her lips into a smile and saw that it was ghastly, forced. But the level gaze of her eyes remained the same. Oddly, her eyes seemed unaffected by the cataclysmic changes taking place in her body. The decision came easily, after all. She would ask her mother to meet her in San Jose for lunch. Looking into her own clear, blue-violet eyes, she gradually felt calmer.

CHAPTER 27

When Amy called her parents in the Oakland hills, her mother answered, hesitating when she heard her daughter's voice. The chilling pause over the line traveled straight to Amy's nervous stomach.

"It's been so long since we've talked, Mum," Amy said quickly into the silence. "I'm dying to see you. I thought we might get together at Renée's." With her voice shaking slightly, she tried to set a date for sometime in the next few days.

This elicited from her mother a small embarrassed-sounding laugh. "You've taken me by surprise, Amy. I'm hosting my garden club on Tuesday and serving tea to the museum docents on Thursday. This is a busy week for me. I guess…I could make it on Friday."

"Not till Friday? That's almost a week away."

"Sorry, Pet, it's the best I can do on such short notice. What's brought this on?"

"I just miss you, that's all. I'd like us to get together once in a while. Without the men around, just you and me."

They set the date for Friday. As Amy hung up the phone, she was so brightened by both nervousness and relief that her nausea was temporarily driven away.

When Friday came, Amy first had to drive Jonas to the university, nine miles in the wrong direction, so the trip to Renee's in San Jose took over an hour. But she had time, having left early.

Traffic was heavy in the city as she drove downtown. Having bolstered herself with a car-sickness pill, she entered the parking lot feeling as if her stomach were stuffed with cotton. Ahead lay an elevator climb to the restaurant, up fourteen floors.

She had planned to say nothing about her dilemma during lunch. First, she would see if she and her mother could return to the old comfortable rapport they had once had.

Isn't this nice, Mum? Just the two of us, meeting for lunch?

Afterward, Amy would suggest that she accompany her mother to her car so they could talk for a moment in private. Here the plan would meet a dreadful unraveling: her mother would look up sharply, seeing that her suspicions about this lunch had been correct after all, and something was wrong.

Beyond this point, Amy had no plans, and would have to deal with whatever happened.

When she entered the building, the orange-and-rust carpet swirled beneath her feet. But the anti-vertigo pill that she had taken worked, fuzzily, through the long elevator ride. At the top, she entered the restaurant foyer and announced herself at the reception desk. Her mother had already arrived and was waiting for her at a window table.

Margaret had changed. Her hair was now frosted with silver and arranged in soft curls around her face. Amy saw that although her hair was beautiful, her face looked older, with her eyes set in deeper wrinkles.

"Mum, how nice you look!" she said, bending to kiss her cheek.

"How are you, dear? You're so thin!"

Prepared for this, Amy slipped casually into her seat as her mother went on.

"For heaven's sake, you're not dieting, are you?"

"No, of course not. I don't think I've actually lost weight. This dress has always been loose-fitting." Then she changed the subject. "How nice you look, Mum, in that suit. I love that pale green."

"Thank you, dear.... How's Jonas these days?"

"He's fine, but terribly busy. Right now he's writing the report for his master's degree. The project itself is almost finished, a beautiful rocket-shaped urn. Part of it is gold-plated...."

Margaret had already opened her menu and was studying it,

cutting Amy off before she could mention Jonas's being invited to the art show. She would have a chance later, she thought. "And how's Daddy?"

"Not too well, dear. He's on medication now for high blood pressure, and his sciatic pain is bad enough that he's considering surgery. He's aged quite a bit recently. It's been a difficult year for him."

There the conversation halted as the waitress approached. They ordered shrimp salads, Amy's without dressing.

"Why, Amy, I thought you said you weren't dieting."

When Amy didn't respond to this, Margaret ordered wine. Amy ordered iced tea.

After the waitress left, Margaret announced that she and Robert were planning to spend the month of June in Hawaii.

"That's wonderful, Mum! Hawaii sounds so lovely. Where will you be staying?"

"We're taking a cruise, staying aboard the ship as it tours the islands. It's simpler that way. We have a nice suite of rooms. Your father wants mainly just to rest."

"Why haven't you been down to see us?"

"I think you know the answer to that." Margaret said this gently, with no anger in her voice. "After what happened with Jonas and the diamond."

Change the subject, came the warning thought, but Amy ignored it. "Really? Surely, Daddy didn't care all that much about the diamond."

"Why not?" Margaret laughed drily. "If you think that, you don't know your father. It mattered enough that he boasted about it to all his friends at the club before offering it to Jonas. Now he's ashamed to let them know what happened. You and Jonas embarrassed him terribly."

Amy paused in buttering a roll and laid it down. She was starting to perspire.

"And not only that, honey, so you'll understand. It was more to him than just losing face. You know you've always been the apple of his eye. He was so proud to be able to give it to you. It was an expression of his love, plain and simple. And you refused it. Jonas practically threw it in his face. Do you understand? I don't wish to hurt you with this, I just want you to understand your father a little."

"And what about Jonas? How about a little understanding for *him*? He created this pearl ring for me, and Daddy made it look cheap! Daddy treats Jonas as if he were insensitive! And he's terribly sensitive! He wants so badly for you to be proud of him, and he's working so hard.... He's just been invited to enter a big crafts show in Los Angeles, called *California Creates*—"

"Amy, stop it," Margaret said quietly.

Amy was caught up short, nearly shaking in her need to tell more.

But her mother spoke first. "It's no use bringing up all those old arguments, Amy. We could have accepted Jonas. He's bright and ambitious, and bent on improving himself. But he's arrogant, with all that noble austerity he flaunts in our faces. This is so foolish, getting into it all over again." Her voice wavered, threatening tears, as Amy stared at her plate in disbelief.

Then Margaret recovered. "If I had known this was the kind of talk you had in mind, Amy, I wouldn't have come."

"I'm sorry, Mother, I had no such intention! I don't know how we got into all this."

Margaret reached across the table to touch her hand.

"Dear, I'm sorry, too. I know why you defend Jonas. Just understand that I must also be loyal to your father. He feels that the two of us are all we have now.... Honey, your hands are so cold!"

"Yes. It's alright. It's the air conditioning."

Amy took a sip of her tea as she glanced out the large window. It was tinted, dulling the city below to dun-colored buildings and hills. She felt dizzyingly high above ground.

"Mum," she began again, "let's talk about you and me. That's really what I came here for. You seem very busy with your social life these days."

Margaret sighed. "Yes, I'm pretty busy with the museum docents' program. I'm also getting involved with my sorority chapter again. I hadn't been active with them for years."

As she glanced across the room, her face froze, then brightened. "Celia! Oh, land, yes, it's Celia! And she sees us! I haven't talked with her for so long!" She lifted her hand to wave, and mouthed the words, "C'mon over!"

Then, evidently having second thoughts, she turned solemn eyes to Amy, as if really seeing her for the first time today, and whispered, "Is it alright with you, dear? I didn't mean to cut into our time together."

But Amy had no time to express her feelings. "It's alright, Mother," she said quietly, as the plump, heavily made up Celia came bustling over in a cloud of flowery scent.

"Maggie!" Celia exclaimed. "It's been ages! How have you been?"

Amy saw a slight flinching on her mother's face at the name Maggie.

"I'm well, Celia. Just not getting around as much as usual, though we'll soon be off for a month in Hawaii." Then, gesturing toward her daughter, she said, "This is our daughter, Amy. You know—I'm always talking about her idyllic mountain life with her genius husband, Jonas."

"Happy to meet you, dear."

Celia's eyes dropped to Amy's hands, which Amy instinctively covered to hide the rings.

"Won't you join us for lunch?" Margaret asked, following this with a quick glance at Amy. "You don't mind, do you, sweetheart?"

Amy hesitated a moment, then said, "Of course not."

Although she was jarred, her thoughts were jumping ahead: she and her mother would still have their private time together at the car.

Celia ordered a chef salad and a martini, and while they waited for their food, Margaret described her club activities. Amy watched her mother pretend to be burdened by them while using them as bragging points. Celia tried to top these with her own social highlights and travels with her live-in mate. They would also be traveling in June—to the Greek Islands.

By the time their food arrived, Amy was becoming queasy, and realized that her nausea pill was wearing off. Picking at her salad greens and ignoring the shrimp, she didn't bother any longer to conceal her rings, but allowed Celia to see them openly. One glance at them, and her mascaraed eyes met Amy's with a look of confusion.

Amy spoke up quickly, asking her mother if she had been shopping for cruise outfits, knowingly bringing up one of Margaret's favorite pastimes.

"Oh, land, yes! Celia! Have you been in the new leisure wear shop on Marsh Lane? Wonderful stuff. Designer copies you'd swear were the originals."

"Do you mean at the corner of Marsh and Haley? I didn't know it had opened yet."

"I was waited on by the nicest young man, who knew more about women's clothes than I do." She laughed lightly. "I only bought an evening wrap. It's sheer, very dressy. I intend to go back. I need more evening things."

"Could we go together, you and I?" Celia asked. "Actually…, maybe we could do it this afternoon, after lunch."

"I'd *love* that! I'm free all day." Then she thought of Amy. "Oh…, dear…, would you like to join us?" Her faltering tone betrayed her reluctance to invite the girl.

Amy realized that her plan for private time with her mother had just been shattered.

My God. This whole trip has been for nothing.

"No, I don't think so, Mother. I need to pick up Jonas when I get home. I might just drive directly to the university when I leave."

While Amy sat numbly, the waitress brought the dessert tray to the table. The two older women pored over it until Celia settled on a chocolate and whipped cream concoction, and Margaret, a small wedge of Key Lime pie. Amy ordered nothing.

When the waitress brought the check, Margaret made a scene, insisting on paying her daughter's bill, which Amy badly wanted to pay herself. In protest, the girl stubbornly laid out a ten-dollar bill, which slipped off the tablecloth and landed on the floor.

Amy stared at it, frozen, until Celia said, "Well, don't just let it lie there." Bending down, she picked it up herself and flopped it on the table.

As the three of them stood up to leave, Amy said, "I think I'll use the ladies' room before my long drive home."

That pleased the two older women. After saying their hasty

goodbyes to Amy, they left the restaurant, laughing and talking with their heads together.

Amy started out stiffly toward the restroom, and partway there broke into a run.

CHAPTER 28

In Cabot's Mill Tavern, sunlight shone through amber windows made of diamond-shaped sections of glass. Bill Santone sat in the warm light, hunched over the bar with his eyes closed. Fully absorbed in the simmering, pain-manufacturing business of his body, he scarcely knew where he was. Sometimes it seemed to him that he was home in bed. His arms itched and stung as they lay before him on the bar, palms up. Inside his shirtsleeves, they were covered with weeping blisters.

But his face was worse. Face skin seemed different to him from other skin, burning more than it itched. He would never have dreamed of scratching it. With eyes closed, he could imagine flames sweeping up past his face. His ears were crusted, as were his cheeks, and his mouth was covered with tiny blisters that felt like pebbles when he rubbed his lips together.

A wave of dizziness swept over him, like the edge of sleep, and he felt he might be slipping off the stool, losing himself horribly—tilting, sliding. But then he caught himself.

Insomnia was the problem, he thought. Badly as he needed rest, he dreaded even crawling into bed at night, knowing that his sleep would be tortured. When he glanced up, he saw the bartender eyeing him. He had been nursing a beer for nearly an hour, and still had an inch left in the glass. Moving an arm, he swept the beer carefully over to his mouth. As long as he drank, he had a right to sit here.

At the other end of the bar, there was a group of men, some of whom Bill knew. From time to time, they looked over at him and grinned.

The laughing hyenas!

Bill saw now that Jeanette was with them, the first he had seen her since the day he had asked her for money and she had flown out of his house in a rage. With her lips set in that smug manner of hers, she leaned out to look at him. Then she rose and started over.

Frizzy black hair. She must've had a permanent.

"What in God's name *happened* to you, Bill? You look awful! Is that poison oak on your face, or something else?" Raising her upper lip in disgust, she bent closer carefully, with her fat hip pressing into his metal stool.

"Poison oak," he muttered, ducking his head slightly between his shoulders. There was no human warmth in her today.

"Why the hell don't you see a doctor?"

He shrugged. "No money. What's the use, anyway? He'd just give me some stinkin' salve that's no better than soda." Bill's fingers unconsciously started scratching his arms. She was watching, so he forced himself to stop.

"You need a bath, Bill."

"Can I come to your trailer and use the shower?"

"Do it at home. Run some water in the sink and wash yourself. It'll make you feel better."

Sensing some kindness in her after all, he nodded, appreciating it.

But then it ended.

"You got it bad, Bill! You need *help*!" Jeanette's voice had sharpened now with anger. "You damn well better wake up and do something!"

"Alright! I know!" He jerked himself up a little straighter. "It's a allergy. There's nothin' you can do but get away from what's causin' it. And I plan to, soon as I'm able. I'm gettin' clean off that hill."

"Oh? Where will you go?"

He took a deep breath, somewhat clearing the clouds in his brain. "Down to L.A. There ain't no poison oak down there, and there's plenty of work. I can make more money down there in a week than I can here in a month."

She studied him curiously. Money stirred her interest, he knew.

"Well, good. You'll need your car, then. You better get it in running condition."

He didn't answer right away. The thought of the car was undoing him again, bringing the blacking-out feeling. After another sip of warm beer, he gingerly wiped his lips on his wrist. "Can you just *lend* me some money?"

"Not another cent. You're in hock to me now more than you'll ever be able to pay."

He nodded. She had money in the bank, so it would have been easy for her to write him a check.

She could even buy me a car if she wanted to.

At the thought, his eyes filled with tears.

"Oh, stop it, Bill, for pity's sake! Clean yourself up! Look at you! You smell awful! And clean up that rat nest of a house. It's no wonder you got poison oak all over yourself."

"But I never go in the weeds! I'm telling you, I never touch the plant!" Crying now, he dabbed at his swollen eyes with a sleeve. "I must be gettin' it from the very air!"

"You're getting it from the stuff in your house. Your clothes, your shoes, your tools. Everything you own must be polluted with it!"

Through his tears, Jeanette's face looked orange. And she made no sense.

"I told you, I never touch the leaves."

"It's the *oil* on the plant that causes the rash, Bill. Anything that touches the plant gets oil on it. And then, when you touch that thing, you get the rash. You don't have to touch the plant directly. Do you understand, for Chrissake? I can't make it any plainer!"

Groaning, he started hugging his arms and had to stop it.

She watched him and grimaced with contempt. "You're a disgrace! For pity's sake, go home and get some sleep!"

"I can't sleep at home."

As he spoke, he was sinking. With his arms folded in his lap, his head was drifting down, turned so that one hot ear felt the merciful coldness of the bar.

"Hey! You can't sleep here."

Dimly, Bill saw the bartender's plaid shirt slide into view.

"I heard ya. I'm leavin'."

The bartender floated away, out of his realm.

★ ★ ★

Bill awoke to morning sunlight in his bedroom, but instead of clinging fitfully to sleep, as he usually did, he struggled at once to get out of bed. On his feet, teetering, he found his legs swollen. Both eyes were nearly shut, so that he peered mistily out through slits. With his head aching, he started for the door, seeking fresh air.

How much beer did that bastard bartender let me drink? And after a couple shots of bourbon.

Jeanette was right, he saw now, as he breathed in the clean, grass-scented air. He was getting worse, and he'd better do something about it. The trouble was, as he peered out at the shining green leaves poking through the duller blackberry, he was surrounded by poison oak. If he could just get rid of it around the house, like Deputy Hunter had said to do, he could give himself a chance to heal. In a few hours, if he had the strength, he could rip it up for ten yards or so in all directions, or even burn it up. He would have to cover his skin completely with clothes.

What did Jeanette say about clothes? If the oil got on them, they could be as dangerous as the leaves?

Twisting his thick neck painfully, he peered into the bedroom at the heaps of soiled clothes lying on the floor. They had to be full of the oil. He could be getting the rash from his very own clothes! But how did the oil get on them in the first place? As he puzzled over that, he turned to gaze outside again.

On the path below, something was moving.

Blinking to clear his eyes, he saw that it was Girlie, head down, skulking along. She paused, no doubt catching wind of him, and remained partly hidden by a coyote bush.

The skinny runt, gettin' along somehow without food from me. Crawlin' through the bushes to come home and sleep in my bed.

Light was suddenly born in him like a shining explosion in his brain.

Damn my eyes! Why didn't I see it? I've been poisoned and made a fool of by Liddie's dog!

All those nights he had rolled and tossed in a bed that was a nest of poison oak! A hoarse cry escaped him that brought all his fury and anguish scraping up out of his chest.

The dog watched him, surprised by his furor but not retreating. With her tongue lolling out, she drew back her slanted little eyes into a squint.

Somehow, he would have to get her inside the house. Stepping aside, he moved away from the door so she would think he was going about his business. Soon he heard her toenails scrabbling to get hold of the high step, and then she was inside.

Before she could head for the bedroom, he grabbed an empty wine bottle by the neck and confronted her. Lurching toward her, he saw her flinch, cowering, rolling her eyes toward the bedroom. But as he lifted the bottle to bring it down on her skull, he paused.

She was baring her sharp teeth, drawing back the skin around her dark gums, with a husky growl from deep inside her throat. With the bottle still raised, he was actually afraid of her.

Then the dog streaked for the door and before he could lower the bottle, she was gone from his sight.

CHAPTER 29

"Country Roads…take me home…to the place…I belo-onng—"

Will was sitting in the stifling cab of his truck, stopped in a line of traffic on Arroyo Road's southbound lane. John Denver music filled the air, pouring out from the battered-looking van in front of him. It was missing its rear doors, so Will could see that it was empty except for some piles of stuff, and had a good view of the longhaired driver.

"West Virginia…mountain mama…take me home…."

In front of the van, there was a line of cars and then the cause of the tie-up—a road crew working with heavy equipment. In the woods around him, every leaf and branch was picking up dust. Will told himself that there would soon be rain to wash it off. With spring barely started, there would still be rain before summer's drought.

Beside the road lay a trench that began a few miles behind Will, at the Cut-off. The utility lines, long vulnerable to falling limbs and trees, were being placed underground. A tardy move, Jonas had said, after years of power outages. Sighing in exasperation, Will stirred in his seat. His shirt was clinging to his chest like a wet dressing.

He could have taken Highway 17 to Santa Cruz, a thought that galled him now. Although he had seen the "Road Work" sign on the freeway, he hadn't driven south lately on Arroyo Road, so he hadn't known how bad the traffic was. He needed to get to the bank, which had closed a few minutes ago.

From the truck cab's open windows, he caught a breath of cooler air, but it brought him little pleasure. Somewhere in the forest, there was a tree that stank. One that he hadn't yet identified was currently hung with fuzzy, greenish blooms. He guessed it to be the offender. The dull, cloying smell seemed intensified by the heat.

As Will drove forward for several car lengths, a bulldozer became visible ahead, twisting and sidling as it worked to uproot a redwood stump. Together with a backhoe, it was preparing a smooth, level path for the smaller trencher, which Will had already passed.

Stopped again, he watched a car further ahead maneuver back and forth to make a tight U-turn into the other lane and escape the line-up by driving north. Will considered trying that, but decided it was too dangerous. There was too much traffic in the other direction.

As he sat waiting, a flagman appeared ahead, stopping both lanes of traffic, while a heavy truck loaded with dirt came lurching out from the woods. It maneuvered the difficult U-turn and slowly rumbled away northward. After it, the line of cars moved forward a good distance.

Just as Will was sighing in relief, the cars were stopped again.

What now?

A short distance ahead, the road turned, obscuring his view. He could see no reason for this stop. Then he noticed that the left lane was empty of traffic. While he puzzled over that, he heard the distant, high-pitched wail of a siren.

In front of Will, the van's driver, who had lain back, suddenly sat upright. Then he surprised Will by opening his door and stepping outside. Thinking of cooler air, Will also opened his door and climbed down onto the road.

As he tucked his damp shirt into his pants, he looked ahead to a few more drivers who had left their vehicles and started walking beside the line of cars.

On legs stiff from sitting so long, Will jogged awkwardly to catch up with the nearest walker.

"What's the problem now?" he asked the man. "Do you know?"

"I think there's been an accident."

"I'm a doctor. Maybe I can help."

As Will spoke, he was already moving again, faster. The siren sounded once more, coming closer now. Then it abruptly stopped.

As Will jogged, he was starting the road's long curve when he saw a jumble of vehicles far ahead. A man was running toward him, talking to the walkers as he passed them.

"Somebody's dead."

Will thought he heard the words, but wasn't sure. Raising a hand, he stopped the runner to ask, "How bad is it?"

The man paused beside him, out of breath. "Bad. A Volkswagen just got creamed. A pickup truck was making a U-turn into the other lane, and the Volks pulled out right after it. But the pickup didn't finish its turn, and the Volks was stuck out there—" The runner had to take a breath. "Then a heavy truck came around the bend and crashed into both of them. The Volks was crushed between the pickup and the dump truck."

The runner was starting again as Will shouted, "What color Volkswagen?"

"I don't know," he called back.

Running faster now, Will tried to think of other Volkswagens he had seen on this road, besides Jonas's gray one. He remembered one that was pale blue.

It's not Jonas. He's too cautious to have tried a thing like that, he reassured himself.

As he neared the wreck, the ambulance's white roof appeared among the vehicles, its red lights still flashing.

Will could glimpse the heavy dump truck, sitting odd-angled on the road. In front of it, the remains of a gray Volkswagen lay crushed against the white pickup truck. The Volk's bent hood was raised. Will had to run past it to see the upper parts of a body lying against it. Then he saw lavender cloth, a pale arm wrongly bent, and blond hair.

A man in a white coat was trying to reach the body, while paramedics were entering the car through its torn roof.

Will struggled to get past a deputy sheriff, who held him back until he said that he was a doctor and a close friend. Then he pushed close enough to ask the paramedics, "Is she dead?"

One young man said, "Yes. We have a doctor here, and he made the determination."

Will stood looking a few seconds longer. Then he turned and stumbled away.

The deputy came over and took his arm, asking, "Are you alright?"

"Yes," Will said, standing straighter. "I'm an M.D., Will McKeen, and I knew the victim. Do you need help identifying the body?"

"No. One of the crew is a friend of Jonas Schumann's, and knew his wife. Her name was Amy Schumann."

"That's right," Will said. "I guess they're sending for Jonas?"

"Two deputies left for the university, and another one headed for his home. They'll track him down."

"Would he..., will he be seeing her here, as she is?" Will spoke, then blew out a breath, wondering if he would be throwing up.

"No, they'll take him right to the morgue."

Will nodded, then asked, "Are you contacting Amy's parents?"

"We have a couple of men looking them up. They thought they'd get information from Jonas. Do the parents live around here?"

"No, they're in Oakland. I don't know their address."

The deputy looked at Will closely. "Are you alone here? You're real pale. Do you need a ride home?"

"No, no. I'm fine. I have my truck here. I can drive myself."

"Her death was instantaneous, the doctor said."

Will nodded again. "Thanks for that."

Back at the truck, he managed the U-turn onto an empty road and drove slowly home.

The first thing he did was call Julia, breaking the news to her as gently as he could, and listening to her crying over the phone. After offering her some weak consolation, he asked her to call him when Jonas came home.

"Couldn't you come over to our place, Will, and wait here? Please. We don't want to be alone right now."

"I don't either. Thanks, Julia, I'll be over."

Moving quickly in the cabin, he prepared for the night with Jonas. After gathering up the pillow and blanket from his bed, he added two cans of beef stew to the bundle and carried it out to the truck.

Julia met him at her door with open arms, and he walked into them as if coming home to warmth and safety. Then Manny joined them, and the three of them clung and cried together.

Afterward, they sat down together at the kitchen table, and Will described what he had seen of the wreck, without divulging too many details.

Then they discussed how Jonas would get through this ordeal.

"He knows he's welcome here, night or day," Julia said. "And I can make his meals for him. He can just eat with us, if he likes."

Will nodded. "Your good food will be a comfort. I have no plans, but just to stay with him as long as he wants me here. He can also bunk at my place, of course."

In a short while, Manny, who was watching at the window, said, "There's a sheriff's car out here, bringing Jonas home. It's taking him back to his house."

Will gathered up his bedding and food from the truck and walked back to the little house as the sheriff's car was leaving. Unable to wave with his arms full, Will nodded to the deputy, who lifted a hand in response.

Standing on the Schumanns' front step, Will freed an arm to knock on the door.

Jonas opened it to him, saying, "I knew you'd come."

CHAPTER 30

Hours after Amy was killed, Will spent a long night with Jonas in the Schumanns' house. As darkness turned the windows black, Jonas wanted all the lights turned on, so the house was filled with light so bright it seemed garish.

At first, Will was concerned that Jonas was not quite facing what had happened, as he refused dinner and sat with his hands in his lap, staring blankly ahead and seeming to take little notice of Will's presence. Will ate, feeling awkward about it, and then spoke softly while he cleaned the cooking pan and his dinner plate and fork. Working in Amy's clean little kitchen, handling pans and dishes that now seemed her personal belongings, he sensed her presence. *This is a special kind of hell.*

When Jonas started talking, it was with a breaking voice and had to do mostly with guilt. "I've been pushing her aside." he said. "I ignored her needs, and just shoved her into the background. How in the hell could I have done that? I thought more of the urn than I did of my own precious wife." Tears finally came, and after a hasty wipe he let them roll down his face. "How could I have hurt her like that?"

Will had learned fast to put his own private grief aside. "You were up against a deadline, Jonas, and the urn was taking all your time and energy. That's understandable. And it was just temporary. You knew it would end when you finished the piece."

Jonas sobbed quietly with his head in his hands.

"Amy always knew that you loved her, Jonas. Think about how you worked to make a plant room for her, with a skylight, and shelves…. And how she loved the pearl ring. The way the two of you took on Hainsford over the ring, you had to have a strong marriage. And that was love, if I ever saw it."

After a while Jonas quieted and sat rocking again. Finally, he looked up dull-eyed and asked if they could have some coffee.

Will would have preferred that they got some sleep, but was unwilling to deny Jonas anything. He found the coffeemaker and coffee and made a small potful.

Then, with caffeine in him, Jonas became more agitated.

"It was all for her," he tried to explain to Will. "Everything I've done…. The whole master's degree…. It was all for her, and our marriage. Our future together."

Will nodded, surprised at this new tack of Jonas's.

Then a grand idea took hold of the youth. "What's the matter with me! Amy's ashes should be placed in the urn! It's almost finished! The timing of her death is providential, don't you see, Will? The show…, even the master's degree! None of that really mattered. They were just a means of keeping me working, not knowing that she was going to die!"

Jonas's red eyes shone with new zeal.

Will tried to imagine Amy's ashes in the heavy, metal urn. Somehow, it seemed unthinkable. *Still, this is me. If it were mine to do….*

Then he had a new thought. "Are you going to ask the Hainsfords if they'll consider using the urn?" he asked. "It's too late to call them tonight."

"I'll ask them in the morning," Jonas said, starting to calm down. "They're coming here anyway. I'll call early, to give them a little time to think about it first."

As Will tried to see the urn through the Hainsfords' eyes, he was afraid that there might be trouble.

★ ★ ★

After a few hours of uneasy sleep on couch cushions spread on the floor, Will awoke with a start in daylight. He couldn't find Jonas anywhere in the house, so he checked outside. There he found him standing in dawn light, with the urn set up on a level redwood stump.

Jonas was taking readings from a light meter, with a camera strapped around his neck. Will saw that the urn seemed completed, with the gold egg on its top, and the six legs spread out on the stump. The whole piece gleamed softly in the early light.

First intending to ask Jonas how he was feeling, instead Will exclaimed, "My Lord, it looks beautiful! You did some polishing on it last night."

Still bent over the light meter, Jonas nodded silently with his disheveled hair falling past his face.

"Did you get any sleep at all?" Will asked.

"No. I tried, for an hour or two. Then I got up."

"Why didn't you wake me? I could've helped!"

Jonas just squinted briefly toward the sun, giving Will a chance to see his face. His eyes were red and swollen, his cheeks dirty with black fingerprints.

"Did you call the Hainsfords and tell them about the urn?" Will asked.

"Yes, I talked with Margaret. She was a little reluctant, but she finally said they'd take a look at it. They'll be here around ten."

Drawing a polishing cloth from his pocket, Jonas gently wiped the egg, which was gathering a film of dew. The sun was rising above the hills with rays bursting softly through the trees.

Then, suddenly, the sunlight touched the golden egg.

"Look at that! That's it!" Jonas exclaimed. "I've got to work fast now." Grabbing the camera, he whipped the cord around his neck. "Damn it, wouldn't you know, I'm getting the shakes!"

He checked the meter once more quickly, and then his lens settings. "My fingers are so sore I can hardly work the damn thing."

Will moved closer, but couldn't find a way to help.

As Jonas steadied the camera on his upraised knee, it slipped, and he just barely caught it.

"Shit!" he muttered furiously. "I can't believe this! Right when the light's perfect. Come on, you son of a bitch!"

Jerking the camera strap, he tried again for a better grip.

Will placed a steadying hand on his shoulder, but Jonas said, "It's okay. I got it now."

Jonas succeeded in taking the first shot.

After advancing the film, he took another. Then he photographed the urn from a higher position and, strengthening as he worked, moved around it for various views. As the sunlight brightened, he changed the camera settings. To capture the egg alone, he set it directly on the stump, its halves opened to reveal the blue enameled top and the softly glowing citrine.

Finally, Jonas put down his camera, reassembled the egg, and closed the urn's bay doors.

While Will carried the egg, Jonas took up the urn and carried it to the house's front stoop, where he set it down.

★ ★ ★

Will and Jonas stepped outside as the silver Cadillac pulled up the driveway and parked. The urn was still sitting on the house's broad stoop, now in full sunlight. Jonas wanted it seen outdoors, he had explained to Will, because the house was in too much of a mess for them to go inside. Will also saw this as Jonas's weak attempt to keep the meeting short.

After the Hainsfords left their car, Margaret's head drooped as she walked slowly, gripping her husband's arm. She was already dressed in black, with her face hidden by a veil.

Robert looked ashen as he enfolded Jonas in an awkward embrace, keeping well back from his uncombed hair.

Then Margaret, who had pulled back her veil, rested her head on Jonas's shoulder and sobbed quietly.

Will, who was close to tears himself, offered Robert his quiet condolences. Then he watched Robert glance down to the waiting urn. The steel gray eyes locked onto it briefly, then looked up to Will with a terrible suspicion.

Will imagined what was going through Robert's mind: *So this is what they've concocted! Will has known all this time what Jonas was doing. In fact, he conspired with Jonas.*

Hainsford said nothing about this for a minute, shifting his feet nervously while he waited for Jonas to finish speaking with his mother-in-law.

Then he ran out of patience. Reaching for her arm, he said, "Margaret, I think you'd better take a look at this."

As she followed her husband's gaze to Jonas's urn, Will saw her swollen eyes grow still. She raised a gloved hand silently to her lips, and then her face crumpled.

"It's alright, dear," Hainsford said. "We don't have to use it. What is this, Jonas? Some kind of cruel joke? Just what did you have in mind here?"

Jonas blinked his eyes, showing only weariness and innocence, as if his brain were lagging a few seconds behind.

"This will never do, you know," Hainsford said, taking another look at the urn. "Never!"

With his lips pressed tightly shut in anger, he shook his head.

Jonas became strangely electrified, speechless but moving, gesturing with his arms in a questioning way.

Will found himself speaking out: "You know, I myself have just recently learned to appreciate contemporary art. If a person stays current with it, as Amy and Jonas have—"

"You *would* defend it, McKeen!" said Hainsford. "Your taste is as cheap and perverted as his."

"Bob," Will said, "would you take a minute and look at it? It's a contemporary piece. You must have known it would be. The metalwork shows great skill, and everything about the design is meaningful. You have to take time to study it. Jonas, I'm going to open the egg to show them. Do you mind?"

"No! Don't do it!" Jonas protested, lifting a hand to stop him. "To hell with them! Why should I have to prove myself to them? Amy liked it. She was intelligent enough to appreciate it...." Tearful again, he stopped in mid-sentence. Then he continued. "Look! Look what you're turning away in your ignorance! Step aside a minute, Will."

Reaching down roughly, Jonas opened a bay door, but then clumsily let it flop back with a bang.

"The container inside here holds the ashes, can you see that? It's pewter, and the body of the urn is bronze. The egg is silver with gold plating. Here, let me show you the egg. It opens. Look at this."

With shaking hands, he picked the egg off its magnet-held perch and unscrewed the halves.

Margaret leaned forward to peer into them with teary eyes. Will saw that she was trying to understand, struggling to relate to art that she considered outrageous.

"I don't give a damn how many metals are in it," Hainsford said. "It's grotesque. What is it? A bird? With an egg on top for a head?"

"It's a rocket shape," Will answered him calmly, "with the egg as the nose cone." He saw that in his weariness, his words didn't seem to make perfect sense. "A rocket and a bird both embody flight. You might consider the flight of the human spirit after death. Isn't that right, Jonas?"

Jonas nodded abstractly.

"The egg is the perfect symbol of an afterlife," Will added.

Suddenly, staring with a furrowed brow into the egg halves, Margaret seemed to give up. Turning away, she sobbed. "I'm sorry," she said brokenly. "We don't want to hurt you, Jonas. It's just that we loved her so. She was our only child, and we'll never have another. We can't put her away in something that's so foreign to us. Don't you see? We had envisioned something beautiful, like a gold and silver vase."

Jonas moved to go inside, but Will reached for his arm.

"Jonas," Will said quietly, "remember you thought it was all predestined? Maybe this was, too. Their rejection…, all part of it. Maybe the urn was meant to be shown."

Jonas spoke dully: "No. No, I don't give a damn what happens to it now." Extending a bare foot, he placed his toes between two of the bird legs and lifted, tilting the urn.

"Jonas, stop!" Will cried.

The egg was falling as Will lunged forward to catch it before it hit the stoop. With his other hand, he reached for the urn, which toppled with a bay door falling open. Seizing it, he set it lurching back heavily onto its legs.

"Take it, would you, Will?" said Jonas. "Do you want it? That's a lot of metal. You can sell it for scrap."

Jonas turned to the house and grappled briefly with the door latch. While the others watched helplessly, he made it inside and closed the door.

After that, the Hainsfords lingered for a few moments before turning awkwardly away. Will remained by the door, refusing to move with them. They had things to do, they said. They seemed to him chastened, possibly ashamed. But they had had their way.

After Will said goodbye at the house, his not accompanying them down the driveway left them in a peculiar aloneness, supporting each other back to their car. Hainsford helped his wife inside, then climbed in, backed the Cadillac in the driveway, and slowly drove away.

Will was now alone with the urn. He sat down beside it and waited a while, listening to insect-buzzing and other strangely normal sounds of the morning.

"Are you alright, Jonas?" he called once through the door, but heard nothing from inside.

Finally, he drew himself to his feet. Lifting the egg carefully in one hand, he bent down to wrap his other arm around the heavy body of the urn. Carrying it with the bird legs dangling, he started slowly down Julia's driveway toward his truck.

★ ★ ★

It took Will several phone calls to the Los Angeles museum to reach the number for the *California Creates* show. Yes, the woman on the line verified for him, they had received Jonas Schumann's entry form. It was there in their files.

"There's been a death in Jonas's family," Will explained, "so he won't be able to send his own piece. I'm a neighbor and a close friend, and I'd like to ship it for him, if that's okay."

"Well, I guess that would be alright." She spoke hesitantly. "I do have his paperwork right here.... Are you going to send it insured?"

"Yes, of course."

She gave Will the address for the entries, and he thanked her.

After spending an hour shopping for tools and materials, he

constructed a wooden box with a screwed-on removable lid. Then he packed the urn carefully, placing the egg in its own small container with foam padding.

It was nearly 6:00 when he rushed the box to the shipping company. While the delivery truck sat in the lot, loaded and ready to go, the clerk ran out and told the driver to wait.

Did Will want the parcel insured, the clerk asked, and for how much?

Will had no idea what it was worth in money. Finally, rushed and desperate, he insured it for twenty-five hundred dollars.

"Holy hell!" the blond, lank-haired driver said, staring in amazement at the heavy box in his arms. "What is it?"

"It's a piece of art work," Will explained. "Sort of a sculpture. It's made of bronze and pewter, and silver and gold. And a gemstone. I'd appreciate it if you'd load it carefully."

"No way! It's riding up front with me! I'm keeping it right beside me on the seat."

Will watched as the driver carefully placed the box and climbed in after it.

The sunset sky was beautiful, Will noticed with sad surprise. Its soft blue and rose seemed somehow appropriate.

Then he watched as the van rumbled quietly and started rolling down the sidewalk ramp into the street.

★ ★ ★

After rejecting Jonas's urn, Amy's parents resumed their original plan for a closed casket that would be interred in the family vault. On the day of the funeral, Will and Jonas sat with the Hainsfords and other mourners in a waiting room outside the main chapel, which was closed off behind a wide, curtained doorway. Soft organ music sounded from behind the curtain, while two ushers stood waiting to guide the mourners to their seats inside.

Will sat straight in his chair, keeping up his facade of strength. Tomorrow, he thought, he would go home and sink into the morass of his own private grief. But this day, still, was Jonas's.

The young man was abstractly scraping at his calloused palm with a thumbnail tough and flat as a quarter. He was wearing an expensive wool suit—black, beside Will's dark gray. As they had shopped together in the men's store, Jonas had stared with surprise at his image in the mirror, a metalsmith-Indian in a dress suit.

The two of them had seen the coffin when they entered the chapel to place their flowers. Among the floral arrangements, the Hainsfords' large pink-and-white spray already lay centered on the coffin's lid. Jonas moved it down slightly to make room for his own white lilies, which he had decorated by interweaving in them a few blooming strands of myrtle.

Will, who would have liked to fill the room with flowers, had brought a small basket of white rosebuds and violets. Having been moved by Margaret's plaintive wish for a gold and silver vase, later he would make a donation to the Hainsfords' suggested charity.

Now, in the waiting room outside the curtain, Amy's parents sat with their friends a short distance from Will and Jonas. Margaret wore a black veil that covered her down to her shoulders. She and Robert had been especially accommodating of Jonas in making the funeral plans and arrangements.

Too late, Will had thought. *Too late now, after all your disdain for him. You've lost not only a daughter, but also a fine young man who could have been a son.*

Julia and Manny were there, Julia dressed in black, with Manny wearing what Will thought was probably his first suit. As he scanned the seated crowd, Will recognized artists he had met at the Christmas fair and speculated that a good half of the audience were Jonas's friends.

After the ushers opened the curtained doorway, one of them headed directly to the Hainsfords, while the other approached Will and Jonas, beckoning them to rise.

Amazing, Will thought as he rose from his seat. *I'm right up front with the chief mourners, just as I should be.*

CHAPTER 31

During the weeks after Amy's death, a malaise of grief and sadness settled over Will's area of Arroyo Road. He tried and failed to reach Terry McCall, who had not attended the funeral and now apparently was not answering his phone.

Jonas had shut himself inside his house, filling out an application for a teaching credential, after telling Will that he would like to try teaching part-time at a University of California. Several times Jonas showed up at Will's cabin at night with his sleeping bag, and the two of them slept peacefully in each other's company.

Each morning, Julia knocked on Jonas's door, unobtrusively checking on him while discussing the day's meals. Jonas finally shopped for food and told her he could feed himself—except for dinner. For that, he still took advantage of her standing invitation.

★ ★ ★

While helping people around her to endure the tragedy, Julia carried a secret that weighed heavily on her mind. She had information that she believed was known only to herself. Although she had wanted to tell it to Will on the day of Amy's death, she had decided to give him a few days to recover from the grief they all shared.

On a morning while Manny was in school, she decided to reveal it to Will. After driving down Arroyo Road, she found him standing outside, staring up into his trees.

"Hello, Will. Are you drawing strength from your redwoods?" She asked.

He smiled. "Yes, and I just enjoy them, you know? I like to spend a little time out here once in a while."

Then he led her inside the cabin and started making them a pot of coffee.

At the table with their cups, Julia eased into her story.

"Will, I hope I won't be causing you more sorrow, but I have something I need to tell you. It's a real dilemma, and I don't know what to do about it."

Will nodded. "Let's hear it. I'll help if I can."

Julia took a breath and began. "Amy had a big problem, before she died. One day, I went over to talk with her and found her very sick, nauseated. She tried to brush it off, but I knew right away what was wrong.... Then, later, she told me the truth. She was pregnant."

She stopped there, concerned about the change in Will. He had drawn back in his chair, looking as if she had struck him in the face.

"Are you alright, Will? I was afraid this would be a shock. But I need your help. Amy wouldn't let me tell Jonas. Imagine, being pregnant and not able to tell your own husband. Now she's gone, and I don't know whether I should tell him, or not."

Will finally spoke, in a strangled-sounding voice. "Don't tell him. Jonas wasn't the father. He's sterile. You didn't know that, I guess.... They were keeping it quiet, but Jonas confided it to me. The baby couldn't have been his."

Julia raised both hands to her mouth, speechless.

Will continued, "But I know whose it was. My God, how awful this is! Remember when Amy fell on the hill, and told Jonas she had just fallen in the gorge?"

"Yes, of course."

"She told us she had fallen up on the hill. But she must have been trying to escape from Santone. When I met her coming down the road with her injuries, I asked her if she had seen Bill up there, but she denied it. She said that she hadn't met him."

Julia caught her breath. "He must have raped her! No wonder she couldn't tell anyone. And with a sterile husband! *Dios Mio!* She was in an impossible situation."

They sat stunned.

Will finally spoke. "I'm thinking, it might be better if we don't tell Jonas. Other than Bill, who won't be talking, apparently no one knows about this but the two of us. Amy didn't want it known. So why should we add to Jonas's misery? If he knew about her rape, it's possible that he would go after Santone and end up ruining his own life. No, I think it's better he doesn't even find out."

Julia nodded and grew more relaxed. "I agree completely. If Jonas is sterile—of course, we mustn't tell him. I'm sure that's what Amy would have wanted."

"That's right. Whatever her reasons, she didn't want him to know she had even gone up the hill."

"Thank you, Will. I'm relieved of my burden. But in a way, I've taken on another. We both will have to live with this, you know."

"Yes. It will be our secret."

"At least, there are two of us to share it. That will be easier than bearing it alone."

After Julia left, Will started up his road. With a rage that grew with each step, he tramped so fast that he had to keep slowing down to settle his heart.

As he climbed higher, with the road narrowing in brush and weeds, he smelled smoke.

★ ★ ★

Gray smoke, thick and acid-sharp to Santone's eyes and nose, rose from the brushfire he was building near his shack. He thought it must have been the poisonous oil in the young green plants that made such smoke—and such heat.

An evil fire, he thought. *Unnatural.*

He couldn't get close to the flames, or the heat became too painful on his blistered flesh. Retreating, he shielded his face. Then he crept back again to poke with a rake at the vines that, in his fevered mind, were twisting and curling like snakes.

Having chased away the dog that had slept in his bed, at last he was eliminating the source of his misery, the plants themselves. As the flames rose again, he imagined Girlie in there, burning and grinning. He endured the heat once more to step in and beat at the mocking face and snapping teeth.

He laid down his rake and bent over groaning, hurting his legs to gather fresh vines. As he rose and reached for the rake again, it was suddenly wrested out of his hands and swung up into the air. A blow struck him across the back, sending him reeling.

He was falling, landing in astonishment on his hands and knees. Looking up, he blinked his swollen eyes to see. Tall jeans and, high above, a reddish beard. It had to be the doctor, lifting Bill's rake to strike him again.

"Don't hit me! I'm hurtin' too bad!"

"You raped her! You raped Amy Schumann! You caught her on the hill, didn't you? I know you did it, you son of a bitch! Get up!" The rake swung again, missing Bill as he ducked lower.

"No, please, please! I'm all swole up with poison oak!"

"She's dead now. She never recovered from what you did to her. Did you even know she died? You might as well have killed her up here!"

With the rake rising again, Bill yelled out in terror, "I'm sorry! I'm sorry I done it!"

Will lowered the rake and leaned in for a closer look at Bill's face. Then he dropped the rake.

"I want you off this hill! You're on my land, damn you! You're here without my permission! I'll give you a week, and then I'll have the sheriff throw you out. Do you hear me? One week!"

At last, Will fell back, ducking to avoid the smoke rising around him. Turning away, he started out with a few steps downhill.

Then he stopped, and stood with his shoulders hunched.

Finally he turned around and called back to Bill. "You're burning poison oak, you fool! The smoke carries the oil, and if you inhale it, it can kill you! Get out of the smoke!"

As Will continued downhill again, his thoughts flew ahead to taking a shower, scrubbing his hair and entire body with soap and destroying his clothes.

Then he heard a distant siren down below, coming south from the Cut-off.

When he reached his path, the firetruck was just turning into his road.

The driver, slowing to maneuver past Will and his truck, stopped to ask, "Can we make it all the way up to the fire?"

"I think you can get close enough with your hoses," Will replied. "There's a man up there burning poison oak. He's sick already, and probably needs an ambulance."

In the Santa Cruz hospital the next day, with a respirator down his throat, Bill Santone died of infection and asphyxiation.

CHAPTER 32

From his usual perch on the edge of his deck, Will watched thin fog drift slowly through the trunks of his giant trees. Everywhere, he saw new beginnings. The reddish trunks were developing more of their pale green sucker growth at their bases. New ferns had also sprung up in the clearing—short, fuzzy stalks with their tops tightly coiled—looking, to Will, more animal than plant.

Winter's red berries had long ago fallen from his madrone tree or been eaten by critters, including Will himself. He had found them disappointingly tasteless. Now the tree had its new beginnings—blossoms, like tiny white bells.

Although he needed to go inside and build a fire, he remained there, counting the jobs that awaited him. He needed to call George, but recent events were too tragic to tell him about, just yet. And Spring had brought him a lot of outside work to do. Blackberry waited to be cut back along the path, and the traces of poison oak in it had to be squirted with weed-killer. When he and Manny had cut up the fallen oak, they had left a few piles of small branches, which he planned to chop up to fit his stove.

The clearing floor was littered with redwood branchlets and needles that he had planned to rake up, but with the recent rains, they had turned a red-orange color that was a treat for his eyes, so he decided there was no need yet to clean them up.

Rising stiffly, he went inside and made coffee.

In the light traffic passing by on Arroyo Road, he usually recognized the sounds of the mail truck and Manny's school bus and ignored the rest. Today, preoccupied with his thoughts, he hadn't heard any vehicle approach, and so was startled by the knock on his door.

Julia, he thought. He hadn't seen her in a week. Maybe she had brought him something delicious.

But he opened it to a short youth with red hair, who exclaimed, "Hey, *hey*! My *man*!"

Will laughed, recognizing the young man from the Christmas art show. Hadn't Jonas called him a goofball?

"Hey, yourself, Jake. No, wait…, it's Gabe. And an Irish name…."

"Gabe Malloy! You're right, I'm an Irish laddie." As Will opened the door wide, Gabe stepped inside and looked around. "Wow! So this is your cabin! It's glorious!"

"Thanks. I like it pretty much, myself." Will started pouring coffee into two mugs.

"Good, I see you're using my mug. And I know the other one, too. It's Phil Lauer's. Another good ceramist. Not as good as me, of course."

Gabe grinned, nosing around and looking at things. "My God, this place is fabulous! I see Lydia's paintings. And look at the plants!" Reaching up, he touched a drooping tendril of Creeping Charlie.

"Yes, the plants were a gift from…Amy." The name floated out painlessly. Will thought it should have hurt him, like thorns on his tongue. But it was more like the slight, risky opening of a closed door.

Gabe sipped his coffee, subdued. "Yeah, Amy. That was awful, wasn't it? I believe you're good friends with Jonas?"

"Yes. I've been good friends with both Jonas and Amy." Her name slipped out again.

Gabe shook his head in a way that spoke of sorrow. Will responded with a nod, and the acknowledgment of grief passed wordlessly between them. Gabe said no more about it, which Will appreciated.

After another sip, Gabe broke into a grin. "I came bearing a gift, Will. I promise you, this is gonna be a surprise!"

"Oh? I could use a surprise. A good one, I hope."

"This isn't from me. It's from your friend and mine, Lydia Bird."

"What? You've been in touch with her again?"

"Yes. Occasionally. Whenever I go down to L.A., I like to keep tabs on her."

He drew a small envelope from his jeans pocket and handed it to Will, who found folded bills inside.

"What's this? Two hundred and forty-five dollars."

"It's the first money you gave her, she said, the night she ran away from Santone. You had paid her for paintings before that, but this money, she considered a loan."

"Why is she returning it? I don't want it back."

"She's happy to be *able* to pay you back, Will. She's proud that way. Next she'll probably start paying you back for the thousand-dollar check."

"Good Lord. Please tell her not to send any more money. I don't need this, and she probably does. Help me out here."

Gabe shook his red head. "You've got to take it, man. Think of her feelings, and just accept it. Don't worry, she can afford it. She actually has a commission inside her bank right now. They've made a nice smooth wall for her in there, and she's painting her flowers on it, for darn good money."

Will was enthralled. "You mean, like a mural?"

"Yeah, sort of. It's really gorgeous. More colorful than her usual, but still subdued enough. You know how she does it. And the flowers are larger. She isn't happy about making them bigger, but they've still got her special touch."

"Good for her!" Will said. "I have news you can give *her*, too. You can tell her she doesn't have to be afraid of Bill Santone anymore."

"You're right! I read about it in the paper. What a fool, to be burning poison oak."

"Yes, well..., he paid for his ignorance." Will paused and said no more about it. Instead, a happy thought occurred to him. "Something else, Gabe. You can tell Lydia I've been seeing her dog on the road. Girlie. She wags her tail, but won't let me touch her yet. I'm going to start carrying around a little ground beef. I think I'll be able to take her in with me eventually."

"Lydia will be glad to hear that, for sure," Gabe said, setting his empty mug in the sink. "I have to get going, Will. I have bisque ware I need to unload, and the kiln will be about cool enough now."

"Before you go, could you just tell me if you've learned anything more about Terry McCall?"

"Oh, yeah, Terry. I saw him yesterday in Cabot's Mill. He's been hauled into the sheriff's office for questioning. They've been picking at his bare bones."

"Damn it!"

"He said they asked more or less the same questions over and over, trying to make him change his story or contradict himself."

"That could confuse anyone, innocent or guilty."

"Then, there's the new murder," Gabe said. "The guy found in a redwood grove near the university."

"I read about it in the *Coastline*. I hope they aren't trying to pin *that* one on Terry."

"He said they'd like to. The M.O. was similar to the one in Wheeler's murder—the guy's head was bashed in. And both men had their wallet stolen, but nothing else. Fortunately for Terry, he has an alibi of sorts. His wife had her knitting club at the house that night, while he tended to their daughters."

"So they're just keeping him on the hook and harassing him?" Will said.

"No, it's worse now—he expects that one of these days when they haul him in, they're just gonna keep him. He and his wife are planning for the time when he'd be gone. Sheila's found a waitress job, but I don't know who would watch the girls."

After Gabe left, Will was in a quandary. *Damn it! Is it really happening? They're finally going to arrest him!*

He decided to call the deputy right away, hoping to catch him at his desk.

Hunter surprised him by answering after the first ring.

Will started out in a foul mood. "Alan, you need to call off persecuting Terry McCall, and release him! You never have had a case against him, and it's time you admitted it! You guys need to either leave the crime unsolved or get to work finding the real killer!"

Hunter was quiet briefly, then made a sharp retort. "Who the hell do you think you're talking to, Will? I've had about enough of this. I have half a mind to charge you with interfering in our work! *We guys,* like you say, are working night and day to keep ingrates like you safe! You'd better not forget it!"

Then the deputy's tone softened. "Look, Will. I know how the situation appears to you. I know how you like Terry and don't think he could be a killer. But now we have another murder, which looks enough like Wheeler's to have been committed by the same killer. It's practically the same M.O., with just the wallet stolen. We already had a lot of circumstantial evidence against Terry, and now this."

"So you want to charge him with *two* murders he didn't commit!"

"You're getting dangerously close, Will."

"This is a travesty of justice, Alan! A mockery!"

With a click, the deputy hung up.

Shaken now, Will replaced the receiver and sat a while, calming down.

Then he got up and walked around in the cabin with his head bent and hands in his pockets. He was surprised at himself. Hunter was right. What was he doing, shouting at a sheriff's deputy and telling him how to do his job? Now he had lost his connection with the sheriff's office.

Worse, he had broken off a friendship that had meant a lot to him.

And what good had it done Terry? None.

CHAPTER 33

Two days later, Will pulled the *Santa Cruz Coastline* from his mailbox and caught a surprising glimpse of color on the newspaper's front page. He hurried into the cabin with it and spread it out on his table. A full-color photo of Jonas's urn took up nearly half of the page.

Astonished, Will read the text. Then he read it all again:

> *Local Artist Wins Top Prize*
>
> An elaborate memorial urn created by Santa Cruz County resident Jonas Schumann has been awarded First Prize and Purchase Award in "California Creates," an exhibit of contemporary crafts currently showing at Los Angeles's Palace Art Museum. Since its opening on April 1st, the exhibit has drawn a large, appreciative crowd and national recognition, according to the gallery director, Meredith Long.
>
> Schumann's prize-winning urn is set in an individual glass case, along with photographs that show it opened and partly disassembled to reveal its finely detailed interior. Uniquely constructed of bronze, pewter, silver, and gold, the urn's shape suggests a rocket ship. Six bird legs of bronze support the body, which has six bay doors that open outward to reveal the pewter vessel inside. For the nose cone, a gold-plated egg sits atop the urn.
>
> The egg opens into two halves. The top half is enameled blue and contains an intricately mounted gemstone, which Schumann, a master's student at UC Santa Cruz, explains is

meant to guide the ship's small spirit world to the stars. The title of the prize-winning urn is "La Vida Segunda," the second life.

Hardly able to contain himself, Will quickly phoned Jonas at home. But the young man didn't answer; he was probably at the university. Next, Will called Julia, who apparently also wasn't home. Manny would be in school.

Damn! I don't have a soul to share this with!

Finally, Will drove to Santa Cruz to pick up the newspapers from San Francisco and San Jose, but neither of them made any mention of the show.

The next evening, Will, Julia, and Manny were gathered in Julia's kitchen to celebrate Jonas's success, awaiting the arrival of the artist himself. Julia had made enchiladas, and Will had brought tequila and other makings for margaritas.

But when Jonas entered, hollow eyed and unsmiling, the evening at once became solemn. Pausing over the newspaper on the table, he turned his sad eyes away.

"We're all so proud of you, Jonas," Julia said softly, and the others agreed.

"How are you doing with your job applications?" Will presently asked, moving the conversation in a more positive direction.

After Jonas briefly described his plans, Julia put the margarita makings away for another day, and they all sat down to the solace of her delicious beef enchiladas.

★ ★ ★

A few days later, Will was sitting on his porch with the magazine section of the *San Francisco Times* spread over his knees. An article had the headline, "Dream of an Afterlife." It contained a photo of the urn, smaller than the one in the *Coastline*, with a lengthier description. The paper was well thumbed, for he had read and reread the article until he had it practically memorized.

Jonas had left home, with all his belongings packed into a brand new Volkswagen bus. Following the opening of *California Creates,* he had been sent an application for part-time teaching at UC Santa Barbara. With it had come an offer to share an apartment there and studio space with another artist. Jonas drove off in the heavily loaded VW bus solemn-faced but with something of his old energy.

To Will, Jonas's departure came as another personal loss. As he gazed about the quiet clearing, he felt as alone as he had when he first arrived at the cabin. His world was falling away, one person at a time.

Then he heard a familiar sound, the school bus puffing as it stopped at his road. Manny.

Will's spirits had already picked up when the boy appeared in the clearing.

"Hello, Will," Manny said, plopping his book bag onto the porch. Lifting his chin glumly toward Will's newspaper, he said, "I see you're reading *that* one again. Humph. 'Dream of an Afterlife.' Jonas would have a fit if he read that."

"How so?" Will asked, rising to get the boy some lemonade.

"Are you kidding? *Dream?* That's so mushy! A good design plus hard work, that's what it was." The boy sat down heavily to wait for his drink.

"What's new?" Will asked, handing him a glass and sitting down comfortably beside him. "I don't suppose you've heard yet from Jonas."

"Yeah, he called last night. He stopped in L.A. to check on Lydia. Said she was up on a stepladder in a bank, painting big flowers. She had a whole wall to paint on."

"I heard about that!" Will said. "I hear she's getting well paid for it."

"I don't know about that, but Jonas said she had another job lined up, in a fancy restaurant. Regular framed paintings, but bigger than her usual ones."

"Why doesn't Jonas ever call *me*? All this news to you and your mother, and nothing to me. What else did he say?"

"We just got the call last night, and I'm supposed to tell you. The rest of it was for Mom, about the little house. Jonas told her to go ahead and rent it out, 'cause he won't be needing it anymore."

That was a blow. *This is it. Get used to it.* Will gazed up into his trees. *It should come as no surprise.*

"Well," he said, "I guess he won't be coming back *here* anymore."

Manny's head swung around. "Are you crazy or something? This is his home! He said he wouldn't need the house anymore because when he comes back, he'll just bunk with you!"

"*What?*" The word burst out, followed by a loud laugh so revealing of his relief that it embarrassed him. "That's like Jonas. He plans to freeload off me." Will couldn't quit chuckling.

"Go ahead and laugh," Manny said. "All you know is the good news. You haven't heard the bad news yet."

Recalling that the boy had arrived in a sullen mood, Will grew serious. "I'm sorry, Manny. What's the bad news?"

"Mom will be getting a new renter right away for the house. Ramiro Jiménez. He had talked to her earlier about it. He's Chicano, like me. He just started teaching in the junior high as a sub, but in the fall he'll be full-time."

Will thought it over. "Are you in any of his classes?"

"Yeah, History. I really don't like him."

"How come?"

"He keeps trying to butter me up. Even the other kids notice it."

"Uh-oh." Will turned to face the boy, finally realizing that the matter was serious.

"Right," Manny said. "He's interested in Mom!"

Stunned, Will could make no reply.

"He's such an ass! He says Mom's land is part of an old Spanish land grant, and I should call myself Spanish instead of Mexican. I told him my grandfather, Manuel, the one I'm named after, was a farmworker. He didn't like that very much."

"Well," Will muttered, "I guess that's the end of my good dinners at your house."

"I don't know. She invited Jiménez over, but he hasn't come yet."

"Has she said anything lately about me?"

"Not a word."

Will just nodded. Gloom started descending over him again. In the silence that settled between them, Manny glanced across the porch to Will's nearly empty wood box.

"How come you aren't chopping firewood? And that looks wet, like rain blew in on it. Why don't you put a tarp over it?"

He looked more closely at Will.

"You don't look too good. You're skinny and pale, and your beard needs…something. Trimming, I guess."

"I know, son, you're right. I'm behind with everything. I've gotten sort of off schedule lately." He studied the veins on his hands and then fingered his beard.

"There was something I wanted to tell you, Manny. What was it…? Oh, yes, I know. When I spoke with Deputy Hunter a while back, he told me that Santone's car had my license plate on it. He had traced it after he talked to Santone, and forgot to tell me. Then I forgot about it, too."

"So?"

"So, I'd like to have the plate back. The funny thing is, though, I was up there when Santone burned his poison oak, and I didn't see any sign of the car."

Now Manny looked interested. "Well, I don't think he could've driven it down your road."

"You're right. It's overgrown even worse at the top. He must have driven it farther back into the woods. Maybe he hid it because Hunter had written down the number of my plate. That's just how childish he was. Poor jerk, he was marooned. He had to hide his car and couldn't get it off the hill."

"It's gotta be up there someplace, and I'll bet I can find it!" Manny's eyes brightened at the thought. "It'll be just like a treasure hunt."

CHAPTER 34

Carrying a small wrench and a screwdriver in his jeans pockets, Manny started up the road to search for Bill Santone's missing car. He broke into a steady run that soon took him beyond the broken pavement and onto the dirt road, where he felt through his sneaker soles a nice resiliency after a recent rain. As he ran past coyote bushes that now lined the road, he leaned forward into a steeper climb. All the while, poison oak kept taking his eye—lots of it—with tiny white blossoms and new reddish leaves, glistening with oil.

Running steadily, he glanced ahead to the steepest part of the hillside, beyond which the climb would grow easier. The road had narrowed to a trail, crowded on both sides by grass and weeds. Not much farther now—maybe thirty yards—and he would see the top of Bill's shack, which sat back on nearly level land at the top.

He took the rise on the balls of his feet, working his calves. Panting hard, he pounded onward until he soared across a gentle slope just below the hilltop. Throwing his head back, he yelled, "Ya-a-hooo!" He had made it running all the way!

Exultant, he had strength enough to run farther, with his legs happy to be freed of the uphill strain. A sudden dip in the ground surprised him, but he leaped over it and landed safely.

This run settled it. In the fall, he would definitely go out for eighth-grade track.

There isn't a kid in school with legs like mine. Those lazy town kids who do all their running on level ground. I ran up a hill that most people work hard just to walk!

But now he had to sit on a rock and rest, to let his hard breathing level out. Gazing about, he tried blowing air out through his lips.

He knew that the car had to be up here someplace. The animal in Bill would have sought a graveyard for his trapped and useless car, the way elephants seek a place to die.

Moving again, he jogged at an easy pace toward Santone's old shack. Signs of the recent burn lay all about—blackened earth with tiny new starts of grass and weeds. The poison oak that must have been thick was coming back. Arriving at the hut, he examined the burnt siding low on the wooden walls.

It a wonder this whole place didn't go up like a torch!

From there, the search for the car became more daunting. The shack sat in rough, rolling ground that looked impassable for a car. To the south, a deep gully dropped so sharply that even a fool like Bill wouldn't have tried it. He wouldn't have driven north either, since that way led to the nearby Cut-off. He had to have kept going east, heading in the direction of Highway 17.

As Manny turned more eastward, he watched his footing as he plodded around toyon and black oaks, fallen branches, poison oak, and occasional good-sized rocks. Gradually, doubt struck him, a beginning nudge of disappointment.

No one could have driven a car through here. But then, Bill was crazy and might have been drunk. He might have forced his car through all this out of sheer meanness.

Suddenly, he caught his foot on a raised tree root that sent him sprawling. Gathering himself up, he rubbed his right knee, which was slightly skinned. As he looked back at the devilish root, he saw near it a flat rock that showed a lighter streak. He stepped back to examine it closely.

Yes! Something big and heavy scraped over this rock!

Despite his burning knee, he laughed at his own cleverness.

Next came another surprise—Bill's muffler! Battered and rusting, it had fallen off the car. Manny lifted the long, awkwardly shaped thing and laid it back down. "I must be getting close!"

Glancing around, he discovered that the woods were changing, with a few eucalyptus trees standing among thickets of toyon and other high brush. It looked like the woods around the Cutoff, which was very close.

Ahead lay a wall of leaves and branches that looked impenetrable.

Surely, Bill couldn't have driven—

There it was! In the leaves! Shining dark metal!

Carefully parting branches, Manny saw Will's license plate. New-looking, it was safe and secure above a dangling rear bumper. The car's front end, as he looked for it, was pushed in and buried in brush. He whistled at his good fortune. The license plate could have been hidden on the car's front end, mashed against a massive eucalyptus trunk.

He took out his tools. With the wrench, he gripped the nut behind the plate, while he loosened it in front with the screwdriver. Then the other nut, and the plate came off. A perfectly good license plate!

Damn! The Doc will be so tickled to get this back.

He laid the plate safely on a rock and studied the wreck, wondering if he could get inside the car. The part of it he could see looked as if somebody had worked it over with a sledgehammer. The trunk wouldn't open. The broken front windows disappeared in projecting shards of glass, so he worked the back door open. After struggling inside the car, he found two whiskey bottles on the floor and another on the rear seat, along with greasy rags and other trash.

Squeezing himself over the top of the front seat, he landed on broken bits of glass, where he turned himself around and perched with great care. In the dim light, he could hardly see the shattered web of windshield, which was close to his head. The glove compartment, low in the car's crumpled front end, looked untouched.

As he tried the compartment door, it sprang open. Reaching in, he dug out crumpled newspaper. Behind that, there were old maps, used paper napkins, faded trading stamps, and a plastic flashlight, which turned out to be dead when he tried to turn it on. Digging deeper into the cavity, he found something flat but soft. Padded. A wallet.

Manny's heart started beating faster. Could Bill have been dumb enough to abandon his wallet along with his car? He tossed it carefully into the back seat, where there was more light, then squeezed himself back there to examine it.

It was leather.

Kind of expensive-looking for Bill.

When he opened it, Manny saw, behind slightly clouded plastic, a dim driver's license with a face on it that was not Santone's. It was a thin face with a quizzical look.

Dennis Wheeler!

Manny recognized the face even before he read the name on the license. He had seen it several times in the *Coastline.*

He started going through the other cards, but abruptly stopped.

Don't touch anything! Fingerprints might matter! Bill must have murdered Dennis Wheeler, and they're going after Terry! This thing's precious! I've gotta get it to the sheriff!

Needing both hands to climb out of the car, he momentarily laid the wallet on the seat, then scrambled out and reached back in for it. Gripping the wallet by its edges, he picked up the license plate and started back over the rough terrain.

As he drew near Bill's shack, he slowed his steps. A new thought occurred to him.

I'm probably covered with poison oak! Besides, Mom should see this.

He looked around, getting his bearings.

Then, instead of continuing downhill toward Will's cabin, he angled north toward Bill's private path, which led to the Cutoff and home.

★ ★ ★

Julia was standing bent over her desk, glancing through a stack of student tests, when Manny came bursting through the front door.

"Slow down! You're making a breeze!" She grabbed for a paper that had blown off the stack. "Close the door behind you!"

"Mom! Forget about that! Wait till you see what I've got! I found Santone's old car, and guess what was in it?"

"Will's license plate?" She walked calmly over to close the door herself.

"*In* the car, Mom! The car was all smashed up, but I got inside it. Look what was in the glove compartment!"

He laid the wallet carefully down on her desk.

"A wallet? Bill left his wallet in the car?" She reached for it tentatively.

"Don't touch it, Mom!" He grabbed her hand. "We mustn't put our fingerprints on it! I carried it all the way here by its edges. It's Dennis Wheeler's wallet!"

"Dennis's wallet was in Bill's car?"

Once again, she reached for it, but Manny held her off. "Let me open it," he said. With a thumbnail, he carefully flipped it open to the driver's license.

"*Dios mío!*" she breathed, leaning closer to study the pointy-featured little face. "Poor little man.... Bill must have murdered him."

She straightened. "We must call Deputy Hunter right away! Get the phone book, and we'll look up the sheriff's office.... No, wait! It's better that we take it to Will."

"Yes, but you know what? I think I'm covered with poison oak! The car was buried in leaves and I know some of it was poison oak."

Julia was already running for the strong soap cake. "Hurry up and shower! Scrub yourself, hard! I'll get you clean clothes."

Within ten minutes, they were in the car.

★ ★ ★

Will was on his porch, lightly pruning his madrone, when the yellow car drove up his road and parked behind the truck. Laying down his pruning shears, he hurried over to meet Julia and Manny.

"Boy, am I glad to see you two!"

"Hey, Will!" Manny called from inside the car. "Wait'll you see what we brought!"

"Something *delicioso,* I hope," Will said. He had recently bought a Spanish dictionary.

"Ha! Better than that!" Manny said.

"Better than *that?* Oh, I know.... You found my license plate. That's good, but not better...."

The boy climbed out carefully, still holding the wallet by its edges, while Julia carried the license plate. When she handed it to Will, he surprised her with a one-armed hug.

"I found something a damn sight better than the license plate!" Manny said.

"Manny!" Julia scolded.

"Look, Will! I got inside Bill's old car! Look what was in the glove compartment!"

The boy carefully lifted the wallet to show Will.

"A wallet? Is it Bill's?" Will asked, leading his guests into the cabin.

"It's Dennis Wheeler's wallet!" Manny exclaimed.

The boy carefully laid the wallet on the counter and opened it to the driver's license. Will leaned in closer to see.

"I'll be damned! It *is* Wheeler's license. Bill had it? My God, he stole this from Wheeler. So he killed him, after all!" Will looked dazedly from Manny to Julia. "Bill's one of the murderers. I've been living right here below him all this time."

"*Dios*, Will," Julia said quietly. "You've been in real danger."

"He came down here and threatened me once, and I called him a son of a bitch, to his face!"

"Wow!" Manny said. "You were mighty lucky, Will."

Carefully closing the wallet, Will said, "I have a plastic bag we can put this in to protect the fingerprints. I hate to say this, Manny, but you should have left the wallet in the car."

"Why?" Manny asked. "It's better for us to turn it in to the sheriff."

"But it's evidence. The sheriff would rather see it where it was found. Don't worry, though. If you hadn't found the wallet, it probably would have just rotted away."

Will carefully lifted the wallet's plastic windows to glimpse Dennis's other cards, then placed the wallet in a small plastic bag.

"Are you going to call the sheriff?" Julia asked.

"Yes. Right now. I'll call Deputy Hunter. He and I have argued for months about this murder. There's a small streak on the wallet that might be dried blood. Let's not say anything about it to Hunter, though. We'll let him discover it for himself."

Manny laughed. "Good idea. He can take credit for *something*."

"Do you think this will clear Terry McCall?" Julia asked.

"Yes, I think so. Maybe not immediately, but the news will certainly cheer him up."

Will dialed Hunter's phone number, which he knew well.

The deputy answered the phone briskly. Then, learning that it was Will, his voice changed. He sounded reluctant to talk.

"Something interesting has happened here, Alan. Manny Harrington just found Dennis Wheeler's wallet in Bill Santone's old car."

Julia and Manny listened quietly to Will's side of the conversation.

"He had abandoned the car, further back on the hill," Will explained. "Manny was looking for the license plate that Bill had stolen from my truck."

Will was silent for a little while as Hunter spoke.

"I hadn't seen the car, either," Will said, "when I was up there just before he died. Manny said Bill had driven it over rough ground and crashed it in some thick brush. I'm guessing that he was trying to hide it because you saw the stolen plate when you were there. Maybe the car itself was stolen. He must have long forgotten about Dennis's wallet.... It was in the glove compartment."

Another pause as Julia and Manny listened, then Will spoke again.

"No, it's really Dennis's wallet. Nobody could have faked it. His driver's license is in it and a bunch of other cards. And I know the site is important. You'll probably want to take a crew up there."

Again, a short silence.

"Don't worry, we've been very protective of fingerprints. While you drive here, I'm going to phone Terry McCall."

The deputy objected to that so loudly that Julia and Manny could hear his scolding voice over the phone.

★ ★ ★

While Will and Julia were still haggling over whether or not to call Terry despite Hunter's objections, the deputy arrived at the door. He was accompanied by another man, whom he introduced as Detective Inspector Warren Talbert.

"You say you've found Dennis Wheeler's wallet?" the detective asked.

With an authoritative air, he pulled protective gloves on over his hands. As he listened to the story of Manny's trip up the hill, he carefully removed the wallet from its plastic bag. First he checked the driver's license.

During this time, Will stole a look at his old friend. Deputy Hunter appeared reticent, with his eyes less than eager to meet Will's.

So that's how it is between us, Will thought, *after all our arguing over Terry's innocence or guilt. I was right all along, and he was wrong. It isn't easy for him now, and it isn't easy for me, either.*

Talbert was already scolding Manny for removing the wallet from the car. "This evidence is contaminated now, do you understand? It's been moved around and handled. You shouldn't have even touched it, Manny."

At first, the boy, who had expected praise, was set back. He looked to his mother, but Julia was unable to help him. Then Manny became stubborn.

"How else could I have known whose it was? I thought it was Bill's, till I saw the driver's license. It was hard as heck to get at the wallet. The front end of the car was so scrunched up, I had to go in through a back door and climb over the seats. I doubt if you guys could even get *in* there."

"Manny volunteered to go up and search for the car," Will explained, "to look for my stolen license plate."

"That's right," Hunter said in a subdued voice. "I saw Bill's car earlier with only one plate on it, which I traced to Will's truck."

"Forget about license plates," the detective said, growing impatient. "The fact remains that the boy should have left the wallet where he found it."

Manny was still defensive. "I brought it down here so we could call Terry and let him know that he was off the hook!"

"Hush, Manny!" Julia scolded.

"*Off the book?*" Talbert was angry now. "What if you tell Terry he's free, and we find his fingerprints on the wallet? What then? We've got to test the evidence before we tell him anything! Some things we have to do by the book!"

"Warren," Hunter said, "I don't think there'd be any harm in just telling Terry we found the wallet. He could be cautioned that he's not free of suspicion, and still give him reason to hope. After all he's been through."

"No way, Deputy." Talbert snapped out the words while he watched Manny pour himself a glass of milk with Julia's help. "Let's get up that hill, and take the boy to show us the way. I'll call in to send a team up there right now, and we'll secure the site."

"How about Bill's shack?" Will asked. "It's on the hill near where he hid the car. I assume you'll want your team to check that out."

"Oh? Of course, yes," the inspector said with a blank look, which said he hadn't thought of it. He covered his error by looking quickly at Manny, who was still drinking his milk. "I suppose you've been in that house already, rooting around."

The boy said calmly, "No. I walked around it, but didn't go inside. I've never been in Bill's shack."

"Inspector," Hunter said, "let me see the wallet, would you please? I thought I saw something on it…."

Talbert sighed impatiently as he drew the wallet back out of the evidence bag, where he had placed it.

"See there," Hunter said, pointing something out to Talbert. "The small brown streak on the leather? I think that could be dried blood."

"You're right, it could be. I didn't see that. Humph. The lab will check it out."

While Talbert used Will's telephone to call the office, Will stepped out onto the porch with Manny to talk privately.

"Don't let Talbert upset you, son. You're still a hero today, no matter what he says."

Manny grinned, then became solemn again as Hunter joined them.

"Alan," Will said quietly, "I'm going to telephone Terry, to tell him that Manny found the wallet. I hope I have your consent."

"Don't do it," Hunter murmured, watching the door. "You'll just make trouble."

"I wouldn't tell him he was free."

Then their conversation was halted as Talbert stepped out onto the porch and steered Manny with him into the clearing.

Hunter had started after them when Will called out softly to him, "Say, Alan?"

The deputy glanced back.

"Breakfast one of these days?"

Hunter's plump face relaxed into a grin. "When?"

"Anytime. This week. I'll call you."

With a nod, the deputy disappeared down the path.

★ ★ ★

"Well, Julia," Will said as they stood together on the porch watching the other three depart, "here we are, alone at last." He let out a long sigh. "It's a relief, to have the men gone and now it's just you and me."

She looked at him, suddenly embarrassed. "Things have been happening so fast, I hardly know what to feel."

"I think I know the cure for that. We ought to be feeling *good.* In fact, I think it's time to celebrate! Let's go inside and I will treat you to some of my new discovery, cafe mocha."

"That sounds interesting, whatever it is."

"Coffee and chocolate," Will said. "Two of my favorite things, together at last. It comes in a powder. I just stir it into hot water. Actually, I use half milk."

Julia took a chair while Will made them each a cup, then seated himself beside her at the table.

"Manny would be happy to see us here together, wouldn't he?" Will asked.

"That boy! I want to tell you, Will, that it's been very embarrassing to me, the way he's kept trying to push us together."

Will sipped his mocha, then grinned. "He told me that you think I'm good-looking."

"Oh! I *knew* it! All that time he spent over here, I wondered what he was telling you about me! That brat! I hope you didn't believe his tales, Will."

"Does that mean you *don't* think I'm good-looking?" he asked slyly.

Julia started to reply, then paused, stymied.

"It's alright with me if you like my looks, Julia. After all, I like yours, a lot. You're very attractive. And not only that, you're a beautiful person altogether."

Manny suddenly appeared at the door, out of breath from running back to the cabin. "Hunter just told me you could go ahead and call Terry! The other guy doesn't know it, but Hunter said it's okay."

"Great!" Julia said, as Manny left to catch up with the men. "Let's call him, Will. It'll be such a pleasure…."

"Okay, we will. But first, I want to tell you more about how lovely you are."

"Oh, Will, stop." She was blushing, finally. "What are you doing?"

Reaching into a pocket, Will drew out a small red velvet box.

Julia looked at the box, then at Will. Then she raised her hands to cover her face.

Will wordlessly opened the box, and held it so she could see. Inside was a gold ring with a diamond set between two smaller rubies.

Her eyes brightened with tears as he slipped it onto her finger, where it fit perfectly.

"Shouldn't I say yes?" she asked. "Is this a proposal?"

"It is if I don't have to get down on my knees."

He cleared his throat. "Julia, *Te casas conmigo?*

"*Dios Mio,* Will!" She laughed gently. *"Si! Si, Si, Si!*

Looking at her hand again, she said, "This is the most beautiful ring I've ever seen! Rubies! I love them! Is it a Jonas masterpiece? I hope it didn't cost you a fortune."

"It cost me a brand new Volkswagen bus."

Then Will stood up, drew Julia to her feet and wrapped her in his arms. After exploring her dimpled cheeks with his kisses, he found her lips.

In a little while, Julia asked, "Shouldn't we make the call now?"
Will released her to pick up the telephone.
"Hello, Terry. This is Will."

About the Author

Esther Escott authored not only *La Vida Segunda*, but also a coming-of-age novel entitled *Plum Bottom*. She also illustrated a child's book, written by Jamison Escott, entitled *The Clockmaker of Mullen*. She lives with her husband in California.

www.amazon.com/author/estherescott
www.mywritingnews.blogspot.com

Made in the USA
Monee, IL
24 December 2021